The Back Up Plan

Elsie McArthur

To my children, without whom this book would never have been written.

CHAPTER 1

Duirinish was a request only stop on the West Highland line; the last one before the service terminated at Kyle of Lochalsh. Only Marsaili and one other passenger remained on board as the train neared the completion of its two-hour journey from Inverness, and she was surprised to see that he had also disembarked. He was pacing the platform now, mobile phone in hand as he tapped furiously at the screen, the hood of his anorak pulled up against the drizzling rain and a rucksack propped against the wall of the tiny wooden shelter. Sighing audibly, he stopped to hold the device up in the air in vain search of a signal. He had to be a tourist, Marsaili assumed, although there weren't usually that many of them around at this time of year. Not ones travelling by rail, at least. The success of the North Coast 500 driving route - Scotland's answer to Route 66 - had brought an influx of visitors to the remote part of the country that Marsaili called home. Most of them, however, visited in the summer, clogging up single track roads with campervans they had no idea how to drive. Not hiking on foot in November, as this man seemed to be planning. Wherever he was heading, public transport wouldn't take him much further, and Marsaili found herself hoping that he had accommodation booked for the night.

She'd just been about to ask if he needed directions when the sudden stutter of a worn-out car engine cut through the silence of the night and made them both jump. Marsaili knew instantly that her mother was approaching. She smiled to herself. Things here seldom changed, and there was something comforting about the familiar noise of Shonagh Mackenzie's old, exhausted, Volkswagen Beetle.

It was only early evening, but the village around them was deserted, its inhabitants having already sought shelter indoors and battened down the hatches for the night. At just approaching 5pm, the sky was already fully dark. It would be another 13 or 14 hours, Marsaili knew, until the sun rose again.

She glanced once more at her fellow passenger, who had now hoisted his rucksack onto his back and had a slightly more purposeful look about him. His phone was in his hand and he seemed to be following Google Maps somewhere. Briefly wondering whether she should offer him a lift, Marsaili grabbed her own bag and headed down the single-track road to meet her mother.

It had been almost a week now since, lying asleep in her Glasgow flat, she had been awoken by her brother's late-night phone call. The unexpected buzzing at 1am had startled Marsaili awake in a panic, her heart in her throat. When she heard the crack in Lachlan's normally steady voice she panicked even more.

"Is it Dad?" she asked urgently, sitting up, throwing her legs out of bed and flicking the bedside lamp on before she'd even come to. "Mum? Are they alright?"

"It's Rowan," her brother almost shouted, the words bursting from his lips in a frenzied rush. "She's had the baby. You've got a niece!"

It took a moment for the information to penetrate her groggy mind, but when it did a wave of relief and joy washed over her. A baby girl! Tears pricked at Marsaili's eyes. She suddenly longed to hear her best friend's voice. "Put Rowan on," she said. "How's she doing?"

"She's asleep," Lachlan replied. "She said she'll call you in the morning. God, sorry, I didn't even realise how late it was; were you asleep?"

"Yes," Marsaili laughed, picturing her brother's face beaming with pride. Lachlan Mackenzie was tall and broad, ruddy skinned and freckled with close cropped brown hair and a wild, rust coloured beard. He looked tough, his arms muscled and his skin weathered from long days at sea hauling fishing nets onto the boat, but underneath this gruff exterior, he was the gentlest soul Marsaili had ever known.

As soon as the phone call ended, she was online and booking her train. Fortunately, she had a few days off work coming up anyway. The theatre, where she worked as a barmaid, was closed as final preparations took place for the Christmas pantomime, and she had just enough money left in her overdraft to scrape together the fare. Less than twenty-four hours later, she was nearly home.

As she opened the gate from the station and stepped out onto the darkened road, Marsaili saw headlights bouncing along towards her, cutting through the darkness and illuminating droplets of rain like little blobs of gold. Her mother accelerated when she spotted her, the car barely reaching a standstill before Shonagh was reaching over the passenger seat and opening the door for her only daughter. "Get in!" She shouted unceremoniously. "It's pissing down!"

Marsaili smiled, clambering into the car and flinging her bag onto the back seat. The rain had indeed intensified, and she could feel her red hair sticking across her face in long, damp tendrils.

Shonagh stared at her daughter for a moment, before tutting audibly.

"Look at you!" she cried, appalled. "You're skin and bone!" She leaned across and squeezed Marsaili's thigh, which was more than ample by anyone's standards, she thought, before kissing her damp cheek.

"Dad's got a seafood pie in the oven, let's get you home and fed." Shonagh threw the car into first gear, the clutch squealing as she executed a speedy three point turn before hurtling back down the road and out through the village.

"How's things, Mum?" Marsaili asked, bracing herself against the dashboard as Shonagh flung the car into a sharp bend. It was dark and the country roads were unlit, but she'd lived here all her life and knew them well. Nonetheless, Shonagh took her eyes off the road for a little bit longer than Marsaili was comfortable with, and she felt her foot involuntarily twitch for the brake.

"What sort of a question's that?" Shonagh replied with an incredulous smile. The older woman was almost sixty, her make-up free face scattered with freckles, and the short curly hair that had once been fiery red now faded to fawn and speckled with silver. "I'm a granny at last!" she exclaimed with a grin.

Marsaili's parents owned an old croft in the middle of a wild and barren moorland, surrounded by rugged fields tossed with heather and craggy boulders. The one and a half storey house lay at the end of a single-track road, with no neighbours in sight. A small, curved bay on its Western side looked out over the sea where Loch Carron flowed into the Inner Sound. As a child, Marsaili had never really thought about how lucky she was to grow up somewhere like this. She'd taken the long summer days for granted; paddling in the sea, rock pooling and playing on the beach with her brothers and their dogs. It wasn't until her adolescence that she'd become bored and began to dream of something more; dreams which eventually drove her south to the bright lights of Glasgow. But recently, whenever she visited, she felt the niggling tug deep in her belly of something that she suspected was homesickness.

Her father squeezed her warmly when they arrived, the comforting smell of homemade fish pie filling the cosy farmhouse kitchen. At six foot four Murdo Mackenzie's' head wasn't far from the ceiling of the small room, and Marsaili enjoyed being dwarfed in his embrace for a moment. She buried her face into the comforting, scratchy material of his knitted sweater, inhaling his familiar scent of sea salt, smoke and whisky.

"Lachlan's been busy," she commented, eyeing up the steaming dish that was sitting on the kitchen table, topped with mounds of mashed potato and melted cheese. Her tummy rumbled, and she realised how long it had been since she'd enjoyed a proper meal that hadn't been cooked using a microwave or a kettle.

"A good haul this week," her father replied with a smile. He held his daughter at arm's length for a moment, looking at her carefully. "Too skinny," he declared eventually. Marsaili rolled her eyes. Squeezing into a size 14, skinny was the last word anyone else would use to describe her, but her parents were feeders and always had been.

"I've already told her!" her mother shouted in response, trudging into the kitchen with Marsaili's bag over her shoulder. "God only knows what she's eating down there."

"I'm eating food mother," Marsaili answered, as she bent down to rub the ears of Fraoch, their old black lab. The ageing dog looked up at her from her wicker basket, cosied into the best spot in the room, right next to the warmth of the kitchen Aga. Her gentle brown eyes were just as Marsaili remembered, but her muzzle seemed greyer than before.

"What kind of food?" Shonagh challenged, grabbing plates from the cupboard and placing them on the table. "All this vegan, gluten free, dairy free, wheat free rubbish that everyone's into these days? I don't know," she sighed, "what's wrong with good, honest, proper food?" Marsaili smiled as her mother continued to rant, not wanting to admit that actually, if it weren't for the generosity of her flatmate she would mostly be surviving on an old bottle of ketchup, some leftover vodka from last Hogmanay, and cream of chicken cup-a-soups from Poundland.

Enveloped in the comforting sound of her parent's chattering, Marsaili sat at the table and gratefully accepted the large portion of fish pie that was spooned up in front of her. Taking a mouthful, she sighed contentedly - the tang of the smoked haddock and mustard balanced out the creaminess of the sauce perfectly. She silently wished that she'd paid more attention during all those years her mother had spent trying in vain to teach her to cook.

They stayed sat around the kitchen table for the rest of the evening. It was the warmest room in the house, with both a wood burner and the heat from the Aga. Marsaili had forgotten how much she enjoyed listening to the sound of the rain pounding against the single glazed windows, whilst they were nestled inside in the warmth. On this exposed outcrop of sandstone, the wind whipped in relentlessly, but the little croft had stood resolutely against it for more than 200 years, and sitting in there, Marsaili felt almost invincible.

With the help of a full belly and the large whisky her father had pressed into her hands later that evening, Marsaili slept in her old single bed as soundly as she could remember sleeping for some time. The wind was howling as the storm outside built, but her mother had placed two hot water bottles under the sheets for her - one at her bum and one at her feet, just like when she was little - and she didn't stir all night. The next day, when her alarm started to ring in the still-darkness of an early winter morning, she found herself poking her toes out from under the duvet the way she had as a child, feeling the chilled air of a home without central heating, and building up the courage to jump out of bed and into her dressing gown and slippers as quickly as possible.

Marsaili arrived downstairs to the smell of bacon sizzling and the sound of the kettle whistling on the stove.

"Morning," her mother smiled as she entered the kitchen, placing a stoneware mug on the table and gesturing for her to sit down. Shonagh was already dressed, accustomed to the long years of early mornings as a fisherman's wife and unable to break the habit. Her husband, however, was still enjoying the long lies that retirement afforded him.

"I'll wake your father soon," Shonagh said. "He could sleep for Scotland these days. Bacon sandwich?"

Marsaili nodded eagerly, taking a long, hot swig of tea. She sat in silence for a while, as her mother cut thick slices of fresh, homemade white bread and slathered them with butter. She topped the bread with three rashers of smoked bacon, fried to a crisp, and a generous dollop of brown sauce.

"I remember how you like it," she said with a smile, as she passed the plate to her daughter. "Although it's long enough since ye've been here."

Marsaili bit into the sandwich hungrily, choosing to ignore the jibe.

"I'll have doubled in size by the time I leave if you carry on like this," she said instead, her voice muffled by the mouthful of bacon and bread.

"Well, you could do with fattening up." Shonagh pinched Marsaili's hip as she passed, making her wince.

Her mother sat in the seat opposite, tapping her wedding ring against the side of her mug - the way she always did when she had something on her mind - as Marsaili continued to eat. The air was suddenly laden and she could feel the question looming before her mother even opened her mouth.

"So," Shonagh began eventually.

"No!" Marsaili declared, before her mother could get any further.

"You don't even know what I was going to say!" Shonagh protested.

"Yes, I do, mother! No, I haven't met any 'nice young men', yes I am still single, no I haven't had any auditions, yes I am still a barmaid and no I haven't thought about throwing in the towel and just becoming a drama teacher instead."

Shonagh sighed. "I just want you to be happy, sweetheart."

"I know mum. But I am happy. Honest!" Marsaili replied, a little too brightly.

CHAPTER 2

It had been over ten years since Marsaili had packed her bags and headed South for Glasgow. Standing back in her old bedroom, she could remember the excitement that had bubbled inside her the day she left. In hindsight, she couldn't help but feel a little guilty. She had set out on her adventure without so much as a thought of how her parents might feel - would they miss her? Worry about her? They'd both lived their whole lives up here, in this small corner of the world - and generations of their families before them - but Marsaili couldn't wait to escape.

She had fallen in love with the city on her very first visit for the University open day. She was instantly overwhelmed by the sheer volume of things to do and see - museums, parks, art galleries, pubs, nightclubs, restaurants... So much that she had never had the opportunity to experience before. Even all these years later, she loved the anonymity the city offered. Having grown up in a place where she was on first name terms with virtually every other resident within a five-mile radius, it was refreshing to be able to walk down the street and for no one to have the slightest idea who she was. It was an opportunity to reinvent herself; to become the person she had always wanted to be.

Had it really worked out that way though? University had been everything she'd dreamed of at first. But then it had become just another assortment of cliques, fuelled by gossip and built on intricate social hierarchies; not all that different from village life, really. Other than a poorly paid job, a shabby rented flat and a few friends, what did she have to show for her great adventure? She couldn't ignore the fact that her thirtieth birthday had been and gone, and her mother's well meant, but tiresome, enquiries into the progress of her career and personal life were becoming harder and harder to ignore.

She thought of Lachlan and Rowan. Her brother and best friend had fallen in love at a teenage party when Rowan and Marsaili were just 15 and Lachlan 17. They'd been inseparable ever since, and Marsaili almost couldn't remember them being apart. She was genuinely over the moon that they now had the little family they'd always dreamed of, but she couldn't help but feel it only highlighted further her own state of perpetual spinsterhood.

And then there was Gregor. Her twin brother, who'd apparently inherited all the sexual magnetism, charisma and effortless charm that Marsaili herself had missed out on. He was a successful lawyer and currently stuck in Edinburgh working on a case, before he was due to jet off on one of his many foreign holidays with one of his many exotic girlfriends.

And whilst she didn't really crave a high-powered career, or a six-figure salary, or a baby (yet, at least) Marsaili did wish that she could excel at *something* when compared to her brothers. She was neither the reliable, stay-at-home earth mother nor the successful, high-powered career woman. So, what was she? The out of work actor with no savings account, no mortgage and no man? It was hard not to feel second (or third) best.

Later that morning, after helping her mother bake a batch of fruit scones and a shepherd's pie to take with them, Marsaili squeezed herself into the backseat of her parents' little yellow car. They were travelling to the nearby village where Lachlan, Rowan and their new baby girl lived. Marsaili hadn't had much time to go shopping, but she'd rushed into Marks and Spencer's on her way to the train station the previous day, and a hastily wrapped packet of pink, flowery sleepsuits was in her grasp.

Plockton was a pretty, waterfront village on the shores of Loch Carron, with the somewhat dubious honour of, supposedly, being the only settlement on Scotland's West coast to actually face East. This quirk of geography meant that the little town enjoyed an unusually mild climate, sheltered as it was from the prevailing Westerly winds, and as a result was known for the conspicuously tropical assortment of palm trees that flourished there. Plockton was popular with tourists due to its picturesque setting, having been used as a location for a number of films and TV shows, and at the height of the summer season you could struggle to find a parking space. On a wet, miserable winter's day like today, however, the streets were deserted and the palm trees sodden and bent beneath the sheets of rain.

Marsaili hoped they weren't going to be intruding. Rowan was the first person she knew who'd had a baby, and she wasn't sure of the protocol for new mothers. Would she mind being ambushed so soon after giving birth? Her parents had assured her they were welcome, but Marsaili wasn't sure whether she'd feel like making polite conversation and eating shepherd's pie with visitors so soon after evacuating an 8lb human from her uterus.

However, as they pulled up to Lachlan and Rowan's cottage, Marsaili noticed a number of familiar cars scattered down the street, and knew that Rowan's family had already beaten them to it. If nothing else, maybe Marsaili could run interference between the competing sets of grandparents.

They let themselves into the little house, the front door having been left unlocked as always, to be confronted by a wall of pink balloons in the porch.

"Hello?" Shonagh called out, hopping excitedly from foot to foot as she pushed her way through the balloons.

Voices were coming from the living room to their left, and a plump, rosy face popped round the door as they approached. Marsaili recognised Rowan's mum immediately.

"Shonagh!"

"Rhona!" The two women embraced, a huddle of squealing, giggling and crying, as a flurry of other bodies exited the room and greeted Marsaili and her Dad. She exchanged pleasantries with Rowan's dad and sister, before Lachlan folded her into a crushing bear hug.

"Sis," he said briefly, planting a kiss on her cheek. "Thanks so much for coming,"

They piled into the cosy living room, squashing on sofas and pulling extra chairs through from the dining room, while the two new grannies rushed off to the kitchen to make pots of tea and squabble politely over which of the home bakes to put out first. Lachlan pulled Marsaili aside before she could sit down.

"Can you do me a favour?" her brother asked. "Rowan's upstairs - we said Callie needed a nap, but really she just wanted to feed her in peace, without Rhona inspecting her latch."

"Callie?"

Lachlan smiled. "Would you go up and check on them for me? Warn Rowan of the coming stampede?"

Creeping upstairs as gently as she could, Marsaili knocked softly on the solid oak door before entering.

"Come in," Rowan called, in a hushed stage whisper.

She was sitting up in bed, surrounded by pillows and with the top of one breast exposed. Her dark hair was pulled up into a messy bun and there were circles under her eyes. She looked exhausted, yet undeniably lovely. A tiny, equally dark-haired little head was nuzzled at her chest, grunting and snuffling contentedly. Rowan looked up and smiled.

Wordlessly, and as quietly as she could, Marsaili moved across the room and embraced her with one arm. "Congratulations," she whispered.

They were still for a moment, neither one speaking, just looking down in awe at this perfect, miraculous new human.

"It still doesn't make sense," Rowan said eventually. Marsaili took a seat in the nursing chair next to the bed, watching enthralled as Callie sleepily nodded from the breast, eyes closed, lips parted, milk dribbling down her tiny dimpled chin.

"I mean I was relatively conscious throughout it all," Rowan continued, "but I still can't quite believe that one minute she was inside me, and the next minute here she is. An actual little person." Rowan smiled at her daughter, seemingly amazed by her very existence. "Do you want to hold her?" she asked.

Hesitant, Marsaili babbled incoherently in response. "She's so peaceful," she managed eventually. "I wouldn't want to wake her."

"Oh, don't worry about that," Rowan said dismissively. "She's milk drunk - nothing in the world could wake her now."

With an impressive one-handed deftness, Rowan swiftly pulled up her nursing bra and clipped it back into place, before leaning forwards and placing the sleeping baby gently into Marsaili's arms.

She really was perfect, Marsaili concluded. A dusting of dark brown curls, long eyelashes brushing her cheeks, ears so thin they were almost see-through. Callie was breathing gently, her little tummy rising and falling rhythmically, and Marsaili had to stifle a yawn.

"It's soporific," Rowan agreed. "Suits you," she added after a pause.

Marsaili rolled her eyes. "Don't you start too," she said. "I'd be happy with a date, never mind a baby." Although there was something undeniably intoxicating about the sweet milky smell and the softness of Callie's downy skin.

"How long do you think we'll be able to get away with hiding up here?" she asked.

"Is your mum here?"

Marsaili nodded.

"About thirty seconds, if we're lucky."

Right on cue, the sound of footsteps and muffled voices could be heard at the bottom of the stairs.

Marsaili turned to Rowan, as she climbed out of bed and quickly transferred Callie into the Moses basket by the window.

"Please don't tell mum I held her first," Marsaili asked.

CHAPTER 3

The few days she had at home passed far too quickly. When it was time to leave, Shonagh drove her to the train station and waited with her until it arrived. As they were parting, she hugged her daughter and cupped her face gently in her hands.

"I worry about you," she said, kissing her cheek. "Please take care of yourself."

Marsaili found a seat by the window just as the train set off, whistling past the loch and disturbing a fishing heron. She watched it take off clumsily and circle once before landing again. It was still early – the train journey South would take most of the day – and the winter sun was only just creeping above the horizon, casting the world in an eerie, pink glow.

Marsaili sighed, her breath briefly fogging up the inside of the train window. It had started to rain again, the clouds gently hugging the tops of the snow-capped hills as they wound their way East through a smattering of sparsely populated villages. She really hoped she would be able to make it back home for Christmas. Lachlan and Rowan were insisting on hosting, despite Shonagh's protestations that it would be too much for them with the new baby. Marsaili wanted nothing more than to spend the festive period with her niece, but she knew from experience that the weather could play havoc with travel plans up here.

She filled the time until they reached Inverness by reading her book and drinking instant coffee from the trolley service, but as they left the city and sped further South, she felt tiredness overcome her. Closing her eyes, Marsaili rested her head against the glass. The next thing she knew, she was being awoken by someone gently shaking her arm.

"Are we in Glasgow?" she asked groggily, dimly registering that the man whose hand was on her shoulder was quite attractive. Nice eyes. She hoped she hadn't been snoring.

"No, Perth," he replied with an apologetic smile. "But we've all got to get off. There's a problem with the train, we need to transfer to another one."

"Oh, OK. Thank you."

Cursing internally, she struggled to drag her battered holdall down from the overhead luggage rack. The handsome stranger didn't bother offering to help, she noticed.

Hoping there wouldn't be too much of a delay, Marsaili stumbled onto the crowded platform and followed her fellow passengers into a new carriage. She was working tonight, and was already cutting it fine. It was the opening night of the pantomime and if previous years were anything to go by, it would be busy. Of all the nights to be running late, this wasn't the one.

Clambering into a seat near the door, she once again threw her case onto the overhead rack. She was grateful to see a conductor approaching.

"Excuse me," she called. "Any idea what sort of time we'll get to Glasgow?"

The grey-haired man sighed and scratched his head, frustrated.

"At this point, your guess is as good as mine. We'll set off as soon as we can, then it should only be about an hour."

In the end, they sat in the station at Perth for another half an hour, then came to an unexplained standstill again about twenty minutes later. Marsaili made a mental note to start saving some of her paltry wage – public transport was a nightmare. She really had to scrape together enough money to buy a not-so-new car.

By the time they got back to Glasgow the train was nearly an hour behind schedule, and Marsaili had just 10 minutes to get across town to the theatre before her call started at 6pm. Her phone had died on the train, so she couldn't even ring ahead to warn them she'd be late.

Running out of the station, Marsaili was confronted by a wall of drizzle and a seemingly endless queue at the taxi rank. December was fast approaching, and the eager shoppers of Glasgow were out in force. Marsaili sighed and looked at her watch. She was never going to make it.

She was only ten minutes late in the end, which, all things considered, she didn't think was too bad. Marsaili ran past the two women in the ticket office with a hurried wave, and thundered straight up the stairs towards the Grand Circle foyer, hoping she would just catch the end of the pre-shift briefing.

She pulled the door open and rushed in, but the room was

empty except for a solitary, tuxedo-wearing figure bent over the kiosk desk opposite. Marsaili approached him from behind, babbling breathlessly as she went.

"Bruce, I'm so sorry I'm late, I was at home for a few days because my brother just had a baby – well, *he* didn't, but his wife did – and my train got delayed, and then my phone died, and…"

But the figure who turned towards her did not have the familiar, rounded face and bald head of her friendly manager. Instead of Bruce's slightly portly, middle aged frame and toothy smile, she was faced with a tall, fair-haired stranger.

The man was eyeing her carefully as her words dried up on her lips. Marsaili hoped the hot flush she suddenly felt in her cheeks could plausibly be explained by the fact she'd taken the stairs two at a time. He was very good looking – a thatch of thick blonde hair sat atop a strong boned, square jawed face, with brown eyes that were watching her intently. She tried to return his gaze as confidently as she could. He seemed to be simultaneously frowning and smirking at her, and Marsaili couldn't decide if the expression was irritating or endearing.

He glanced down at the call sheet in his hands. "Mar-say-lee, I presume?"

"It's Marsaili actually," she corrected, although the look he gave her made her wish she hadn't spoken. "Like in, *parsley*," she finished lamely, resorting to the rhyme she used to use in primary school. It still wasn't quite right, but it was the closest English sound she'd ever been able to come up with

His lips twitched slightly and he almost looked as if he were about to laugh, before he composed himself and carefully adjusted the cuffs of his shirt instead. She noticed he was wearing smart silver cufflinks, rather than the cheap, button-fastening shirts Bruce wore.

"*Marsaili*, sorry," he said, managing a decent enough attempt at the correct pronunciation. He had a very well-spoken accent, like Hugh Grant in that film where he played the Prime Minister, Marsaili thought. Or any film, for that matter.

"That's ok," Marsaili mustered up a smile. "I'm sorry I'm late, it's just…"

"Just don't let it happen again," he interrupted, with a dismissive wave of his hand. One of those posh signet rings encircled his pinkie finger - gold, with an onyx stone set in it. He looked her up and down, taking in her flustered and slightly bedraggled appearance. She self-consciously ran her hand over her unruly copper curls and tucked them behind her ears, trying in vain to look slightly more put together.

"You'd better hurry and get yourself tidied up," he said brusquely. "We've got a big audience tonight. You're in the Gallery bar, with Caitriona."

Marsaili paused, suppressing the internal eye roll she felt at the mention of her colleague.

"Well? What are you waiting for? Off you go."

"Yes, sir," Marsaili replied sharply, in a slightly more sarcastic tone than she had intended. He suddenly looked abashed, and opened his mouth as if he were about to say something, before obviously thinking better of it and extending a hand instead.

"Will Hunter," he said, clearing his throat nervously. "I'm sorry; I should have introduced myself properly. I'm the new manager. I've been sent up from the parent company in London."

"Nice to meet you, Will," Marsaili replied. His hands were large and warm, and his brown eyes met hers once more, unblinking.

"Nice to meet you, Marsaili."

The one bonus of being in the Gallery on opening night was that her shift flew in. For once, the theatre was practically sold out, and by the time Marsaili made it up to the bar the first customers already had drinks in hand. Caitriona was bent down stocking the fridges as Marsaili bustled into the room, hurriedly tying her apron before throwing her hair up into a messy bun.

"There you are!" Caitriona exclaimed brightly as she stood up. "Waited till all the hard work was done before you decided to show up?"

Half opened boxes and crates littered the floor behind the bar. Carrying all of that up single-handedly from the basement storeroom would have taken multiple trips, yet miraculously, Caitriona didn't seem to have a drop of sweat on her.

Flicking her long blonde hair over one shoulder, Caitriona winked one perfectly outlined eye at her. "Never mind," she said. "I got some of the lads to give me a hand." She laughed, a childish giggle, like water bubbling up from a drain.

Marsaili rolled her own naked eyes in response, grinning

unconvincingly. No matter how much she tried, she just couldn't take to Caitriona. Deep down she knew that a lot of it was just down to good old-fashioned jealousy, but this knowledge didn't help her actually get on with the girl any better.

Thankfully, they were spared much further opportunity to chat due to a sudden influx of customers. The Gallery, occupying the uppermost floor of the old theatre, offered the cheapest seats in the house. As a result, it also tended to attract the rowdier clientele, and tonight was no exception. The people of Glasgow were kicking off their Christmas festivities with gusto, and Marsaili and Caitriona were kept busy providing them with fuel for their merriment.

They were afforded some respite as the ushers gathered the last few hardcore drinkers and accompanied them to their seats in time for the curtain going up. In a rare moment of camaraderie, Marsaili and Caitriona closed the doors and slumped onto a nearby bench side by side.

"Time for a quick coffee before we re-stock?" Caitriona asked.

"Please," Marsaili replied, surprised. It wasn't like Cat to offer. "Cream and one sugar."

Caitriona poured them both a coffee and sat back down beside her. She crossed her slender legs and tapped one perfectly manicured nail against the edge of her cup as she waited for the coffee to cool.

"So," Caitriona began, "been to any auditions lately?"

Marsaili sighed. This was another stumbling block in any attempt at friendship with Caitriona. While lots of staff at the theatre were ultimately aspiring for a more creative role within the entertainment industry, she and Caitriona were both actors, both female, and both around the same age. Marsaili actually suspected Caitriona was older than she was, but she hid it with her superior hair and makeup skills. Not to mention being at least three dress sizes smaller, four inches taller and infinitely prettier. Marsaili hated herself for it, but once again she couldn't help but draw comparisons, and find herself lacking.

"Not had anything in a while," she replied. In truth, she was beginning to wonder how much longer she could even call herself an 'actor'. Since leaving university with her degree in Theatre Studies she had only a handful of paid jobs to her name, and most of them were just promotional work rather than genuine 'acting'. One very exciting (but unpaid) performance at the Edinburgh Fringe three years ago had been the highlight of her non-existent career so far.

"How about you?" she asked, preparing herself for the inevitable surge of jealousy.

Caitriona sighed melodramatically and stretched out her long legs, taking a leisurely sip from her coffee before replying.

"Oh, you know, nothing much," she purred. "Just a couple of voice over jobs, an audition for an advert. My agent says BBC Scotland might want to see me for a new sitcom pilot they're working on."

Marsaili took a moment to suppress the rising bubble of envy in her chest. "Nothing much" sounded like a veritable landslide of opportunities to her. She would have given her right arm just for an agent.

"That's great," she managed, saved from having to say anything further by the sudden creaking of the bar room doors. A dark-haired head peered into the room and broke into a grin when he saw her.

"There you are!" Forbes cried, and Marsaili bounded out of her seat to greet him.

Marsaili and Forbes had both started at the theatre on the same day and had been firm friends ever since. Forbes (real name Graham – he thought Forbes made a much more dashing and sophisticated stage name) was an accomplished, classically trained opera singer. He was also one of the most popular drag acts at Glasgow's longest running gay club. Although his performing career was going from strength to strength, he still supplemented his income with a few shifts behind the bar at the theatre now and then.

"How did you get on up in teuchter-ville?" he asked with a glint in his eye. "Any gorgeous farmers catch your eye?"

"There are no gorgeous farmers where I grew up, Forbes," Marsaili replied. "There are hardly any people there at all, which is why I left."

"Well never mind that," Forbes continued, pulling her to one side, "have you met the latest addition to our own resident man candy? Lush or what!?"

"Who? Will?" Marsaili asked, trying to sound as if she hadn't noticed how handsome he was. Objectively, at least. And being handsome was no cure for being obnoxious or rude.

"Yes Will! Magnificent Will, the blonde Adonis!" Forbes swooned dramatically, and Marsaili rolled her eyes at him.

"I didn't think he'd be your type," Marsaili said, busying herself with rearranging the sugar packets in their little cubby holes. "Seemed like he had a bit of a stick up his arse to me."

"Oh, I kind of like his whole strict school teacher vibe. Crisp suit, smartly combed hair – just makes me want to mess him up a little bit." Forbes raised his eyebrows suggestively.

Just then the bar room door creaked open again. As if their conversation had summoned him, Forbes and Marsaili turned to see a perfectly combed blonde head enter the room. Instantly, she felt the colour rise in her cheeks.

Will paused for a moment and glanced down at his watch, one eyebrow raised, before speaking. "On a break already?" he asked. "You've only been here half an hour."

Marsaili looked down at her coffee cup, unsure of what to say but feeling her face grow even redder. She and Forbes were propping up the bar, Marsaili with a drink in hand, clearly skiving. She risked a glance to her left. Where had Caitriona gone?

"Oh Will, that was my fault! I told her she could take a break while I cracked on with things here." Caitriona suddenly popped up from behind the bar, sighing and blowing a wisp of hair out of her eyes in a way that managed to make it look like she had been scrubbing the bloody floors down there. Marsaili noticed that an extra button on her shirt had come undone, offering a tantalising glimpse of her firm, tanned cleavage.

Will had clearly noticed too, as now it was his turn to blush. Flustered, he averted his gaze and coughed nervously before speaking. "Thank you, Caitriona, but I expect everybody to pull their weight equally around here. Marsaili," he stumbled over her name once again, "coffee break is over now, I think. And for you, Forbes."

"Aye aye, cap'n," Forbes declared, with a wicked grin and in his campest voice. Did he actually *wink* at him?

As Forbes followed their new boss out of the bar, he couldn't help turning back mischievously to show Marsaili his appreciation of Will's backside. She stifled a giggle as the door slammed shut behind them.

"You're welcome!" Caitriona chimed. Marsaili grimaced

again, before grabbing a glass and starting on the interval orders, wishing that the double Scotch she was pouring was actually for her.

CHAPTER 4

The twenty-minute interval passed in a whirl of shouted orders, spilt drinks and broken glasses. By the time the last few stragglers had been herded back to their seats, a frazzled Marsaili was standing in a puddle of red wine, an armful of empty glasses clasped to her chest. Caitriona was behind the bar, hands on her hips, her appearance still amazingly - but unsurprisingly - flawless.

"Well," she said with a sigh, "at least the tips were good!" She reached behind her and jangled the almost full tip jar. There were even one or two notes in there, Marsaili noticed. That was at least one perk of working with Caitriona - she certainly knew how to charm the punters.

"That definitely helps!" Marsaili clattered glasses onto the bar as Caitriona started filling the dishwasher. They laboured in silence for a while, before Caitriona suddenly asked, "Are you going to the party tonight?"

It took a moment for Marsaili to click. Having missed the briefing, she'd forgotten all about the customary opening night party.

Her heart simultaneously rose and fell. Opening night parties were always good fun - and, more importantly, free - but in her hurry she hadn't picked up anything to wear. All she had were the black jeans she was wearing - which now smelled strongly of red wine - and the crumpled tee shirt and scarf she'd been travelling in all day. And her hair was a mess.

"Um," she hesitated, "I'm not sure. I'd kind of forgotten to be honest. I haven't brought any clean clothes."

"Oh, that doesn't matter!" Caitriona chirped, locking the bar doors behind them as they headed downstairs to restock. "I've only got something casual to throw on, you'll be fine as you are. It'll be a laugh!"

Marsaili shrugged. After a glass or two of free wine, she probably wouldn't care what she looked like anyway. And it was always worth going to these things - the panto cast and crew would be in residence for a couple of months. It was good to get to know a few faces, and there was always the possibility of a bit of networking with some slightly more successful thespians.

"OK," she relented. "I'm on the matinee shift tomorrow

though, so I'll only be able to stay for a couple."

Two hours later, the last bus long forgotten, she and Forbes were traipsing arm in arm down the aisle of the stalls. Marsaili had been for a pee and he had been outside for a cigarette.

"Dum dum da-dum, dum dum da-dum!" Forbes sang, as he marched her ceremoniously between the seats. She giggled, clinging on to him. She'd had rather more than a couple by now and was feeling quite merry. They were heading back to the bar for one more before last orders were called.

"Can I give you away when you get married?" Forbes asked.

"Forbes! That's my dad's job!"

"Yeah, I know, but at the rate you're going…"

"What's that supposed to mean?" Marsaili slapped his arm playfully. "You're not exactly flooded with offers yourself," she retorted.

"I know, but I'm not the settling down type, darling," Forbes replied with a flourish.

"Maybe I'm not the settling down type either?" Marsaili said, unconvincingly. Her parents had been happily married for decades, and she had always assumed that one day, she would find a lasting relationship like that too. It just wasn't proving to be quite as straightforward as she'd expected.

Forbes paused, looking her up and down, his eyebrows raised. "Sweetheart please, those hips are just made for childbearing!"

Marsaili gasped in mock outrage, and slapped him a little harder than intended. They were both giggling loudly as they made their way through the crowd and back up to the bar.

They squeezed into a pair of empty stools and ordered two more glasses of wine. Their poor colleagues, who had drawn the short straw of working the after-show shift, looked harried and overheated. Morag, a middle-aged woman who worked 9-5 in the council housing offices, eyed Marsaili carefully.

"Don't you think you've had enough?" she asked, placing the glasses in front of them anyway.

"Just one more Morag! Then I'll be heading home, Girl Guide's promise." Marsaili held up three fingers of her right hand in a little salute. Morag smiled ruefully in response, shaking her head and giving Marsaili a look that she suspected was normally reserved for her rebellious teenage daughter.

Marsaili took a long sip from her glass and surveyed the room. The free wine on offer was just the cheap house Merlot, but after the first glass it didn't seem quite so acidic. By now, she was actually quite enjoying it.

The crowd had thinned slightly, with most of the theatre staff making their excuses and heading for home. A lot of the dancers were still there though, along with a few of the more recognisable faces. The panto was always a good gig for local celebrities, and this year was no exception. A stand-up comedian, who'd recently made the step up onto national TV via a few Channel 4 panel shows, was playing the resident Dame, and a young actor who portrayed a bit of a lothario on a long running Glasgow based soap opera was Prince Charming. Marsaili couldn't help but notice he was having a rather animated conversation with Caitriona - whose "something casual" had turned out to be skin tight jeans, heels and a clingy, cleavage-enhancing top - at the other end of the bar.

"Not bad," Forbes interrupted, following her stare, "if you're into the dark haired, boyish type."

He was cute, Marsaili conceded, if a little young. Probably only early twenties. He looked Italian; all dark hair and stubble, with olive skin and vivid blue eyes. Stocky and well-built, he was casually dressed in a hoodie and faded jeans. He was laughing at something Caitriona had said and little dimples creased his cheeks as he smiled. Clearly, her charms were having the desired effect.

"Personally, however, I still prefer our very own, brooding, Christian-Gray-come-to-life," Forbes continued, gazing over at Will. Their new manager was hovering by the door of the bar, watching the proceedings and fidgeting with his suit.

"No thanks," Marsaili declared, downing the last of her wine. "I'm swearing off men for now," she slurred. Maybe that last glass hadn't been such a good idea after all. "I'm concentrating on my career!"

"As a barmaid?" Forbes asked, a quizzical expression on his face.

"No! As an actress!" she declared, exasperated. "This year's nearly gone, and next year is going to be my year! I am going to find myself an agent and get at least one decent, paid acting job."

"And if you don't?" Forbes asked.

"Then I'll give it up, accept my fate, and take a full-time job in a call centre," she said morosely. Just the thought of it made her heart sink.

"You're getting maudlin now, darling," Forbes said. "Time to go home, I think." With one arm wrapped protectively around her shoulders, he led her out of the bar. Marsaili's head was suddenly thick and swimming, crowding her with images of new babies and all her happily married, successful friends and family.

They stumbled past Will at the door and Marsaili could feel his eyes following them. Prick, she thought. Judgemental, stuck up, pretentious prick.

Once outside, the cold air hit her and Marsaili began to feel even worse. Her stomach churned, and she realised she hadn't eaten since the bacon sandwich her mum had given her in the kitchen at home that morning, which now felt like years ago. Thinking of her mum suddenly made her want to cry.

Forbes fastened her coat for her, as if she were a child, and wrapped her up in his oversized scarf. She didn't resist. "You can give me it back tomorrow," he said.

He then phoned each of them a taxi - they lived at opposite ends of town - and moved away to light a cigarette while Marsaili rested against the wall of the theatre. She was grateful - the smell of the smoke would definitely have made her throw up.

"Are you OK?" The sudden intrusion of a well-spoken voice forced her to open her eyes. Will was watching her, two mellow brown pools beneath a furrowed pair of blonde eyebrows.

"I'm fine," she replied, closing her eyes and leaning back once more against the cool brick exterior of the theatre.

"How are you getting home?"

"Forbes called me a taxi," she slurred. At the mention of his name, her friend came scurrying back.

"Are you going with her?" Will asked. "Someone should make sure she gets home OK." For God's sake, Marsaili thought, I'm not a bloody child. And I'm not even that drunk! But she didn't have the energy to voice her objections.

"No, I'm West End. She's East," Forbes replied with a shrug. "She'll be fine, she's a big girl." Marsaili silently thanked her friend for confirming her status as a fully-fledged, Functioning Adult.

Will, however, remained unconvinced. He sighed and

checked his watch, seemingly torn about something. "If you can give me ten minutes…" he started.

Just at that moment, the theatre doors opened again and they were joined outside by someone else. It was the young, swarthy soap star. He smiled at them, those dimples once again creasing his cheeks.

"Chilly night," he called, rubbing his bare hands together as his breath frosted in the air. "Don't suppose any of you are heading towards Dennistoun?"

"She is!" Forbes replied with glee, gesturing towards Marsaili.

"Brilliant! Mind if I jump in?" he asked, jogging towards them without waiting for a response, his hands trust deep in his pockets.

"Of course she doesn't!" Forbes replied, before Marsaili even had a chance to open her mouth.

"Euan," the soap star introduced himself. "Euan Campbell."

"Mackenzie. Marsaili Mackenzie," Marsaili responded in a growling voice, giving her best Sean Connery impression. Will caught her eye. Was she imagining it, or did he smirk at her?

Just at that moment, the first taxi appeared and Euan and Marsaili were unceremoniously bundled into it. "Now, straight home you two!" Forbes trilled. "No stopping off for a nightcap!" He waved them off, a wide grin on his face, clearly delighted with how the evening's events had unfolded.

CHAPTER 5

Her eyelids had turned to sandpaper. She forced them apart just enough to peer around the room, her head throbbing as everything lurched ominously to one side. Relief flooding over her, Marsaili took in her surroundings. She was on the sofa in her living room, face down and, from what she could tell, fully clothed. She waited a few moments for everything to come back into focus, before rolling gently onto her back, kicking off her shoes and closing her eyes again. The blinds of the bay window opposite were open, but mercifully it was still dark outside. There was no sign of movement from elsewhere in the flat, so she figured it was still early. Isla was always up and getting ready for school well before 7am. Marsaili couldn't risk looking at her phone to check the exact time - the light from the screen would definitely blind her.

She tried to fall back asleep, praying that when she next awoke, she would feel sober enough to at least stumble into the kitchen and get a glass of water, but sleep wouldn't come. Instead, her mind was feverishly running over and over the events of the night before.

She'd made a fool of herself. She'd drank too much and embarrassed herself in front of her new boss, whom she hadn't exactly got off to a good start with in the first place. Will would be perfectly justified in thinking she was nothing but an unreliable slob with a drinking problem based on last night's behaviour.

And then she'd been whisked off into that taxi with Euan, thanks to Forbes, bundling her off as if she were one of the Sabine women. Euan had chatted away with the careless ease of someone accustomed to making small talk, while Marsaili sat in silence, staring very hard at the back of the taxi driver's head and trying to concentrate on not...

Oh shit...

She had been sick. Violently and profusely sick. She wasn't sure if she'd made it out in time, but she remembered Euan suddenly stopping mid-sentence and shouting at the taxi driver to pull over as she lunged for the door handle. He'd even got out and come around to her side of the car to check she was ok. Congratulating herself on yet another excellent display of responsible adulting, sleep finally enveloped her.

She awoke what felt like two minutes later to the sound of the kettle boiling.

"Good morning sunshine!" Isla called from the adjoining kitchen.

Marsaili's flatmate was a morning person. They'd co-habited since university, and no matter how drunk she'd been the night before or how late they'd stumbled home, Isla was always up at sparrow fart, a cup of tea in her hand and a smile on her face. As much as she loved her friend, Marsaili cursed herself for not having managed to stumble the last few feet to the sanctuary of her bedroom.

She sat up groggily, rubbing her head and noticing with gratitude that Isla had already placed a pint glass of cold water and two paracetamols on the coffee table in front of her.

"Cup of tea and toast with peanut butter, *pour madam*," she said teasingly as she entered with a tray in her hands.

Isla was as pretty as her demeanour was cheerful; petite with a short white blonde bob and rosy cheeks. She looked angelic, but her heavenly exterior belied the fiercely competitive extreme sports person that lay beneath; someone who mountain biked, surfed and rock climbed *for fun*. Marsaili had always liked the idea of being adventurous and outdoorsy, but could never quite muster up the energy for it. A walk with the dog culminating in a few beers at a country pub was about as close as she got.

Isla was already showered and dressed for work, and smiled at Marsaili as she placed the toast and tea in front of her. "Good night?" she asked.

Marsaili swallowed the pills, her throat parched, and took a long swig of tea before she answered. "Up to a point."

Isla sat down opposite her, crossing her legs and taking a slice of toast for herself. She fixed her friend with an unblinking stare, eyebrows raised. "What happened?"

Marsaili paused for a minute and contemplated the toast. She took a slice and nibbled tentatively at a corner. When her gag reflex remained untriggered, she followed it up with more tea, as she filled Isla in on the events of the previous night.

"You'll win him round," Isla counselled, when Marsaili told

her about the terrible first impression she'd made on her new boss. "Everyone loves you; you're impossible not to love."

Marsaili rolled her eyes. "The evidence would suggest I am in fact all too possible not to love," she said.

Isla tutted. "That doesn't explain why you were so late getting home. Where were you?"

Moving on to the events of the opening night party, and her taxi journey home with Euan, Isla interrupted her suddenly.

"Wait," she said, her blue eyes round. "Euan Campbell? Off the telly? He's gorgeous!"

"I know!" Marsaili said. "And I puked on him!"

Her friend laughed. "It's not funny!" Marsaili protested. "I have to see him virtually every day for the next two months."

"Maybe it was endearing?" Isla offered. "Some men like the whole damsel in distress thing. Maybe it made you seem vulnerable?"

"Well even if it did, I can assure you it wasn't the endearing kind of vulnerable," Marsaili replied. "More the 'so drunk she can't stand up and will probably puke on your shoes' kind of vulnerable."

"I'm sure it wasn't as bad as you remember." Isla said with a smile, as she started clearing up the plates and cups from the coffee table. "I need to get going. Are you remembering I won't be home tonight? I'm off to see Findlay for the weekend. We're going abseiling."

Findlay was Isla's boyfriend. They'd met at university, on a night out in Edinburgh. Marsaili had taken a few girls through on the bus to go out clubbing with Gregor and some of his friends. Findlay and Gregor knew each other through the university rock climbing club, and it didn't take long for Isla and Findlay to bond over their shared love of the outdoors. The irony of it was laughable - Marsaili had managed to get her two best friends partnered off via her brothers, directly or indirectly, and yet they'd never introduced her to anyone she was even remotely interested in herself. As soon as Gregor or Lachlan befriended a gay opera fan, she was sure she would be able to tell Forbes that she'd found him his soulmate.

Findlay was a pilot in the RAF now, stationed at a base down in England. Isla spent most of her weekends driving up and down the M6 to see him.

"Yeah, I remembered." Marsaili flopped back onto the couch, silently relieved she'd have the flat to herself for a few days. She didn't feel like very good company at the minute.

Marsaili made it to the theatre a full twenty minutes before her shift started. She entered via stage door, wound her way through the props and backdrops that littered the backstage area and into front of house. The theatre was deserted, and she stood at the Grand Circle balcony for a moment to drink it in.

She'd initially applied for a job here, all those years ago, because she naively thought it would be a good networking opportunity. She imagined she'd be here for six months or so before she was introduced to some director or casting agent who would take one look at her and declare, "You! I must have you immediately! You are my Lady Macbeth!" before whisking her off on a worldwide tour leading to rave reviews, critical acclaim, and ultimately - of course - a Tony award. Clearly, it didn't work out that way.

She still adored it though. The slightly unloved and neglected old building charmed her, even if she was just front of house rather than centre stage. Unpopulated and in the middle of the day, as it was now, with the lights dim and the safety curtain dropped, it all looked a bit dingy and tacky. You could see the peeling paint and the uncleaned light fittings, the tattered fabric around the edges of the seats. But set the backdrops and turn on the lights and suddenly the place was transformed into a glittering, marvellous, magical auditorium, capable of transporting you anywhere in the world, anywhere in time, even, just for the price of a ticket.

"I wasn't sure we'd be seeing you today." A clipped English accent spoke behind her. She turned abruptly, startled from her thoughts, to find herself nose to chest with Will. She tried to step back, but the balustrade was directly behind her. Stumbling, Will put out a hand to steady her.

"How are you?" he asked. His charcoal three-piece suit was immaculate, a crisp and freshly ironed white shirt beneath it, and his thick straw-coloured hair combed to one side. He could have stepped out of a fifties spy novel.

"Fine thanks," Marsaili answered, though it came out as a croak. He was still standing very close to her, one hand gently cupping her elbow. She was glad she'd managed to shower and (hopefully) didn't smell of stale alcohol or vomit. Will, she couldn't help but notice, smelled of something sharp and fresh.

"Good," Will cleared his throat in that slightly awkward way he had. "Look, I think we got off on the wrong foot yesterday…"

"There you are!" A dark, stubbled figure bounded into the auditorium. Will jumped at the interruption, stepping back from her and releasing her elbow. "My taxi buddy! You were a little worse for wear last night. How are you feeling?" Euan smiled at her, all dimpled cheeks and blue eyes. He was noticeably shorter than Will, dressed in what seemed to be the same crumpled hoody, faded jeans and scuffed Converse trainers from the night before. It made him look youthful and carefree, next to Will's business like Proper Grown Up.

"Surprisingly well, all things considered," Marsaili managed to smile back. "I'm really sorry if I embarrassed myself last night…"

"Relax," Euan dismissed her with a wave of his hand. "Happens to the best of us! You were charming, in a very drunken and apologetic way." He smiled again. He really was very good looking. "Fancy making it up to me?"

"How do you mean?" Marsaili asked. Will was watching their exchange awkwardly, hovering nearby as if he didn't quite know how to extricate himself.

"A drink? After the show tonight?" Euan asked.

"Yeah, sure," Marsaili replied without thinking. "Most of us head over to the pub across the road at the end of our shift…"

"Um, Actually," Euan interrupted. Was Marsaili imagining it, or did he look shy all of a sudden? "I meant just us," he elaborated, his voice lowered. "I thought maybe we could pick up where we left off?"

"Oh… really?" Marsaili was dumbfounded. What could this charming, attractive young TV star want with her? Surely, he could have his pick of fit, lithe dancers and panto groupies?

"Yes," Euan laughed at her dubious expression. "I think you're very… interesting."

Marsaili wondered what on earth she'd been saying to him in that taxi last night. Still, it was the best offer she'd had in a long time.

"That'd be lovely," she said, conscious of Will standing beside her. "I'll meet you at stage door?"

"Perfect! Must dash, I'm due in makeup." He squeezed her arm lightly before heading round to the dressing rooms.

"Break a leg!" she called after him.

When Marsaili turned around, Will was still watching her.

30

"Um, OK, well…" he paused, rocking his weight from foot to foot. "You'd better go and get changed or you'll be late again. Have a good shift." And with that he trotted off, back down the stairs to his office.

CHAPTER 6

Almost immediately, Marsaili regretted accepting Euan's invitation. She had at least showered today and made her hair look halfway presentable, but she was wearing yet another boring top, scarf and jeans combo with an old pair of retro Puma trainers, and had only rubbed a bit of tinted moisturiser onto her face before leaving the flat. Hardly appropriate for a date - if that's what it was? - with a local TV star.

Was it really a date? Marsaili wondered, as she fastened the buttons on her work shirt. Generally speaking, a man didn't ask a woman he'd only just met out for a drink, on their own, if all he wanted was to be friends. Her memory of last night was sketchy at best, but she didn't think there'd been much chance for any meaningful conversation - let alone flirting - before she'd so rudely interrupted their taxi journey with her projectile vomiting. What could she possibly have done to appear so alluring? And hadn't she seen him, not fifteen minutes before, looking very cosy at the bar with Caitriona?

Maybe he was living up to the reputation of the playboy lothario he portrayed on TV, and just lining up a few possible conquests to tide him over the cold winter months, Marsaili thought. Sex was off the menu tonight, she decided. Not that she normally slept with people on first dates. Well, not often at least. If he was just looking for another notch on his bedpost, she wouldn't be daft enough to oblige.

Will seemed determined not to make eye contact with her. Only two other members of staff were present at the briefing, and he managed to focus his attention entirely on them alone. Marsaili felt invisible. The audience figures had dropped dramatically following opening night, and today they were operating on a skeleton staff. She would be manning the Stalls bar alone, and was silently relieved that she would be able to spend the afternoon lost in her own thoughts.

The Pantheon Theatre was over a hundred years old, and once upon a time had been the centre of Glasgow's music hall entertainment scene. But in latter years the theatre had been in decline. As the city had grown, the little corner occupied by The

Pantheon had become increasingly isolated from the main pedestrian shopping precincts, restaurants and car parks. About six months ago, with profits as low as they had ever been, the local council made the decision to sell to an umbrella company which ran some of the biggest theatres in London; that was where Will had been sent from. Maybe it was a demotion for him, Marsaili wondered. It would certainly explain the chip on his shoulder.

At the time of sale, arrangements were already in place for the annual panto, but once it was over and the new year arrived, the parent company had plans for a major refurbishment and overhaul of their spring and summer programme. Marsaili assumed that, while the work was going on, she would probably spend a few weeks mopping floors and manning stage door to give access to the workmen and decorators. Easy money, at least. And she hoped it would give her plenty of time to execute her own life-refurbishment plan - from stage door she would be able to make phone calls to agents and touring companies, maybe line up a few auditions. If she got on Will's good side (and saved some cash) they might even let her use the theatre as a setting for some arty new headshots. Her old ones were about three years out of date now.

As she headed to the office to collect her float, Marsaili was pleased to see Bruce. He smiled at her ruefully from behind a mountain of paperwork.

"How's things?" she enquired.

"Living the dream," Bruce responded, managing another tired grin. He had been employed by the council for years and was kept on during the takeover, but it looked like the stress of the transition was taking its toll. Marsaili made a mental note to bring him a coffee once the show had started.

The first punters arrived soon after she opened the bar, and Marsaili was kept busy with a steady stream of orders for teas, coffees, soft drinks and bags of sweets. Given the early hour, and the fact that the schools hadn't broken up for the Christmas holidays yet, today's audience mainly consisted of pensioners and flustered groups of mums with toddlers.

As she heard the first strains of the overture filtering through from the auditorium, Marsaili poured two coffees into paper cups, popped on some lids, and locked the bar doors before setting off to find Bruce.

Her hands were full as she approached the tiny office, so she called out to warn him of her entry. "Special delivery!" she cried, in her best high-pitched Avon lady voice, before bumping the door open with her bum and entering the room backwards.

But when she turned around, Bruce wasn't there. Sat behind the desk, pen in hand, Will was looking at her, bewildered. She stared back at him, silently cursing her bad luck.

"Is this actually all you do around here?" he asked. "Drink coffee?" Marsaili couldn't tell if his tone was teasing or admonishing.

"It's not for me," she answered defensively, before looking down at the two cups in her hand. "Well, they're not *both* for me. I brought one for Bruce. I thought he looked stressed."

"Yeah well he should be stressed, the state these accounts are in," Will dropped the pen he was holding and stretched back in his seat, pressing the heels of his hands against both eyes. He looked exhausted too.

"It's not like we're exactly rushed off our feet down there you know," Marsaili replied, at a loss for anything else to say.

Will brushed both hands through his hair, messing up his neat side parting. "I'm sorry," he sighed, not bothering to smooth the flaxen tufts back into submission. He'd taken his suit jacket off, leaving his waistcoat exposed, and the top button of his shirt was undone. Somehow the combined effect made Marsaili find him even more attractive than when they'd first met, despite the bags under his eyes. She shoved the though to the back of her mind – no good could come from fancying her boss.

"It was nice of you to think of him," Will said, "but he's gone to the bank to drop off the takings from last night."

Marsaili nodded, surprised by his apology. "Well… do you drink coffee?" she asked, gesturing with the now ownerless cup. "Shame for it to go to waste."

Will narrowed his eyes at her, half smiling. "What's in it?" he asked.

"Nothing, just black."

"Perfect," he said, an uncharacteristic grin spreading across his face. He kicked the chair out from opposite him and nodded at it. Taking this as an invitation to sit, Marsaili perched on the edge of the proffered seat and passed him the warm cup. Will took the lid off and swallowed half of it in one go. He laughed apologetically.

"Sorry," he said. "Haven't stopped all morning. Didn't realise until now how thirsty I was."

Marsaili smiled and took a sip from her own sweet, milky coffee. This simple, friendly conversation was making her inexplicably nervous, and suddenly it felt quite awkward to be sitting together in his tiny, broom cupboard office, so close their knees were almost touching.

"Are you settling in OK?" she asked, struggling for anything more original to say.

"Not bad," he answered. "There's lots to do, but Bruce seems up to the challenge. Once we've got panto out of the way and these books are in order, we should be ready to start planning for the refurb and get the new programme for next year sorted."

Marsaili nodded.

"You're one of the few people left on a contract here aren't you?" Will asked. "Bruce said most of the staff were casual these days. Is this your only job?"

It was an innocent enough question - this kind of work was a second job for most people. A bit of extra pocket money to put towards holidays or Christmas presents for the kids. But Marsaili couldn't help but feel the sting behind it, as if he were judging her, and her lack of meaningful career. In her thirties, and still 'just a barmaid'.

"I'm an actor, actually," she said, with as much confidence as she could muster.

"Really?" Will's eyebrows raised. "Anything I would have seen you in?"

Another question she hated. Everyone asked it when you said you were an actor, as if they thought they were being terribly original and witty.

"Not unless you visited Santa's grotto at Hamley's in the St Enoch centre last year, where you would have had the good fortune of seeing me in my starring role as Kandi Kane, Santa's head elf," Marsaili answered, deadpan.

Will paused for a moment before laughing, and she softened in return. If nothing else, she could at least take the piss out of herself.

"Well, you make a mean coffee," he said, dredging the last of his cup, "and I'm sure you were a very lovely elf." He smiled, holding her gaze for just a little longer than Marsaili thought was necessary.

"Marsaili," he said it as if it were a question, leaning forward in his chair and pronouncing it carefully, looking to her for approval to make sure he got it right this time. "I couldn't help but overhear that you're going out for a drink with Euan Campbell tonight. I know it's none of my business, but I don't think it's a very good idea. You should know that…"

"Pardon me?" Marsaili interrupted, her temper instantly flaring. "Who exactly do you think you are?" she continued, not giving him a chance to respond. "Did they let you dictate the personal lives of your employees in your last job? Because that's not going to fly here, let me tell you - *everyone's* at it here." It was true - Marsaili had never worked anywhere more incestuous in her life. "The only way you get a say in who I date, is if I'm dating you," she said, feeling her face flush red at the unintended implication. Will just stared at her, open-mouthed. She ploughed on regardless, talking over her embarrassment. "Well, you're right – it *is* none of your business, and there's nothing in my contract to state who I am and am not allowed to go for a bloody drink with."

She stood up, banging her knee on his desk as she went. Gathering up the empty cups and ignoring Will's stunned expression, Marsaili swept out of the room. "I'll be sure not to abandon my post again," she threw back at him, "I am nothing if not professional." She let the door slam shut behind her, leaving Will gaping at her back.

CHAPTER 7

Marsaili knew, even before she'd made it back to the bar, that this was a major cock up. She'd shouted at her boss, somehow mentioned the possibility of dating him, and simultaneously suggested that all the staff were shagging each other. She was mortified.

"My mistake," Will answered shortly, in response to her stammered attempt at an apology when he appeared to cash up her till at the end of the shift. "I'll be sure not to interfere in your personal life again."

Thankfully, Bruce was on call for the evening performance. The Friday night audience numbers were healthy, and the crowd was lively. Marsaili was pleased for the distraction. She enjoyed these types of evenings best - the bar was busy, the customers were merry, the shift passed quickly and she didn't have a chance to mull over her catastrophic tantrum at Will. It felt like no time at all before the show was over and, at just after 10pm, she found herself hanging around at stage door.

Euan had popped out to see her as soon as the curtain went down, still in his Prince Charming tights and thick stage makeup. Marsaili had to try really hard not to let her gaze drop below his waist - up close, those tights left little to the imagination.

He'd said hello quickly before running back to his dressing room to shower and change. As she paced back and forth in the narrow corridor, Marsaili couldn't decide if she was excited or not - part of her wished she could just go home and crawl into bed. Her stomach was churning, but she wasn't sure if it was first date nerves or residual guilt over the way she had spoken to Will.

"Hello, Beautiful." Out of nowhere, Euan had reappeared. He bounded up behind her and grabbed her gently around the waist, planting a kiss on her cheek. Marsaili jumped in surprise and noticed one or two of the female dancers eyeing her suspiciously.

She turned and smiled, trying not to read too much into it. Maybe he was just the overly affectionate, luvvie type? She'd met a few of them before. Maybe he was actually gay, and this really was just a friendly drink? Maybe he wanted to ask her to set him up with Forbes?

"Where to?" Marsaili asked brightly.

"Follow me," he replied with a smile.

Without asking, Euan tucked her hand into his arm and led her up towards Buchanan Street. It was a crisp, frosty winter's evening and the city was pleasantly busy with revellers and late-night shoppers. They crossed the river and wound their way underneath the garish lights of the Christmas Market at St Enoch Square, until they reached the sophisticated, understated decorations of the city's designer shopping district.

"There's a nice place at the top of Princes Square with an extended license," Euan explained.

Marsaili stopped, looking down at the scuffed toes of her trainers and the tattered ends of Forbes' oversized scarf (which she'd forgotten to return). Princes Square was an upmarket, trendy indoor shopping centre, home to an assortment of tasteful restaurants and bars. Marsaili looked more suited to a cider and blackcurrant in some dingy student pub, rather than prosecco and canapes in a posh bar.

"Euan I'm not dressed for that, they'll never let me in..." she started.

Euan smiled. "Don't be silly," he said, taking her arm again and leading her back up the street. "I know the manager; I drink in there all the time. You'll be fine."

They climbed onto the escalators and travelled all the way to the top of the square in silence. Marsaili was watching the ascent of the supersized Christmas tree beside them, which sparkled and shone all the way from the floor to the ceiling, four storeys up, when she felt Euan's hand sneak up beneath the hem of her jacket and press protectively into the bare skin at the small of her back. It stayed there as they were greeted warmly by the Maître' D, with whom Euan was on first name terms, and led to a private booth towards the rear of the bar.

Ever the gentleman, Euan took her coat and scarf and passed them to the waitress, who whisked them off to some hidden VIP cloakroom. Marsaili slid into the booth and was surprised when, rather than sitting opposite her as she expected, Euan slid in beside her. He sat so close that their legs were touching.

By now, all doubts had vanished from Marsaili's mind - this was definitely a date. He smiled at her as the waitress returned with their menus, displaying white teeth, dimples and an attractive smattering of stubble.

"So, what would you recommend?" Marsaili asked, wincing when her voice came out a couple of octaves higher than she had expected.

"Depends - what's your usual poison?"

"Well, when I can't get any cheap merlot…" she answered with a smile, "I'm a whisky girl."

"Really?" Euan looked impressed. "A curvaceous redhead who drinks Scotch? Next thing you'll be telling me you love Die Hard movies and WWF." He leaned closer and pinched her arm playfully. "Are you real?" he asked.

She knew it was a line, but despite herself, Marsaili giggled. He was laying it on thick, but she couldn't help but be flattered. "Blame it on growing up in a house full of men. I was practically raised on the stuff," she explained.

"Hmmmmm," Euan mumbled in response. The hand that had pinched her remained on her arm, and his fingertips we're now dancing gently up and down her skin. "Well, I can't claim to know that much about whisky, so I guess you should be the one making the recommendations."

Marsaili looked through the menu carefully, painfully aware of Euan's piercing blue eyes watching her every move, and when the waitress eventually returned, she ordered them both a double Balvenie. It was more than Marsaili would normally spend on a week's shopping, but she'd decided to make the most of being wined and dined.

"No ice," she emphasised to the waitress. "Just a little jug of water."

Euan nodded his head appreciatively when he took his first sip. "Nice," he said. "Very smooth."

"No ice - that's the secret," Marsaili explained. "It freezes your taste buds and kills the flavours. A wee splash of room temperature water is all you need. Just enough to open everything up a little." She took another sip herself and felt the amber liquid worm its way down her throat and into her tummy, warming her insides and making her feel more confident. Here she was, in a fancy bar, drinking expensive whisky with a handsome stranger who seemed inexplicably into her. It was a dream come true.

"So, where do you come from?" Euan asked. "Your name's Gaelic, I'm guessing? You don't sound like your typical Weegie." Marsaili smiled. Everyone back home thought she'd lost her accent over the years, while people in the city couldn't mistake her distinctive, Wester Ross lilt. Euan listened attentively as she described her parents' croft house, halfway between Kyle of Lochalsh and Plockton, looking out over the Inner Sound towards the Cuilllins of Skye.

"Sounds very pretty," he said when she'd finished. He had a habit of watching very carefully when she spoke, not once interrupting, as if she were the most interesting creature in the world. "I don't think I've ever made it any further north than Dundee."

"Where's home for you?" Marsaili asked.

"Oh, I am a Glasgow boy, born and bred. Lived here all my life." Euan told her a little about his family and childhood. He'd grown up in a high rise flat to the North of the city. His mother was a single parent and his older brother had died of an overdose at just seventeen.

"Thankfully, I fell in with a youth drama group in the area," he said, swirling the last few golden drops of whisky around in his glass and watching the legs dribble slowly down the insides. "I think it probably saved my life if I'm honest - I was heading down the same road as my brother; I'd been in trouble with the police a few times. I was lucky. That youth group helped me make something of my life, and I managed to get a scholarship to go to drama school down in London. From there, I haven't looked back." He shrugged in a matter of fact sort of way, as if his rags-to-riches tale was nothing special.

"Oh God, I'm so sorry," Marsaili said, "that's just awful." She automatically reached a consoling hand towards him, and was surprised when he grabbed it and intertwined his fingers with hers. The whisky had flushed her cheeks and made her head fuzzy. "Your mother must be so proud of you now though?" she asked with a smile.

Euan nodded sadly. He was absentmindedly rubbing the back of Marsaili's hand with his thumb. "I'm sure she would be," he said, "but she died a few years ago. Cancer."

Marsaili squeezed his hand even harder. "Oh Euan, I'm so sorry…" she didn't know what else to say. She couldn't bear the thought of one day losing her parents, not to mention her brothers as well. He must be so lonely.

"It's been just me ever since," he finished, echoing her thoughts. He placed his other hand on top of hers. "Thank you for listening," he whispered. "I don't often bring it up, but for some reason I feel like I can talk to you…"

Before Marsaili knew what was happening, his lips were brushing hers. It was barely a kiss - just a gentle grazing of their lips, the slight scratch of his stubble on her chin - but it was simultaneously tender and erotic. His mouth hovered by hers, uncertain, his breath warm against her cheek as he rested his forehead in her hair.

"I'm sorry," he whispered, nuzzling her neck. "I shouldn't have done that; we've only just met. But I couldn't help myself…"

"No, it's OK," Marsaili assured him, one hand on his cheek. He pulled back to look at her, and she smiled at him. He moved slowly closer in return. This time his other arm found its way around her waist, and there was nothing gentle about the kiss.

Hidden in the darkened booth, Euan's hands caught in the curls of her hair, Marsaili soon forgot her earlier promise to herself. Life's too short, she thought, the tragic ends of Euan's mother and brother echoing in her thoughts. She needed to stop overthinking everything and just enjoy herself, and in her wildest dreams she couldn't have created a more gorgeous man to enjoy herself with.

They stumbled back down the escalators at closing time, wrapped up in each other, and as they fell out into the cool night air Euan pressed her up against the wall of the building, his hands inside her coat, their breath fogging up the darkness around them. He kissed her neck and Marsaili felt a delicious shiver snake all the way down her body. She ran her hands through his hair as he pulled away from her.

"You've no idea how much I want you," he murmured. She kissed him more deeply in response, every fibre of her body urging her to give into the temptation.

"We shouldn't…" she whispered half-heartedly. Euan paused, stroking her hair.

"You're right," he said suddenly, taking a step back and folding Marsaili's coat around her. She couldn't help but feel a bit disappointed - she had expected him to be a little more persuasive.

Euan smiled at her and kissed her gently on the nose. Marsaili tried not to let her disappointment show on her face.

"Let's get you home," he said.

When the taxi pulled up outside Marsaili's tenement block, Euan got out and held the door open for her. He pulled her in for one last kiss.

"I'll see you tomorrow," he whispered. "Sweet dreams."

Marsaili turned and waved from the top of the steps as she let herself in. Sweet dreams indeed, she thought. Things were suddenly looking up.

CHAPTER 8

When she awoke the next morning, Marsaili remained in bed, ensconced under her duvet with her eyes closed, not wanting to break the spell. Had last night really happened? Euan Campbell, the gorgeous soap star that women all over the country fantasised about, fancied *her*.

Marsaili grabbed her phone from her bedside table and flicked through her contacts. Yup, there it was - right between her dad's seldom used mobile and Forbes' contact details, was Euan's phone number. He'd tapped it in for her in the taxi, and even put a little kiss after his name.

Marsaili couldn't help but feel a small, petty thrill of delight at the thought that it was Caitriona who had been chatting him up in the bar two nights ago, and now it was Marsaili who had snogged him and got his phone number. *Shove your BBC sitcom up your arse*, she thought devilishly.

Padding into the kitchen, Marsaili flicked the kettle on and wished Isla was home. Her mood had changed so drastically since the previous morning, and she was desperate for someone to gossip with.

She made a cup of tea and wandered into the living room, luxuriating in the joy of a lazy Saturday morning. She wasn't working until the evening call, so the whole day stretched ahead of her to do with as she pleased.

Marsaili curled up on the sofa and looked at the clock. It was just coming up for 9am, and she briefly wondered if it was too early to phone Rowan, before remembering that Rowan had a new-born baby. She was pretty sure that her day would have started long before 9am.

Leaving her mobile out of temptation's reach, Marsaili reached for the landline instead and dialled her brother's number from memory. It was Lachlan who answered, and she could hear screaming in the background.

"Morning!" Marsaili announced cheerfully. "How's things?"

Lachlan sighed and lowered his voice. "If someone doesn't get me back on a fishing boat soon, I may lose my mind."

Marsaili laughed. "Enjoying paternity leave then?" she asked. She could hear Rowan in the background now, shushing rhythmically along with Callie's cries.

"They tell you it's going to be magical, and it is… Some of the time. Then there's the night feeds, the colic, the endless bouncing, the *nappies*… I can't even figure out where half of it comes from, she's so tiny but there's so much…" Lachlan tailed off. "Are you wanting Rowan?" he asked, stifling a yawn.

"If she's available," Marsaili replied. She heard Lachlan call for his wife, and there was a slight rumble followed by more crying, as phones and babies were exchanged.

"Hey Marsaili," Rowan sounded every bit as tired as her husband. "How are you?"

"Better than you, I'm guessing." Just this brief snapshot of life at her brother and sister-in-law's home was enough to make Marsaili forget her occasional jealousy of their domestic bliss. Instead she felt unashamedly decadent and grateful for being able to lie in until 9am and then lounge around in her underwear drinking tea. "How's my gorgeous wee niece?"

"Grumpy, windy, constantly hungry and pretty much always awake. Sleep is for the weak, apparently." Rowan yawned. "But then eventually you get a burp out of her, and she gives you the most adorable little milky smile, falls asleep, and you don't even care that she's just puked all over the carpet for the fiftieth time. It's all worth it."

Marsaili smiled. Rowan may have sounded exhausted and stressed, but she knew her friend wouldn't change it for the world.

"Is my brother looking after you both?" she asked. Although she couldn't see her, she could tell Rowan was rolling her eyes.

"He's trying," she said, "But he hasn't got a clue, bless him. A force ten squall doesn't faze him, but a ten-day old baby has him utterly beside himself." Rowan lowered her voice. "Do you know the other day he actually put her sleepsuit on upside down? He was prattling away, telling me how clever it was that they'd left a little hole at the crotch to make nappy changing easier, and that it had inbuilt scratch mitts. I almost didn't have the heart to tell him the 'scratch mitts' were the feet and that hole was where her neck was supposed to go!" Marsaili couldn't help but laugh.

"Come on then," Rowan continued, changing the subject. "What's going on with you? You must have something exciting to tell me or you wouldn't have rung at this hour, so spill. I need to live vicariously through you."

Taking her time over the most interesting details, Marsaili filled her friend in on everything that had happened since they had said goodbye just a couple of days before.

"Euan Campbell!?" Rowan declared incredulously. "From *Dear Green Place*? Oh my God he's so sexy!"

"I know," Marsaili giggled. "And he's so sweet, nothing like you'd expect. He's not full of himself or anything, he's really down to earth and, well... *normal.* And he's had such a difficult life," Marsaili proceeded to summarise Euan's tragic backstory.

"So, when are you seeing him again?" Rowan asked excitedly.

"I don't know," Marsaili replied. "We exchanged numbers but I don't want to text him yet. I don't want to seem desperate."

"Let him simmer," Rowan agreed. "I'm sure he'll come running."

Marsaili smiled to herself, hoping that her friend was right. It was so long since she'd met someone she was even remotely interested in, she worried that she'd forgotten how to play the game.

"I'll keep you posted as soon as I hear anything," Marsaili promised.

"You'd better," Rowan warned. "The most exciting thing I have to look forward to today is a baby massage class. I'm dragging Lachlan along too - wish me luck!"

The two women said goodbye, Marsaili smiling at the image of Lachlan trapped in a room full of babies and mummies, listening to twinkly music whilst up to his elbows in essential oils.

Finishing off her tea, Marsaili headed to the bathroom to shower and get dressed, successfully managing not to think about Euan for at least two consecutive minutes. However, as she was drying her hair, a sudden vibration from the bedside table caught her attention

1 new message.

The notification blinked up at her. She almost didn't want to click on it, for fear of the disappointment if it wasn't him.

Morning beautiful xxx

It was only when she caught sight of her reflection in the mirror that Marsaili realised she was grinning like an idiot.

Marsaili seemed to float through the rest of her day, catching up on trashy TV and pampering herself before she headed into work. After a few polite, friendly messages back and forth, Euan eventually asked her out for another drink after the show that night. Marsaili promptly jumped back into the shower and made sure her legs were smoothly shaved. There was no harm in being prepared, she told herself. It didn't mean she was going to sleep with him.

When she arrived at the theatre that evening, Marsaili was dressed in black jeans and an emerald green slash neck jumper, which she always felt complimented her fair, freckly skin and red hair. The titian locks themselves had been tamed into submission for a change, and hung down her back in long, thick waves. She was even wearing mascara, which by her usual standards was positively glamorous.

A group of dancers were standing at stage door smoking as she approached. Marsaili smiled to them as she passed, and noticed a tall girl with dark hair glaring at her. Before she had time to consider what she had done to offend her, Marsaili was distracted by a familiar voice.

"Hey, Beautiful!"

Euan was coming out of stage door. He pushed through the dancers and hugged her. "Wow, look at you!" he said, holding her at arm's length. Marsaili smiled, pleased she'd gone the extra mile; but her pleasure was short lived when she noticed the crestfallen look on his face.

"Oh, I'm sorry, I hope you didn't go to all this effort on my account," Euan said.

"How come?" she asked, trying not to let her voice betray her disappointment.

Euan sighed; his eyes downcast. "I'm afraid I'm going to have to take a rain check on our plans for this evening. I need to meet up with my agent, and this is the only time we both have available."

Marsaili forced a cheery smile onto her face, biting back her desire to point out that, actually, he hadn't had this time available. He'd made plans with her.

"No problem," she said instead, as breezily as possible. "We can catch up some other time."

"I knew you'd understand," Euan replied with a smile. "I've got to get to make up, I'll text you later." With that he placed a chaste kiss on her cheek and disappeared back inside.

When Marsaili looked back around, the dark-haired dancer

was still watching her. This time, instead of a glare, she was smirking at her. She turned to one of her companions and whispered something, at which they all giggled.

Shocked to discover that tears were now inexplicably stinging the back of her eyes, Marsaili hurried through the main doors and into the loos.

CHAPTER 9

Marsaili shut herself in a cubicle and took a few deep breaths, furiously blinking back the tears that had sprung from nowhere. What was she playing at? One date and she was crying over him in the toilets? That wasn't her.

It wasn't until she went to rub her eyes that she remembered she was wearing makeup. Letting herself out of the cubicle, Marsaili ran some water in the sink and attempted to fix the worst of the damage, wishing she had face wipes with her so she could just take the damn stuff off. Stupid idea, dolling herself up for some bloody man.

Disappointment started to turn to annoyance. Who the hell has business meetings at ten o'clock at night? It was a brush off; it had to be. So be it, she thought. If he's not interested then he's not worth getting myself upset over. Plenty more fish in the sea.

Taking one last deep breath, Marsaili exited into the foyer and started up the stairs. Coming towards her in the opposite direction was Will.

She prepared a polite smile on her lips, hoping to get past with just a brief nod and a grunt hello. He was the last person she wanted to speak to right now.

Will inclined his head in greeting as they passed, not really catching her eye, but then suddenly stopped and grazed her elbow gently with the tips of his fingers, halting her in her tracks.

"Are you alright?" he asked, concerned.

"Yes," Marsaili replied, startled. She was cursed with the kind of skin that turned instantly blotchy and eyes that went puffy after just a few tears, but she hadn't really been crying, not properly. Surely, he couldn't tell?

"You look different?" he asked.

"Oh," Marsaili tried to brush it aside. "I just straightened my hair, and, you know…" she gestured to her face.

"No, it's not that," Will said, "I mean, you look lovely, but…" he stopped, and Marsaili felt herself colour at the unexpected compliment.

"Um, I'm sorry, what I meant was, you look… very smart. For work, you know. Very… presentable. Anyway, sorry, I must, um…" he trailed off again, gesturing vaguely over his shoulder with one hand before turning abruptly and heading off down the stairs.

Marsaili stood watching his back as he left. He really was the most contrary man she had ever met.

Forbes teased her when he saw her, of course. She'd expected nothing less.

"Ooooh, who are you making the special effort for?" he cooed. "The last time you straightened your hair and put some slap on your face dinosaurs still roamed the earth!"

They were working together in the Upper Circle, and as Forbes had been on for the matinee shift the bar was already well stocked. No customers had arrived yet, and while they were alone, he leaned over the bar, talking in a stage whisper. "Not trying to impress anyone, are we? Say, a tall, handsome, blonde hunk of upper-class totty?"

"Forbes, stop it," Marsaili answered dismissively. As much as she loved Forbes, she wasn't in the mood for his teasing tonight.

"What!?" Forbes protested. "I've seen the way he looks at you, you know," he continued mysteriously.

"What do you mean?" Marsaili asked. Forbes smiled; a wicked, knowing grin.

"He tries to hide it, but I've seen him, glancing over at you when he thinks no one can see. His eyes full of pent up desire and moody longing," Forbes was enjoying himself now, getting into his role as romantic storyteller. "It's as if he's Romeo and you're Juliet. Or Heathcliff and Cathy!" Forbes laughed. Of course, he was still taking the piss.

"Very funny," Marsaili said with a roll of her eyes.

"Can you imagine!?" he hooted. "Although even if Will really was into you," the glint was back in his eyes now. "It wouldn't matter, would it? Because you've sworn off men, remember?" Forbes was grinning at her, and not for the first time Marsaili wished she weren't so transparent.

"Who told you?" She asked with a sigh.

"Are you kidding? *Everyone* knows, sweetheart. You're the talk of the steamie! I must give myself some credit of course, for being the Fairy Godmother who whisked you both away in your pumpkin carriage the other night."

"The pumpkin carriage that I then proceeded to throw up in?" Marsaili asked.

Forbes' eyes widened as she told him everything that had happened in the past couple of days.

"And then," Marsaili finished, "when I come into work this evening, he cancels on me. Some lame excuse about having to see his agent. So yes, in answer to your previous question, I have sworn off men. For good, this time."

"Oh, sweetheart, don't give up so easily!" Forbes declared. "So, he's had to cancel one date - these things happen."

"I don't know," she said. "It just seems a bit… convenient. I don't think I believe him."

"You're just being paranoid!" Forbes declared with a flourish. "It's been so long since you've dated that you've convinced yourself every man out there is a no good, double crossing liar waiting to break your heart."

"It's not been *that* long…" Marsaili protested meekly.

"Just give him a chance," Forbes said softly, taking her hand in his. She was touched by his unusually gentle demeanour. "Trust your Fairy Godmother - what's the worst that could happen?"

As it turned out, Euan had text her before she'd even finished her shift. The message was waiting for her, the little blue light on her phone winking at her promisingly as she dug her handbag out of her locker.

So sorry I've had to cancel tonight. I'll make it up to you xxx

Deciding that she had nothing to lose, Marsaili took Forbes' advice.

Is that a promise? she replied, hoping it came across as playful rather than demanding.

When her phone buzzed and she read Euan's reply, Marsaili was astonished to find that emojis could make her blush.

CHAPTER 10

With Isla still away visiting Findlay, Marsaili decided to make the most of having the following day off and the flat to herself. She set up camp on the living room floor and surrounded herself with everything she needed - her last batch of headshots, her laptop, Isla's printer, a big pad of paper, envelopes, pens and highlighters. And a pot of tea and some chocolate digestives. The latter were Isla's, technically, but Marsaili was sure she wouldn't mind.

She started off on Google, searching for every talent and casting agent in Glasgow and Edinburgh and jotting down their details on her notepad. She'd contacted most of them in the past, but it had been a few years, and in the first flush of post-graduation excitement she had turned her nose up at some of them. Even if they were just extras agencies, anything that got her some paying work and more experience to include on her CV was worth it. Artistic integrity could wait until she had more options.

Next, she spent some time padding out her CV. It had been a year or so since her last acting job - an unpaid part in a student short film - so she tried to make what she did have sound a bit more impressive, without blatantly lying about anything. Then she typed up a covering letter, emphasising her *'long-standing professional connections with the iconic Pantheon Theatre in Glasgow'*, hoping that it might conceivably be misconstrued as performance connections, rather than hospitality.

Before she knew it, it was midday. Marsaili was still sat in her pyjamas, surrounded by scribbled sheets of paper, a cold cup of tea in her hands and biscuit crumbs all over her top when the buzzing of the flat's intercom forced her from her nest.

"Hello?" she called, not doing a very good job of hiding the frustration in her voice. If this was another bloody parcel for the downstairs neighbour she would scream. As one of the few inhabitants of their block who was home a lot during the day, Marsaili had become a sort of informal sorting office. She should start charging.

"Hey, it's me!" The cheerful baritone of her twin, Gregor, greeted her, and Marsaili suddenly remembered that they'd made plans to go out for lunch that day. He'd travelled through from

Edinburgh to take her out, and here she was not even showered yet.

"Hey, come on up," she replied, trying to sound relaxed.

She unlatched the door so that he could let himself in, and returned to the mess in the living room.

"What on earth are you doing?" Gregor asked when he found her. "I thought we were going for lunch?" He checked his watch - a TAG Heuer. One of many, Marsaili knew. He collected them. "I made reservations for 1pm."

"I know, I'm sorry. I won't be much longer. If you help, we'll be twice as fast," Marsaili nodded to the floor opposite her.

With a sigh, Gregor removed his designer blazer and draped it over the back of the sofa. Marsaili smiled at him. "Thank you," she said sweetly as he sat down, cross legged.

Despite being twins, Marsaili and Gregor weren't particularly alike. Where her hair was auburn, his was dark, almost black, although they shared the same unruly curls. Gregor wore his hair a little longer than the partners at his law firm would have liked, and it turned over the collar of his carefully ironed Thomas Pink shirt. When he was rock climbing, he had to wear a hairband to keep it out of his eyes.

"What are you doing, anyway?" he asked, looking at his sister. "And thanks for going to all this effort on my behalf," he added, nodding at her oversized, faded pyjama top that declared in bold letters 'EAT, SLEEP, SNOOZE, REPEAT'.

"Sorry, I forgot," Marsaili admitted with a shrug. "I'm canvassing agents, trying to get my career back on track."

Gregor nodded. He'd never really understood how she could live from hand to mouth the way she did, or why she didn't just give it up and get a real job with a steady pay check.

"You're on stamp duty," Marsaili instructed, passing him a book of second-class stamps and a stack of handwritten envelopes.

Gregor dutifully worked his way through the pile, grateful that stamps no longer had to be licked to make them stick.

"What exactly are you hoping will come of this?" he asked tentatively. They had argued about Marsaili's career choices in the past, and he wasn't keen to fall out again.

"Just work," she replied. "Any work. Or maybe that I'll be picked up by an agent. I'll dress up as a crisp packet and dance down Sauchiehall Street if it pays, I don't care. I just need something to get me started."

"But where do you see it all going?" In spite of himself, Gregor persisted. He had nothing against actors, or barmaids for that matter, but it frustrated him to see his sister waste her potential. She was bright and intelligent. When they were kids, it was Marsaili who had always done well at school and in her exams. But then after graduation, she seemed to stagnate. "Is that really what you want to be doing for the rest of your life?" he asked.

"Well not that specifically, obviously," Marsaili stopped stuffing her current envelope and frowned at her brother, exasperated. "But everyone has to start somewhere. Gigs like that are stepping stone, that's all."

"It's just… and please, don't bite my head off," Gregor began. "We've already been out of uni for ten years. Do you not think if you were going to become a West End star, you'd be at least heading in that direction by now?"

Marsaili sighed. "Look, I know I'm probably never going to be famous; I'm not stupid. But there's lots of options out there - extras work, theatre in education, voiceovers. I've just not pushed myself enough recently. I need to get back out there and give it another go."

"Is that really what you want though?" Gregor persisted. "Performing shows about bullying in school halls, spending your life travelling in a van with sweaty college graduates, living out of a suitcase?"

Marsaili just shrugged again in response. "What would you prefer?" she asked. "That I spend my days in a depressing, windowless cubicle, cold calling people and trying to sell them insurance or mobile phone upgrades?"

"No, of course not," Gregor replied. "But there are other things to life, you know. A job isn't the be all and end all."
Marsaili rolled her eyes. "That's easy to say when you've got your dream job and you're earning big bucks doing it," she said.
"Fair point," Gregor conceded. "But what will you do if it doesn't all work out like you've planned? What's the back-up plan?"

Marsaili sighed again. She didn't want to fall out with her brother, but all the enthusiasm she had woken up with that morning was being sapped from her.

"I don't have a back-up plan," she admitted. "This is it. This is the only plan. There's just nothing else I can see myself doing."

Gregor shrugged, as she passed him the last pile of addressed envelopes. "Fair enough," he said with a sigh. "If nothing else, I admire your commitment."

Gregor treated her to lunch at a fancy grill house in the West End. They ate steaks, drank too much whisky and made a conscious effort not to spend any more time discussing their differing careers. Marsaili showed him pictures of Callie, and Gregor promised he would be going home for Christmas. He'd been too busy to make the long journey North since she'd been born, and was yet to meet his only niece.

"And will you be bringing a little piece of arm candy with you this year?" Marsaili teased. A string of girls had slept beneath the eaves in Gregor's old room over the years.

Her brother smiled slowly. "Actually," he said, "I will be bringing someone home this year."

"Surprise surprise," Marsaili responded.

"This one's different," Gregor said slowly. "She's… special."

"Why?" Marsaili scoffed. "What is she? A hyper-flexible yoga instructor with no gag reflex?"

Gregor ignored the jab. "She's a lawyer, actually. We met at work. And I think this could really be something serious."

"Wow," Marsaili said, genuinely taken aback. "I don't know what to say. Have you been tamed at last?"

Gregor laughed, twirling the stem of his nosing glass in his fingers. "Maybe," he said eventually. "I think you'll like her."

Marsaili couldn't help but roll her eyes. Most of Gregor's previous conquests made Katie Price look like an Oxford professor. Lawyer or not, she couldn't imagine this one being any different.

"What about you?" Gregor asked. "Any 'arm candy' on the go?"

Now it was Marsaili's turn to smile. "Actually, dearest brother, I do." She gave him the PG rated summary of her date with Euan, withholding for now the details of his minor celebrity status.

"It's early days," she finished. "But he's nice."

"About time," Gregor replied with a smile.

They finished the last of their whiskies and Gregor paid the bill. Marsaili walked with him to the train station just as dusk was starting to fall.

"Thanks for coming through," she said as they hugged farewell. "And for helping me with my envelopes. And for lunch."

"No worries," Gregor replied. "Just promise me one thing," he said.

"What?"

"Think about what I said, Marsaili. I don't want to fight," he added quickly, "but I can't bear seeing you waste your potential. I'm not saying you should get a job that you hate, but… just think about what other options you might have. You've got so much to offer. You're still living like a student; I don't want you to wake up one day and realise that life has passed you by."

Marsaili pursed her lips, forcing herself to nod.

"I'll think about it," she promised, although deep down she hoped that by Christmas, she might be able to tell him that the back-up plan wasn't going to be necessary.

CHAPTER 11

"And a black coffee," the elderly gentleman said with a smile, guddling in his pocket for his faded leather wallet. His wife was with him, and as he ordered their drinks, she found a seat at the rear of the bar. Checking over his shoulder to make sure that she was out of earshot, he leaned conspiratorially over the worktop to Marsaili.

"And pop a double brandy in it, would you? Every year she makes me come to the bloody pantomime, and this is the only way I can get through it!" His eyes twinkled as he spoke, and Marsaili had to suppress a laugh.

She fastened the lid down securely on his paper cup and passed him the two coffees, one with cream and sugar and one with the illicit brandy. He slipped her a pound coin and a wink as he took them from the counter. Marsaili smiled - it was another quiet matinee and the bar was virtually empty. The elderly man joined his wife at the small table, and as Marsaili watched he took her hand gently in his gnarled, arthritic fingers. The woman was clearly dressed up for their day out, all soft white curls, powder and shimmery pink lipstick. She smiled at him as he spoke to her.

Marsaili smiled, trying not to make it too obvious that she was watching them. After all those years, he still took his wife to the panto every Christmas, just because he knew it would make her happy. Marsaili hoped that she would grow old with someone like that, and the image of Euan as an older man briefly flitted through her mind - salt and pepper hair, a little paunch and glasses, but still handsome, with wrinkles around his playful blue eyes.

As if on cue, she felt her phone buzz in the pocket of her apron. She shouldn't really have it on her during her shift, but practically everyone did. Checking that no one else was around, she snuck it out under the cover of the bar and clicked on the message icon.

About to take to the stage. Give me a wave from the back! xxx

Marsaili grinned. She hadn't seen much of the pantomime yet, other than tiny snippets as she snuck through the auditorium to take the hidden shortcuts between the bars and the office or staff room. She'd spent much of the previous evening texting Euan, and had agreed that if it was a quiet shift, she would come in and watch a bit during her coffee break. He seemed very keen for her to see him in action.

She tapped out a quick reply and popped her phone back in her pocket. The elderly couple were taking their coffee cups and heading through to the auditorium, and Marsaili checked the clock. Ten minutes until curtain up - if she got everything ready for interval now, she would be able to take her break early, and maybe even extend it a little if no one was around to notice.

A few more customers wandered into the bar for sweets, soft drinks and coffees, but Marsaili was able to get two more pots of coffee made and ready on the warming plates, and the sweet racks refilled before the overture was finished. She locked the bar doors and headed through to the auditorium just as the curtains were going up.

This year's pantomime was *Cinderella*, and the action opened with the ubiquitous heroine sweeping the floors. When it came to the theatre, Marsaili wasn't fussy about what she watched; one of the main perks of her job was the complimentary tickets she was able to make use of to indulge her favourite hobby. She could get lost in any live show, from musical theatre, to Cirque du Soleil, to Shakespeare. The magic of a live performance never failed to enthral her, and as the ugly sisters made their entrance - to rapturous applause - and began quipping back and forth, she found herself laughing and getting absorbed in the familiar story. Yes, it was cheesy and the jokes were predictable, but that was the joy of panto. It wasn't meant to be sophisticated.

After the first song and dance number, Marsaili unexpectedly felt her heart start to beat a little faster and her tongue stick to the roof of her mouth. Stage right, Euan had just made his entrance, in full Prince Charming get-up, accompanied by his comic foil, Chester the Jester. The room was suddenly full of wolf whistles and cheers, and hidden in the darkness Marsaili blushed and smiled to herself.

Euan looked classically, dashingly handsome; a chiselled chin, his shirt unfastened just enough to show the smooth, firm skin and dusting of dark hair at the top of his pecs. He paused centre stage as the wolf whistles continued, smiling knowingly and raising a suggestive eyebrow at the audience. Marsaili knew he wouldn't be able to see her in the dazzle of the stage lights, but she childishly looked out for some private signal from him nonetheless. He was clearly loving the attention, and for a moment he didn't look anything like the Euan she was beginning to know - the slightly scruffy, humble orphan from an impoverished background. Here, he looked every inch the confident, gorgeous, leading man.

Engrossed in the performance, the time ticked away much faster than Marsaili had realised. It wasn't until Prince Charming and Cinders had sang their first love song - Euan turned out to have a lovely, smooth, tenor voice with just enough vibrato - and shared their first kiss (Marsaili tried not to feel too jealous at that, or to notice how tightly Euan clung on to the waist of the pretty young blonde playing Cinderella) that she suddenly noticed the ushers making their silent entrance with the ice cream trays, ready for the interval. Grateful that she had no pre-ordered drinks to prepare, Marsaili crept from her seat in the back row and trotted briskly back to the bar.

As she filled paper cups with coffee and dished out bags of sweets, Marsaili wondered if the customers noticed that the barmaid seemed particularly happy that day. She certainly felt as if she was smiling more, and had more pleasant conversation to make with the few people who ventured out of their seats for something other than a Cornetto. Euan really was very good, she thought, even if the role of Prince Charming didn't demand much in the way of dramatic flair. He was chivalrous, sweet, funny and most of all, handsome. The perfect romantic interest. She couldn't believe her luck.

The elderly gentleman she had served earlier returned, having left his wife in the auditorium. Marsaili guessed she would be tucking into an ice cream while he acquired some more illicit alcohol.

"Enjoying the show?" Marsaili asked with a smile. He rolled his eyes in return.

"Better than last year's, but that's not really saying much," he said, although his eyes crinkled as he spoke. Marsaili suspected he enjoyed this annual tradition rather more than he wanted to let on.

"Same again?"

He nodded, and Marsaili poured the double brandy into the bottom of a paper cup before splashing the coffee on top. The elderly man slipped her another pound coin, accompanied by a little wink.

By the time she'd re-stocked and swept and mopped the barroom floor, Will was making his way round to cash up the tills.

They hadn't spoken much following her little outburst in his office the other day, which Marsaili was still embarrassed about. She smiled as he entered, hoping her good mood might prove to be infectious.

"You seem very chirpy today," Will commented, as he stuffed the meagre profits into a padded envelope and handed Marsaili back her float.

She smiled and nodded in response, eager to be finished as quickly as possible. As compensation for cancelling their drinks on Saturday night, Euan was taking her out for dinner between the matinee and evening performances. They didn't have much time, so they were only going to the all you can eat Chinese buffet down the road, but Marsaili was still keen to freshen up and put on some makeup before she met him.

"Did you have a nice weekend?" Will asked. He seemed to be making a concerted effort to be friendly.

"Yes, thank you," Marsaili responded, following his lead. "My twin brother came through from Edinburgh and we went out for steak and whisky."

Will looked surprised. "Steak and whisky?" he echoed. "A girl after my own heart." He smiled approvingly.

"How about you?" Marsaili enquired.

Will sighed heavily. "Spent most of it on the phone to my soon-to-be ex-wife's lawyer so…" he shrugged, as if to indicate the inevitable shittiness of the situation.

"Oh, I'm sorry," Marsaili said. She hadn't realised he was married.

Will smiled ruefully. "Steak and whisky would definitely have been better," he said.

They considered each other for a moment, before Will picked up his keys and gestured to the door. "I'm sure I'll manage to piece together some semblance of a social life eventually," he said, making his way out of the bar.

The words were out of Marsaili's mouth before she could stop herself from saying them.

"If you ever need anyone to show you around," she started, before stopping as her brain suddenly caught up with what her mouth was doing. "I mean, I was new here once too. I know what it's like. If you ever wanted to, I wouldn't mind showing you the sights…" she trailed off, realising that it would inevitably sound like she was - albeit very awkwardly - asking him on a date.

"Oh," Will looked stunned. "Thank you. I must say, you're all very kind. Caitriona's already offered to do the same."

"Oh, never mind then," she said, a little too brightly. "I'm sure Cat will show you a good time."

She turned away and busied herself wiping the bar for the umpteenth time, not turning back until she heard the sound of Will's departing footsteps and the doors swinging shut behind him.

CHAPTER 12

The main problem with a date at a buffet restaurant, Marsaili reflected, was choosing what to eat. She remembered going out for Chinese buffets with her last long-term boyfriend, when they had already reached the stage of being so comfortable with each other that they both ate until their stomachs were bursting, before rolling home to curl up together on the sofa, watch movies and share a tub of Ben and Jerry's. Part of her missed that. Although it was hardly the stuff of romance novels, there was something lovely about being so secure in your relationship that you didn't feel self-conscious or constantly worry about what the other person thought of you.

But this was only a second date, and therefore an entirely different situation altogether. Not only was there the issue of garlic breath or getting spring onions stuck in her teeth, but she didn't want to look either greedy or restrictive about her diet. Hoping that she would strike the balance of seeming relaxed and carefree whilst also being relatively health conscious, she opted for stir fried veg, noodles and chicken with cashew nuts. She bypassed the chips and deep-fried prawn toast - which was actually her favourite - but promised herself that she would come back for a slice of cheesecake from the dessert table.

Euan was already back at the table when she sat down, a huge pile of food on his plate and a pint of lager by his elbow. He clearly had no worries about what was or was not appropriate date food. He smiled at her briefly before tearing into some tempura prawns.

"So, what did you think?" he asked, his mouth full.

"I thought you were great," Marsaili replied honestly. "The female members of the audience certainly loved you," she said, with what she hoped was a suggestive smile.

Euan didn't seem to notice what she was implying. "What about the song?" he pressed instead. "Did you like it? Singing was never really my thing, but they gave me a voice coach and I think it's worked out OK."

"You have a lovely voice," Marsaili agreed. "Very Michael Buble."

The conversation continued along that vein for a while, Euan asking about specific parts of the show and Marsaili agreeing with his assessment of his performance. She couldn't help but think how different this felt from their last date. He was nowhere near as attentive or affectionate, and seemed more interested in his food and critiquing himself rather than listening to her. It must be the timing, Marsaili thought. They'd squeezed this meal in at the last minute, sandwiched between performances. It was only natural he had other things on his mind.

"I'm actually an actor as well," Marsaili said eventually, when the conversation moved on to the second act and she had to confess that she wasn't able to watch any of that.

"Really?" Euan asked. He looked surprised. "Who's your agent?"

"I don't have one," she confessed. "To be honest, I haven't had much work at all. But I'm going to give it one last push. I spent yesterday sending out my head shots to some more agents, so keep your fingers crossed for me!"

"Did you send anything to Eileen Kennedy?" he asked, shovelling another forkful of fried rice into his mouth.

Marsaili silently racked her brain. She thought the name sounded familiar, but she'd been through so many websites that she couldn't be sure.

"Um, maybe…"

"Do you have any of your head shots on you?" Euan was suddenly very business-like, firing questions at her one after the other. She shook her head.

"Eileen's my agent," he explained, taking a long swig from his pint glass before wiping his hands on his jeans. "If you give me one of your head shots, I'll pass it on if you like? She'll pay more attention to it if it comes from someone she already knows."

"Are you serious?" Marsaili was overwhelmed. This would easily be her most promising opportunity ever. "That's not why I went out with you," she said in a hurry, anxious that he might think she was only interested in taking advantage of his connections. In their industry, nepotism was a powerful force.

"I know," Euan smiled, and for the first time that day he reached across and took her hand in his. "Honestly, I'd be happy to help. I know how hard it is to get a break in this business."

Marsaili squeezed his hand in silent gratitude. Not only was he gorgeous - if you ignored that piece of spring onion currently stuck in his teeth - but he was generous and thoughtful too.

Euan was looking at her intently. "We could pop round to your flat and pick up a head shot after the show tonight?" he suggested. "My understudy's doing the matinee tomorrow, so I don't need to hurry home…" The unspoken possibility hung in the air between them, making Marsaili blush and her tummy somersault. The mood had suddenly swung back in a much more un-business-like direction.

"What a good idea," she replied.

Later that night, as the last of the performers made their way home from stage door and the lights in the theatre went out, Marsaili and Euan decided to walk back to Marsaili's flat. It was a long way from the theatre and normally Marsaili would take the bus, but it was a beautiful winter's night and the cold gave them a convenient excuse to walk with their arms wrapped around each other, Marsaili's hand slipped into the back pocket of Euan's jeans.

He twirled her hair around his fingers as they walked and talked. Every so often their footsteps slowed and he drew her into his arms for a lingering kiss.

By the time they were climbing the steps to Marsaili's top floor flat the tension had become almost unbearable. Marsaili found herself giggling as she fumbled with the key, her hands suddenly trembling.

"My flatmate will be asleep," she whispered, "she has school in the morning."

"How old is your flatmate?" Euan mumbled, his hands snaking around her waist and his breath warm against her neck.

"She's a teacher, silly," Marsaili replied, squirming out of his reach and into the darkness of the hallway.

No sooner was the door closed behind them than Euan's mouth found hers, urgent and hungry. He pressed her against the wall and Marsaili dropped her handbag, her arms snaking up around his neck instead. All pretence forgotten, they hastily fumbled with scarves and heavy winter coats, their cold fingers clumsy against the buttons.

"Shhhhhhh…" Marsaili whispered, giggling as they stumbled across the hallway and fell into her bedroom door. Euan's hands were already under her tee shirt, deliciously cool against her skin. He whipped her top expertly up and over her head in one deft movement, and then his hands were in her hair again as they collapsed together onto her bed.

"Do you have...?" Euan asked.

"Top drawer," Marsaili replied, lying back while Euan leant over her and rifled quickly through her bedside table. She smiled as she watched him, enjoying the view. His shirt had ridden up across his stomach, and the taut muscles of his torso were clearly visible beneath the dark smattering of hair that covered his skin.

Having located what he required, Euan turned back to her and smiled. His hair was tousled and he was looking at her in a way that made Marsaili's insides melt. He stroked her forehead with the back of his hand as he leaned over her.

"Now," he whispered, his fingers running from her hairline and tracing a trail over her nose, her lips and her chin, down her neck, over her collarbone and towards the lacy edge of her bra. "You must try to be very, very quiet..."

CHAPTER 13

The voices woke her - the deep rumbling of a male baritone coming from the kitchen, punctuated every now and then by a high pitched, girlish giggle. Thinking that Findlay must be visiting, Marsaili rolled over groggily, stretching out in a starfish like she always did and enjoying the coolness of the sheets on the other side of the bed. Just as she was settling off to sleep again, she realised that Isla had only returned from her most recent visit down south the previous day. Why would Findlay have come up here so soon?

And then she remembered that, for once, the other side of her bed should have been neither cool nor empty. Simultaneously curious and worried, she rolled out of bed and pulled on a pair of pyjama shorts and a vest. She roughly combed her fingers through her hair and, hoping that she looked attractively dishevelled, ventured out in search of the muffled voices.

She found them in the kitchen; Isla and Euan standing opposite one another, leaning against the cabinets and enjoying an animated conversation. Isla was already dressed for school, and Euan was wearing his clothes from the previous night. They were both drinking coffee and there was a tray laid on the counter, complete with a teapot, mug, jug of milk, toast and jam.

"There you are!" Euan exclaimed, noticing her in the doorway. He put his mug down and greeted her with a kiss and a hug. "Morning, Beautiful."

"Morning," Marsaili responded. Isla was grinning at her from behind Euan's turned back, her eyes nearly bursting out of their sockets. She was mouthing something and pointing at him excitedly, and looked as if she were about to start jumping up and down on the spot.

"I was just making you breakfast," Euan was saying. "Your lovely flatmate here was kind enough to lend me a hand." He gestured towards Isla and Marsaili thought she saw her friend blush. Isla *never* blushed.

"You didn't need to do that," she said, touched once again by his thoughtfulness, and trying to ignore Isla's gaping, open-mouthed impression of an over-excited goldfish. "I thought we might go out for breakfast? There's a great wee deli down the road."

Euan looked abashed, inhaling through gritted teeth. "Sorry, but I can't. I'm afraid I have to scoot off." He continued in a rush, rubbing her shoulder with one hand in a conciliatory manner. "I know I said I had the morning off, but my understudy called in sick. I need to run home and get showered and changed before I go in. Duty calls!" He kissed her cheek and was wriggling into his jacket before Marsaili had a chance to say anything else.

"Are you working tonight?" he asked, heading for the front door as he spoke. She shook her head, following him into the hall.

"Not tonight," she said. "I'm helping Isla's class rehearse for their Christmas concert."

"That's a pity," he said, his face downcast. "I was thinking I could treat you to a late drink and then maybe we could head back here…?" Euan's voice trailed off suggestively, as he squeezed her hip and pulled her in for a more passionate kiss.

"You could still come over here after, if you like?" she suggested.

"Is that a promise?" Euan murmured in her ear, making her skin go all tingly and the hairs on the back of her neck stick up.

Marsaili was shutting the door behind him as Isla emerged into the hallway.

"Oh. My. *God!*" she squealed, waving her hands in the air like a giddy schoolgirl. "That really was him! *Euan Campbell!* And you slept with him!?" Marsaili felt her cheeks colouring as she drifted back into the kitchen for a cup of tea.

"Maybe…" she said with a smile, gripping the mug with both hands and blowing on the hot, golden brown liquid. "He's lovely, Isla. Really, really lovely."

"I know!" Isla took up position opposite her in the kitchen, her eyes still agog. "But I didn't expect him to wander out of your bedroom on a random Tuesday morning. I nearly choked on my bloody cornflakes!"

Marsaili laughed. "What were you two talking about? Did he say anything about me?"

Isla ran a hand over her shiny little bob, although it was sitting perfectly as always and there was not a stray hair in sight. "He was very polite. He introduced himself, explained he had to run off earlier than expected and that he wanted to take you breakfast in bed before he left. I gave him a hand finding what he needed." Isla downed the last of her coffee. "Are you sure you're still ok for helping out at rehearsals tonight? I need to get the scripts photocopied and handed out first thing. Some of the P7s are developing a serious attitude problem, so no doubt there will be tantrums to deal with when the boys find out they have to wear makeup and put tea towels on their heads." She gathered up her things and headed for the door.

It was only after Isla had left, laden down with props, scripts, music scores and programmes, that Marsaili realised she hadn't given Euan her headshots.

CHAPTER 14

Much to her surprise, Marsaili actually quite enjoyed helping out at Isla's school. She arrived just before 3pm, as children were scurrying to and fro collecting lunch boxes and coats. The friendly lady at the office buzzed her through the secure entrance and gave her directions to the staffroom.

The minute she stepped through the doors, she was flooded with memories. Primary schools didn't vary that much, it would seem. The walls were papered in brightly coloured milskin, decorated with children's paintings, stories and photographs of them working. The unique but instantly familiar smell invaded her nostrils; a mixture of cooking odours, rubber soled shoes, wax crayons, paper and paint. Marsaili could almost imagine that if she closed her eyes, she would find herself back in her old one room school, with a view over the loch and its resident otters.

This school, however, was in the centre of Glasgow, and there wasn't even a potted plant outside the windows, let alone water or wildlife. The playground was a field of concrete, painted with hopscotch grids and snakes and ladders. The building itself was focused around a double height central well, with the game's hall at the bottom. Infant classrooms crowded the perimeter, with sandpits, water trays and painting shirts scattered haphazardly outside their doors. The senior classes were on the floor above, with a balustrade looking down onto the hall below.

The hall itself was currently home to a large, slightly lopsided Christmas tree, and a platform which had been constructed at one end as a makeshift stage. The sounds echoed around Marsaili as she took everything in - children chattering, teacher's voices rising over the din and shoes squeaking on the linoleum floor. There was something comforting about the familiarity of it all.

"Who are you?" A small voice made Marsaili turn, startled. A little girl was looking up at her, her shirt collar grubby and her tie askew. She had wild brown hair that her mother had clearly tried to contain in two French plaits, but the bobbles had worked themselves loose and frizzy tendrils now framed her face. Marsaili smiled at her.

"My name's Marsaili. I'm here to see Miss Munro."

The girl screwed up her face. "I can't do my laces," she said matter-of-factly. She held her foot out and tapped it on the floor to demonstrate, one pair of laces flapping from side to side.

"Oh! Would you like me to…?" Marsaili asked.

The little girl looked at her with an expression of mild disdain. Bemused, Marsaili knelt down and quickly fixed the offending lace. "There you…" she began, but the child was already scampering off without a backwards glance.

The bell rang then, and suddenly the hall was filled with children thundering out of classrooms, tearing down the stairs and across corridors and out into the playground. Pushing through the crowds like a salmon swimming upstream, Marsaili found the staff room and hung her coat and bag on the pegs, slightly disappointed at the banal normality of it. She'd always imagined illicit, clandestine activities taking place behind the staffroom doors, but found instead just a small kitchenette, some slightly tatty chairs and tables and a sink full of dirty coffee mugs.

Marsaili was found loitering in there by an older man with greying temples and a beard. When she explained why she was here he collared a passing pupil and made him show her upstairs to Isla's classroom.

The scene within could best be described as organised chaos. Youngsters were scattered everywhere, some still small and child-like, some taller and clearly on the brink of adolescence, whilst others occupied that awkward space between the two, all gangly and spotty and uncomfortable in their own skin. Marsaili spotted Isla talking animatedly to a crowd of the taller, more confident looking ones - undoubtedly the top tier of the social hierarchy, she thought. School could be pretty ruthless when it came to friendships, from what Marsaili remembered.

The floor was covered in long rolls of paper that were obviously in the middle of being painted as backdrops, depicting various half-finished scenes from the nativity. Marsaili picked her way around them carefully to join Isla at the front of the class, who glanced in her direction and raised her eyebrows briefly in greeting. Isla issued some instructions and sent the group of pupils their separate ways before turning to Marsaili and flashing an exhausted smile.

"Thank God you're here," she said. "Today has been mental."

Marsaili smiled. "It certainly looks that way," she said, gesturing to the general mayhem that reigned all around them.

"What, this? This is nothing," Isla said. Marsaili shuddered to think how much worse it could get.

"Now, how do you feel about taking half a dozen kids down to the hall to block out the first act?"

Marsaili panicked. "No, you never mentioned anything about being on my own? I thought I was just here to help you!"

"Oh, come on, they're just kids!" Isla pleaded. Marsaili looked around her, struggling not to feel intimidated. Some of these 'kids' were taller than she was.

"You'll be fine," Isla continued. "I need to stay up here with the stage crew to get the backdrops and props finished. If I leave them unattended with free access to paint and staple guns God only knows what I'll come back to. All you'll be doing is running through some basics with the principals. Please? They're good kids! And they were very excited when I told them a real-life actor was going to be working with them."

Marsaili pondered for a moment, before coming to the conclusion that there was no reasonable way to talk herself out of this. How difficult could half a dozen twelve-year olds be?

"Fine," she sighed, a touch more melodramatically than was necessary.

As it turned out, the kids were actually really good fun. She fielded the usual questions about whether or not she'd been on TV - they didn't seem too impressed when she admitted that no, she hadn't - and did a few warm ups before running through the first act. It was basic nativity fodder, but the kids were sparky and enthusiastic, and the more she worked with them the more she remembered why she'd fallen in love with performing in the first place.

Having attended such a small, isolated primary school, drama had formed a very small part of the curriculum; with no specialist teachers around, it kind of fell by the wayside, with the exception of their own annual nativity. The nearest theatre was in Inverness, and her mum took her for the first time when she was twelve. They'd watched *A Midsummer Night's Dream* and from then on Marsaili had known exactly what she wanted to do when she grew up.

It was all going smoothly, until Joseph and the angel Gabriel got into an animated debate over which of them had got their lines wrong. Marsaili attempted to interrupt them, but their arguing only intensified.

"Oy!" she found herself declaring loudly, jumping slightly when her voice echoed around the hall. The two boys stopped abruptly, both looking at her and frowning uncertainly. "Cut it out," she said. "That is not how co-stars speak to each other. Be respectful please."

Noticing that Joseph was looking over her shoulder, Marsaili turned to find Isla watching them. She had a stern look on her face, but the raised eyebrow that she flashed at Marsaili told her that she was amused.

"I'm very disappointed to hear that our guest has had to speak to you two about your behaviour," Isla lectured in her best teacher-voice. She paused to let her words sink in, and the two boys looked suitably chastised. "Time's up for today, go back to class and get your bags packed. No more nonsense tomorrow, thank you."

The children scurried off, and Isla hovered for a moment before following. She smiled at Marsaili. "You'd make a good teacher," she said with a wink.

Marsaili didn't have time to dismiss the suggestion before Isla turned and followed the children up the stairs. It wasn't the first time someone had said this to her, but there was something so cliché about the failed actor becoming a drama teacher that she could never even bring herself to consider it. The words *those that can't do, teach* would have haunted her forever.

As she was heading back to the staffroom to gather her coat and bags, Marsaili felt her phone buzz in her back pocket. She pulled it out excitedly, certain that it would be Euan confirming their plans for that evening. She should have time to pick up some wine on her way home, shower and shave her legs before he arrived.

Opening up the message, it took Marsaili a second or two to realise that it didn't say what she was expecting it to say. Confused, she stopped and read it again more carefully.

Hey, Beautiful. So sorry to let you down, I can't make tonight. Something's come up. I'll explain tomorrow. Exx

Marsaili stared at the screen for a few seconds longer, until the disappointment really settled in. He'd stood her up. Again. And with another half-assed excuse, too. Disappointment turned to anger, and she flung her phone into her handbag without bothering to type out a reply. *Fuck him,* she thought.

By the time Isla had appeared, Marsaili's anger was simmering just enough to be visible. It didn't take her friend long to figure out what had happened.

"Don't make excuses for him," Marsaili said, before Isla could say anything. "I don't want to hear it right now."

Isla regarded her carefully for a minute, clearly debating what would be the right thing to say.

"Pub?" she asked eventually.

Marsaili smiled. "You read my mind."

CHAPTER 15

The following day, grateful for a break from the theatre - and Euan - Marsaili decided to go for a walk around the city centre. After a spot of half-hearted window shopping along Buchanan Street, she plodded home in the dark, fed up and finding herself unexpectedly yearning for home. The city she loved so much, even with its cheery Christmas lights and bustling with people, suddenly felt lonely and unwelcoming. She wanted to be eating freshly caught seafood at her parent's kitchen table, with her brothers, Rowan and Callie for company.

Her heart lifted momentarily when, after a long walk home, the front door caught on a pile of envelopes scattered over the doormat. Marsaili pushed the door wider with her shoulder, bent down and scooped them up into her arms. There were some Christmas cards, a bank statement for Isla, and a few addressed to Marsaili. She tore them open before she could chicken out.

It wasn't good news. *Thank you for your enquiry, however our books are full at this time. We have enclosed your head shots to return to you.*

The exact words varied, but the sentiment was the same. *Thanks, but no thanks.*

So, when Euan eventually called, after a conciliatory glass of wine and a cry in the bathroom, Marsaili was already feeling a little delicate. She stared at the buzzing mobile for a few seconds before swiping right to answer.

"Hello?" she answered wearily.

"Hey Beautiful!" Euan replied. "What's the matter?" he asked, her tone immediately evident.

Before she had a chance to think about it, Marsaili found herself explaining the news of her rejections to Euan. Part of her wanted to challenge him on his absence the previous night, but a bigger part was just happy to have a sympathetic ear to offload to.

Euan listened quietly, and made consoling noises at all the right places. "Would you like some company tonight?" he asked. "I can come over after the show?"

Marsaili sighed, the thought of losing herself in the comfort of his arms overwhelming. "Yes please," she whispered.

Euan arrived after 11pm, when Isla was long since in bed. Marsaili greeted him at the door in her pyjamas and he swept her instantly into his arms. They made love again, without the frantic excitement of their first time together. It was slow and gentle, as if Euan knew instinctively exactly what her exhausted body and mind needed.

"I'm sorry," he murmured after. She was lying with her head on his chest, feeling the comforting, rhythmic pulse of his heartbeat against her cheek.

"Why?" Marsaili asked, lifting her face to look at him.

"About last night - cancelling on you like that. You remember my understudy, the one who wasn't well?" Euan asked. "Turns out he was taken into hospital. He's been… struggling, a bit. He hurt himself. On purpose." Euan paused, his fingers lightly stroking Marsaili's upper arm. "I know it was late, but he called me from A&E. He doesn't have any family nearby and I didn't want him to be on his own…"

"You don't have to explain," she interrupted, sitting up to face him. "Is he going to be OK?"

Euan smiled and stroked her hair. "He's fine. Took too many painkillers and then realised he regretted it. He's getting help."

Marsaili kissed him. "Not a lot of guys would pass up a night of sex for a night sitting on a plastic chair surrounded by drunks in A&E."

"Luckily I'm not like other guys," Euan replied, kissing her back.

Marsaili lay back down, nestling her head against his chest and feeling the dark hairs tickle her cheek. Euan wrapped his arm around her and laid his chin on her head, tracing gentle circles around her shoulder with his fingertips.

"I've never even thought about who I'd ring in an emergency," Marsaili said, realising that she had no family nearby, either. It had never seemed like too much of a concern before. "I suppose it'd be Isla, or Forbes. What about you?" she asked. "You've never mentioned any other family. - aunts or uncles or cousins?"

He smiled sadly, shaking his head. "Nope, just me."

"What do you normally do for Christmas?"

"I've spent it on my own a few times," he admitted. "It's not too bad, especially when I'm working. The performances on

Christmas Eve and Boxing Day are a good distraction. Other years I've spent with girlfriends, when I've been seeing someone." His face dropped suddenly, embarrassed. "Oh, please don't think I was fishing, I don't expect you to invite me along or anything..."

"No, it's OK," Marsaili reassured him. "I know we've not been seeing each other for long, and my parent's house is miles away, but if you didn't feel like being alone and were up for the drive… I mean, you'd be more than welcome. If you wanted to," she repeated.

Euan smiled, one hand tracing her jawline and cupping her chin. "I'd love to," he smiled, kissing her softly on the lips.

CHAPTER 16

Marsaili eyed her reflection uncertainly. The shop assistant had talked her into it, and it had seemed a good idea at the time, but now she wasn't so sure. Her usual "party night" attire hadn't changed much in the last 10 years - mid height heels, and an A-line dress of some description; something that would disguise her broad hips and highlight her relatively slender waist. This dress disguised *nothing*.

It was black, which was the only forgiving thing about it. The thick bodycon material started at her knees, clinging so tightly that she felt like a mermaid trying to walk on land. From there it clung to her hips - accentuating them to almost ridiculous proportions - skimmed over her tummy unforgivingly and shoved her boobs up a good three inches higher than their usual position. The neckline plunged into a deep v and the straps wrapped around her shoulders Bardot style, which admittedly she did like, although it made it difficult to raise her arms much above ninety degrees.

It was too much, she decided. It was the work Christmas party, not a Hollywood premier. But it was also the very first time she and Euan would be seen out together as a couple, and just a week ago he had accepted her invitation to spend Christmas with her family. Surely if there were a time to push the boat out this was it?

Just as Marsaili was guddling through her wardrobe to size up some other options, Isla burst into her room with an audible gasp of admiration.

"Where did you get that?" she asked incredulously.

"In an over-priced, overly-trendy shop on Buchanan Street that I had no business being in," Marsaili replied. "Will you help me with the zip? You need to be a bloody contortionist to reach the thing…"

"No!" Isla declared, practically wrestling her away from the wardrobe door. "No way am I letting you take that off. It's stunning!" She held her at arm's length and forced her to do an awkward twirl. "Euan is going to lose his mind when he sees you in that."

"Do you think?" Marsaili ran her hands self-consciously over her hips, pulling and tugging at the material. "I don't think it's very me; it's too over the top. I don't want everyone thinking I'm trying to be sexy just because I've finally got a boyfriend."

Isla raised her eyebrows. "Are we at the boyfriend and girlfriend stage already?" Marsaili immediately regretted the slip of the tongue.

"Nothing official," she corrected herself. "You know what I mean; suddenly I get a regular shag and I'm dressing up like a contestant on *Love Island*. It doesn't seem a bit pathetic?"

"First of all," Isla chided, "you are not pathetic. People are allowed to try different styles, and frankly I think it's about time you ventured out of your comfort zone slightly." She marched her over to the mirror and started fumbling with her unruly curls, pinning and teasing and spraying with hairspray. "And secondly," Isla continued, "if you do have a great *boyfriend* who makes you feel sexy and attractive, then why shouldn't you flaunt it? Anyone else in your position would."

Marsaili's hair was now swept up from her shoulders and twisted into an elegant, but relaxed, chignon. A few tendrils escaped from the knot and framed her face, which was screwed up, unconvinced. "I don't look like me," she said.

"So what?" Isla retorted. "This *is* you; maybe just a different version to the one you're used to." Isla reached for some bronzer and dusted it over her shoulders and collarbone, before taking a heavier hand to the eye makeup Marsaili had already applied. She resisted half-heartedly, but knew it was futile. Isla was better with this stuff than she would ever be. And maybe she was right. Wouldn't it be fun, just for one evening, to dress up like a sex kitten and head out on the town with a gorgeous man on her arm? She could be confident, and elegant, and sexy. Or at least she could pretend she was.

The party night was being held on a boat berthed on the River Clyde. The taxi drew up outside and Marsaili clambered onto the cobbled pavement awkwardly, already dreading the walk down the wobbly pontoon and into the venue itself. The heels she had borrowed from Isla were, by her standard, precariously high. She could feel muscles popping out in the back of her calves that she had never even known existed.

Euan had agreed to meet her outside, and Marsaili scanned the figures bustling beneath the fairy lights anxiously. Eventually she spotted him, talking animatedly to a group of girls who looked to be about eighteen. They were clamouring around him, giggling and posing for selfies. Groupies, Marsaili realised. She hovered uncertainly for a moment, unsure of whether or not to interrupt.

In the end, Euan spotted her first. He glanced up from signing an autograph for a blonde-haired teen in a leopard print miniskirt and his gaze alighted briefly upon her. At first, he looked away, before recognition flashed in his eyes and he glanced back with one eyebrow raised. Making his excuses, he gently but urgently extracted himself from the now disappointed crowd of teenagers.

"Marsaili?"

She just smiled in response, her cheeks flushing at both the barely hidden lust in his eyes, and the stares of the autograph hunters that were now focused on her. He kissed her hungrily. "You look amazing," he breathed into her neck. "Do we have to stay? 'Cos right now all I want to do is take you home and rip that dress off you…"

Marsaili laughed, pushing him gently away. "I didn't spend a week's wages on this outfit for it to spend the night on my bedroom floor," she replied. "But once it's done some dancing, you can rip it as much as you like…"

He kissed her again, and led her by the hand into the warmth and the pounding music of the boat.

Typically, the first person they met inside was Caitriona. She was checking her coat into the cloakroom and chatting to some of the dancers when she gave Marsaili an incredulous double take. It didn't take long for Caitriona's eyes to drift to where Euan's arm was snuggled protectively around Marsaili's waist. She barely bothered to hide her shock, before embracing them both with an insincere squeal.

"Oh my God you guys!!! How am I just finding out about this?" She planted kisses on both of their cheeks, grasping both sides of Euan's face as she lingered just a little longer than necessary. "How long has this been going on?"

Marsaili wanted the ground to swallow her up. She had expected to revel in being on the arm of, arguably, the most desirable man in the room tonight. Instead she just felt self-conscious at the fact that everyone seemed so utterly astounded that they were even together in the first place.

"A few weeks," Euan answered with a smile, charming as always.

Caitriona squeezed Marsaili's arm. "Good for you!" she exclaimed, as if Marsaili were a small child who had just managed to tie her own shoelaces. She grimaced in response and pressed her lips together in what she hoped passed as a smile.

Reading the atmosphere perfectly, Euan politely excused them both and led Marsaili over to the bar. "Nice to know you're doing your bit for charity by going out with me," she remarked.

"Would you stop?" Euan scolded her. "She's just jealous."

"Because she wants to date you? Of course she does, everyone does." Right now, Marsaili wished she'd taken Euan up on his offer of going home. At least when it was just the two of them, she didn't have to worry about half the room questioning what someone as gorgeous as him was doing with someone as average as her.

"No," Euan replied. "She's jealous because she's no longer the most beautiful girl in the room." He pulled her close to him and kissed her, and Marsaili thawed slightly. The whisky he bought her, and the one that followed it, took care of the rest, so that by the time she found Forbes on the dance floor she was positively merry.

"Darling!" he sang, embracing and chinking their glasses of prosecco before taking in her appearance. He gave a low whistle. "Look. At. You! You could be a backup dancer in one of my drag shows!"

Right on cue, *Shut Up and Dance* by Walk the Moon came on. She grabbed Forbes' hand and he twirled her round, the two of them singing, swaying and bouncing to the beat. The song merged into another and Marsaili lost herself in the rhythm, so that all she was aware of was the movement of her body and the comforting thud of the bass line as it reverberated through her. When the music eventually transitioned to cheesy Christmas tunes, she and Forbes retreated to the bar to refresh their drinks.

There was no sign of Euan, but as they pressed through the crowd Marsaili found herself queued up alongside his understudy. She smiled at him, feeling emboldened by the drink in her belly and the pounding music in her ears. He looked well.

"Hi," she shouted over the din. He nodded politely, but clearly didn't recognise her. "I'm Marsaili," she continued. "Euan's girlfriend." It was the first time she'd said it out loud, and she suppressed a small giggle. Technically they hadn't said it to each other yet, but in one week he was going to be spending Christmas with her family. Surely that was where things were heading?

The understudy glanced around awkwardly, looking uncomfortable. "Good to see you up and about," she said, but his expression was still confused. "I'm the one that got stood up so he could look after you when you weren't well," she added, hoping it sounded jokey and light-hearted. A flash of worry passed over his face, and he hesitated before speaking.

"I wasn't sick," he said. "You must be thinking of someone else."

"Yes, you were," Marsaili laughed. "You're his understudy. He went to visit you in A&E."

"Nope." He shook his head, looking uncomfortable. "I mean, yes, I am his understudy. But I wasn't in hospital. You must be confused." Giving up on his place in the queue, the understudy changed his mind and disappeared into the toilets before she could respond.

"There you are," a hand suddenly found her waist, as a familiar voice whispered in her ears. "I saw you doing your thing on the dancefloor. Is it time to go now? I don't think I can contain myself much longer…" Euan's mouth found her earlobe and nibbled it suggestively.

Marsaili turned on him, barely holding back the tears. "Fuck you," she muttered, pushing her way through the crowd and into the drizzling winter's night.

CHAPTER 17

Stumbling out into the darkness, Marsaili forgot about the precarious walkway that led back across the river to dry land. She rushed onto it blindly, and in her haste caught one of her heels between the wooden slats. Before she could do anything to prevent it, she stumbled and fell. Her ankle twisted painfully, followed by her knees thumping against the deck as she crumpled to the ground. Letting go of her handbag in order to break her fall, there was nothing Marsaili could do to stop it falling from her grasp and sliding between the chain link barrier, tumbling into the murk of the Clyde below. She cried out, both in pain and frustration, before burying her head in her hands and sobbing.

Suddenly Marsaili felt the gangway sway gently, and glanced behind her in the futile hope that Euan might have come after her. However, all she saw were the twinkling fairy lights draped along the roofline of the boat and the shadowy figures dancing behind the frosted windows. Ashamed of the state she was in, and wondering how on earth she was going to get home without cash, keys, her phone or a bank card, she started to gather herself together to move out of the way of whoever was approaching from land. But before she could reach her feet, the approaching footsteps unexpectedly sped up. Keeping her head down, Marsaili stumbled aside to let them pass.

The figure came to a standstill next to her, and Marsaili cursed under her breath, not looking up. "I'm fine," she muttered.

"You don't look it," came the reply. Marsaili lifted her head. Of course, she thought, as her eyes met the now familiar brown-eyed gaze of her new boss. Yet another brilliant encounter to add to the list, she thought - off my tits, falling over drunk. Again.

"What on earth happened?" Will asked, his tone more concerned than reproachful. He was taking off his jacket, and Marsaili watched him for a moment. It was the first time she'd seen him out of formal wear; he was dressed in jeans, with a checked shirt and a tweed blazer. He was still wearing cufflinks and the shirt was neatly tucked in, but compared to his usual attire he looked positively casual. Even his hair was gelled up in a tousled, carefree manner, rather than combed into his usual neat side parting.

The tweed jacket found its way around her shoulders, and then Will was crouching, looking into her bloodshot eyes and holding her by the upper arms.

"Are you ok?" he repeated again, before shaking her gently. He was frowning and paused a moment, before raising his voice slightly. "Has someone given you something?"

That woke her from her dazed state. Angrily, Marsaili shook free of his grasp. "What? No, I haven't taken anything! Do you think I'm a bloody junkie!?" She stepped away from him, forgetting about her twisted ankle and wincing involuntarily as she put her weight on it. Will caught her by the elbow.

"I know you're not a junkie," he said gently. Marsaili had expected him to be angry, and the patience in his voice surprised her. "I was just worried in case someone had spiked your drink."

She sniffed, pulling his jacket tighter around her and feeling thankful for its warmth. "No," she said quietly. "I was just leaving and I fell," she broke off, hoping he would assume her tears were only of pain, rather than humiliation. "My handbag's gone into the river," she finished, matter-of-factly.

"Oh." Will seemed unsure of what to say next. "And you've obviously hurt yourself.". Marsaili saw him looking down at her legs, and for the first time noticed that her knees were scraped and bleeding. "Well," Will continued, "we'd better get you home."

"No," Marsaili panicked, starting to take his jacket back off. The last thing she wanted was his sympathy, or yet another reason to make him think she couldn't take care of herself. "It's fine. I can walk home from here." She handed the jacket back to him and leant on the handrail to try and hobble back down the gangway. She'd figure out how to get home, and have a good cry, once Will was safely out of sight and earshot.

"Have a good evening," Marsaili called out as she set off, trying to limp as little as possible. But a second or two later she felt the tell-tale bob of the gangway as Will strode quickly after her.

"No arguments," he said, taking her firmly by the waist. Marsaili was surprised by his strength. The tweed blazer was once again wrapped around her shoulders, as he turned her to face him before folding it firmly over her middle. "You're bleeding, limping, and the contents of your purse are currently floating downstream. And since there are clearly no pockets in that dress, I'm guessing that means you have no phone, no money, and no keys." Marsaili looked down at her battered knees, unable to argue. "I'm taking you home," Will repeated, in a tone that would broach no argument. "Now lean on my shoulder."

Marsaili did as she was instructed, and with Will half crouching and with one hand under her armpit, Marsaili leaned on him as he supported her weight down the gangway. She was too tired, too drunk and too sad to argue. It was comforting to let him take control of the situation, even if the sober part of her mind knew she'd be even more mortified the next time she had to see him. Maybe it would be easier just to quit and take that job in a call centre after all.

Not long after they'd stepped back onto dry land, a taxi approached from under the bridge. Mercifully its light was on, and Will hailed it with a wave of his hand. The driver seemed to hesitate at the thought of letting this drunk, dishevelled girl into his taxi, but the well-spoken, well-dressed man who accompanied her must have calmed his fears.

Sitting in the back of the cab as it bumped its way along the Clydeside Expressway, it took Marsaili a moment or two to realise Will's arm was still around her shoulder. Even when she did, she was surprised to find that she didn't want it to move. Instead, she let her head flop against his shoulder while the rhythm of the taxi lulled her into an almost-sleep.

When they came to a stop, Marsaili was surprised to look out of the window and see not the familiar sandstone of her tenement, but instead the glassy frontage of a modern hotel. Will was paying the driver, before he stepped out and came around the outside to open her door, like a chauffeur in an old black and white movie.

Marsaili stared at him incredulously. "Why are we here?" she asked, barely contained indignation giving her words an icy edge.

"We buzzed at your flat for ages; there was no answer." Will held his hands out apologetically. Marsaili fought through the fuzz of her drink-addled brain; she must have really fallen asleep. Suddenly the taxi driver piped up, seemingly keen to reassure her that she was not about to be raped and mutilated by her impeccably mannered, posh-boy boss.

"He's right, hen. Alexandra Parade, top floor? All the lights were out." Then Marsaili remembered; Isla was spending the night at her mum's before the two of them went for a spa day tomorrow as a pre-Christmas treat. With Marsaili's keys currently at the bottom of the Clyde, they had no way of getting her inside.

Will was still watching her, his eyebrows raised. "I don't expect you to sleep in my room," he explained. "We'll get you a room of your own for tonight, then tomorrow we'll figure out a way of getting you back into your flat."

With one glance back at the taxi driver, who nodded encouragingly, Marsaili took Will's hand and reluctantly let him help her out of the taxi and into the brightly lit foyer of the hotel.

CHAPTER 18

Will tapped his credit card impatiently against the counter top, as the night porter desperately scrolled through the reservations on his computer screen. "You're sure you've absolutely nothing available?" he asked for the third time.

"I'm sorry sir - it's a week before Christmas and I'm afraid we're all booked up. Party nights and what have you." He shrugged. "There's a Travel Lodge about five minutes away, if you want to try there?" Will sighed and closed his eyes, while Marsaili stood helplessly on her good leg, trying to ignore the throbbing pain in her knees and ankle. She felt like a child whose parents had forgotten to pick her up from school.

"No, it's fine," Will said eventually. "Thank you for your help. Come on," he scooped his arm around her once again and half carried her to the lifts.

"There's a sofa in my room," he explained, pressing the button with one hand and keeping the other wrapped firmly about her waist. "You can take the bed."

If she'd thought about it, Marsaili would have expected the hotel room of a single bachelor recently relocated to a new city to have been somewhat disorganised, perhaps with takeaway containers, empty beer bottles and dirty clothes littering the surfaces. Certainly, that's what it would have looked like if Gregor or Lachlan had been staying there. But Will's room had none of these things. Instead, it smelt of the same crisp, slightly sweet aftershave he wore, and the shelves and tabletops were neatly organised; a fresh suit hang on the end of the doorless wardrobe, a cufflink box lay open on the desk next to the TV, and his neatly polished work shoes were tucked in a cubby behind the door. The room was comfortably proportioned and, as Will had promised, boasted a squashy leather sofa in front of the floor to ceiling windows that looked out over the city. It was here that he deposited her, before excusing himself into the bathroom.

It was certainly a cut above any hotel room Marsaili had ever stayed in. They were eight storeys up, and she took a moment to enjoy the twinkling carpet of lights that spread out before her, forgetting for a second all of her problems with Euan, or the aching pain in her legs and ankle.

Will announced his return to the room with his customary cough, and Marsaili saw that he was carrying a little travel first aid kit in his hand. He seemed awkward suddenly; all his self-assurance from earlier had vanished. "Never travel without it," he said, holding up the tin and giving it a little shake. Marsaili managed a smile in response.

"I'm so sorry about all of this," she started, feeling embarrassment rise in her chest as the effects of the alcohol she had consumed earlier began to wear off.

"Don't think of it," Will said. "These things happen." He smiled and she met his eyes properly for the first time all evening, noticing how they crinkled at the edges.

Without asking, Will knelt down on the floor before her and started to untie the straps of the ridiculously high heels she had borrowed from Isla. He was silent for a while as he ran his hands gently but firmly over the swollen ankle, around the top of her foot and back up the lower section of her calf. Marsaili felt her pulse quickening in her chest; his hands were warm and slightly rough, which she hadn't expected. He looked up at her suddenly. "Not broken," he said with a smile.

"How do you know?" Marsaili asked, her words husky and breathless.

"I played rugby at uni," Will explained, intently focused on finding the right size of bandage from his little tin. "A shoulder injury put paid to any hopes of turning pro, so I did a little bit of coaching and some first aid training. It'll swell up, and you'll probably have a nasty bruise, but it's definitely not broken."

He located the bandage he wanted and pulled her foot back into his lap, deftly wrapping it so it was supportive without being constricting. He then removed some antiseptic spray and wipes and gently cleaned her knees. Marsaili knew that she should object - there was nothing stopping her from doing that herself, after all - but she was enjoying the excuse to feel his hands on her bare skin.

When he was done, Will helped her into the bathroom and hung up one of his shirts on the back of the door, before giving her some privacy to change. Marsaili saw her reflection for the first time all evening and started; if she'd gone out looking like Marilyn Monroe, she'd come back looking like Bet Lynch.

With a sigh, she washed her face and scrubbed off most of

the makeup, before unpinning her hair and letting it fall loose about her shoulders. It took some effort to wriggle out of the bodycon dress while balanced on one foot, but she eventually managed and slipped gratefully into the cool material of Will's crisp, clean shirt. It came almost down to her knees and covered more of her modesty than the dress had, but she kept her bra and pants on nonetheless.

By the time Marsaili crept back into the main room, Will had changed too. He was wearing a pair of checked pyjama bottoms and an Oxford University hoodie. Something about the combination seemed strangely normal; Marsaili would almost have been less surprised to find him in a smoking jacket and slippers.

The shirt and jeans he'd been wearing earlier were neatly hung back in the wardrobe, and the polished brown shoes had been placed parallel to the identical black ones in the cubby behind the door. He was sitting on the sofa, looking out at the view of the city, and it was only then that it dawned on her that he hadn't even made it into the party.

"I'm sorry I ruined your night," she said, crossing the room unsteadily towards him.

"Don't be silly," he said, standing up and helping her onto the sofa. "Truth be told I didn't want to go to the bloody party in the first place. That's why I was so late; took most of the night to talk myself into it. Then Caitriona text to see where I was and I figured it was a poor show for me to be so conspicuously absent, so I'd better get my arse down there." He paused for a moment, looking unsure of himself. "If I'm honest, I'm not entirely disappointed to have missed it. Big parties, lots of people, alcohol… not really my thing."

Will pulled a blanket down from the back of the couch and laid it over Marsaili's knees, propping her injured foot up on a pillow.

"Caitriona will be disappointed though," Marsaili said, watching him carefully as he crossed the room and flicked on the kettle.

"What do you mean?"

Marsaili laughed. "Oh, come on," she said. "You really don't know? She's been throwing herself at you since you arrived!"

Will smirked, an expression that suited him enormously. His dishevelled hair had flopped across his forehead, and he peered at her from under the yellow curtain. "Well, I did wonder," he admitted. "But isn't she like that with everyone? And besides, I'm her boss…"

he let the sentence trail off, as the bubbling of the kettle rose to a crescendo and the switch flicked off. He took his time making the drinks, eventually placing a warm cup of tea and a packet of shortbread biscuits in Marsaili's hands. "It wouldn't be appropriate," he finished.

"I don't think she'd let that stop her, somehow," Marsaili said. "She definitely has you firmly in her crosshairs at the minute."

Will settled himself on the sofa beside her, crossing his long legs and taking a sip from his mug. "If she does, I think that's only because you got to Euan Campbell first."

Marsaili dunked a piece of shortbread in her tea. "If Caitriona wants Euan Campbell, she's welcome to him," she muttered.

At first Will said nothing. When their eyes eventually met, he held her gaze for a moment too long. "I did try to warn you," he said quietly.

Marsaili sighed, remembering how angry she'd been that day in his office, thinking he was telling her off. Had he really just been looking out for her all along? "You did," she admitted. "And I was rude to you. Sorry about that - turns out you were right. He's a liar and a shitebag."

Will laughed. "Sorry," he added in a hurry, seeing the annoyance flash in her eyes. "I'm not laughing at you. You just get very Scottish when you're angry; my mum would be mortified if I spoke like that."

Marsaili glared at him again. "What's that supposed to mean?"

"Sorry," he repeated, patting her outstretched leg in a conciliatory manner. It was a perfectly innocent gesture, but it set Marsaili's heart racing again. "I seem to have a habit of unintentionally insulting you. I don't mean to." He was smiling. His hand remained on her leg. "It's just, up here you all seem to swear with much more charm and ease than we do down South. I quite like it actually. I find it very endearing."

He held her gaze again, his hand still warm on her shinbone. "But your mother wouldn't approve?" Marsaili asked.

"Indeed, she would not," he replied.

They looked at each other, neither one moving. Then Will's thumb started to rub her calf, very gently. "I was disappointed when I heard you were going out with Euan. You're too good for him."

"He is a shitebag," Marsaili replied, her eyes never leaving his.
"And you are definitely not."

"I don't think so."

"Me neither."

For a moment the air was laden with unspoken possibility, before a sudden buzz from the coffee table made them both jump. Will's phone was vibrating, bouncing up and down in little bursts on the glass. With an exaggerated sigh, he grinned at her, leaning over to turn it off. Marsaili could feel her heart thumping in anticipation, but as he saw the caller ID on the screen his face dropped. Excusing himself, Will vanished into the bathroom before answering, from where Marsaili could hear the murmurings of a hushed, but urgent, conversation.

By the time he returned, she was sound asleep.

CHAPTER 19

As silently as she could, Marsaili swung her legs out of bed. It was still early, and the room was dark. All that could be heard was the gentle whoosh of passing traffic from the street below, and the quite rumbling of Will's snores.

She could see him on the sofa, his back turned to her, one long leg tossed over the armrest. Watching him for a moment, she realised that he must have carried her onto the bed while she slept. Marsaili said a silent prayer of thanks for the mystery phone call that had interrupted them last night. No matter how attractive she found him, or how much she'd wanted to in the moment, getting off with her boss would definitely have been a Very Bad Idea.

Rubbing her sore ankle, she was contemplating how best to make her escape when Will suddenly snorted loudly and sat bolt upright in bed. Marsaili jumped. He looked around for a moment, bewildered, running a hand through his tousled hair. His eyes eventually picked out her shape in the darkness.

"Good morning," he croaked. He didn't seem surprised, or disappointed for that matter, to see her. He let out a little laugh as he yawned and rubbed his eyes. "I thought for a moment..." he began, but stopped uncertainly.

"I was just going to get going," Marsaili explained. "Thanks for letting me sleep it off here," she said, unsteadily rising to her feet. "I really appreciate it. I'll get your shirt dry cleaned before I bring it back to you..."

Will flicked the light on, dazzling her suddenly. "You don't have to go," he said, standing and crossing the room to her. Despite the excellent job he had done of bandaging her ankle, Marsaili was still a little wobbly on it, and as she tried to take a step had little choice but to accept the outstretched hand he offered her. They held each other at arm's length for a moment.

"I think it's best if I do," Marsaili said quietly.

Will sighed, letting go of her hand and rubbing his eyes wearily. "Yes, I suppose it is," he said. "But at least let me drive you?"

Marsaili started to protest, before he pointed out the exact dilemma she had been considering before he woke up - she had no shoes, no suitable clothing, and was unable to walk unsupported.

Will insisted on ordering some room service breakfast before they left, on account of it being a Sunday morning and their chances of finding a locksmith that could let her into her flat at 6am being fairly slim. They sat together on the sofa, close but not touching, eating croissants and sharing a large cafetiere of coffee. Will flicked the TV onto Sky News as they fell into a surprisingly easy conversation.

"I'll have to pay you back for this," Marsaili said, gesturing to the generous tray of pastries, conserves, ham and cheese. Will shrugged in response and shook his head. "Not at all. It's just nice to have someone to share it with for a change."

"Did you actually go to Oxford?" she asked, nodding at his hoodie.

"I did indeed," he said modestly. "Third generation; it had very little to do with my academic ability and far more to do with the generous donation my great-great grandfather had left the college in his will."

Marsaili smiled. Part of her wished he had been snooty about it, instead of self-deprecating. That would have made it much easier to dislike him. "What did you study?" she asked.

"Law. Third generation of that too, but I'm the first one to jack it in after graduation. Mummy and Daddy weren't too happy about that," he said with a rueful smile.

"My twin brother's a solicitor," Marsaili said. She told him more about her own family; how different she and her brothers were, her overbearing but well-intentioned mother, and the happy home they'd been lucky enough to grow up in.

"Sounds nice," Will replied, and she nodded. Not for the first time, Marsaili was reminded of how privileged her upbringing had been. Not financially or materially, but in the ways that really mattered.

Will, on the other hand, seemed to have wanted for nothing in material terms. He'd been raised in a posh area of London, and from the sounds of things his early years seemed to have consisted mainly of nannies and boarding schools. He was an only child, and seemed envious of the bond she had with her siblings.

"My godfather was a theatre producer," he was explaining now, "so even this job is really just the result of nepotism at its finest.

91

He got me into management when I was floundering after uni."

"And what brought you up here?" Marsaili asked. "Did you draw the short straw?"

He laughed, pouring them both a top up from the cafetiere. "Would you believe I volunteered?"

"Never! You went North of the wall through *choice*?"

He nodded. "Decided to take my chances among the wildlings."

"And how have the wildlings been treating you?" she asked, buttering a croissant and leaving a dusting of flaky crumbs all over the floor.

Will smiled. "They've been very welcoming. Although I may not always have been the best at reciprocating," he admitted with a shrug. "You may not have noticed since I hide it so well, but I can be a bit… awkward, at times." He grinned, making it clear he was poking fun at himself, and Marsaili smiled back. Try as she might, she couldn't help but notice how the early morning light from the hotel room window struck the dusting of golden stubble along his jawline. She wanted to reach out and run her fingers along it.

"I tend to enjoy more solitary pursuits, anyway," he continued. "Running, hillwalking, climbing - that sort of thing. I spent a bit of time up North before my contract started, actually."

Marsaili's ears perked up. "Whereabouts?" she asked. "I grew up in the Highlands, on the West coast."

Will smiled that slow, languid grin that she was beginning to like so much. "I thought you sounded a little different from everyone else around here. You've got that lovely lilt in your voice." He kept his eyes on hers, and Marsaili smiled self-consciously. "I spent a couple of days wild camping around Duirinish. It's in the middle of nowhere –" he paused, obviously having spotted Marsaili's incredulous expression. "Do you know it?"

"I spent the first 18 years of my life there!" Marsaili replied. "Wait a minute – did you say the weekend before you started at the theatre?" Will nodded. She squinted at him, suddenly remembering the tall, hooded stranger who'd disembarked the train with her the last time she'd travelled home. Could it have been him? she wondered. But Will spoke before she could.

"You're the girl on the train," he said, his voice almost a whisper. "I noticed you – I thought you looked like a proper

Highlander. All that wild red hair." He was watching her intently again, and Marsaili blushed as she tucked a stray curl behind one ear, only for it to pop straight back out again.

"I hated it when I was younger," she said self-consciously. "Begged my mum to let me dye it, but she never would."

"Good," Will said simply. "It's beautiful."

Marsaili shifted under his gaze. It would have been so easy to give into the temptation to kiss him, so she changed the subject instead. "You wild camped?" she asked. "In November?"

Will laughed; if it had been a come-on, and he was insulted by her rejection, he didn't let it show. *Just because he pays you a compliment doesn't mean he fancies you*, she scolded herself.

"There's no such thing as bad weather," Will was saying, "only the wrong clothes. It's not so bad if you're prepared."

Marsaili knew it was probably a stupid idea to say what was on the tip of her tongue, but eventually her curiosity overwhelmed her.

"Is your wife into all that outdoorsy stuff too?"

"Ex-wife" Will clarified, his expression clouding over. "And no, not really. Like I said, it's something I usually do alone."

Marsaili nodded. "It must be tough; going through a divorce."

"It's certainly not fun," Will said, sighing. "I've tried my best to make it work; that was her on the phone last night, actually. But I don't know anymore..." his words trailed off, and he seemed to retreat within himself once again.

"Maybe you can fix it?" Marsaili began. She didn't know what else to say. And part of her, she realised, wanted to know whether he was truly single or not.

"It doesn't matter," Will interrupted, rising abruptly from the sofa. "I think we should get you home now."

Will's car was parked in the multi-storey car park attached to the hotel. Once she was safely buckled into the classic e-type Jaguar, Marsaili focused her energy on looking out of the window and giving occasional directions. The Sunday morning traffic was light and they moved through the city with ease. She was wearing one of Will's zippy tops over the white cotton shirt he'd lent her, and a pair of his jogging bottoms with the toggle pulled as tight as it would go around her waist. A pair of thick hiking socks finished the ensemble. She couldn't wait to get home, have a bath, and try to forget that the last twenty-four hours had ever happened.

Before they'd left the hotel, Will had rung ahead and arranged for a locksmith to meet them. With the self-assured air of a Proper Grown Up, he explained the situation, and promised that Marsaili would be able to provide evidence that she was a resident of the property as soon as they'd gained entry. She did, Will paid the man before she even had a chance to object, and before she knew it, they were alone once again.

They hovered awkwardly in the hallway of her flat. "Thank you for everything you've done," Marsaili said. "I really do appreciate it. And I will pay you back."

"It's OK; I know where you live now," he tried jokingly, but the smile didn't reach his eyes. His hair was neatly combed once more, and he was back to looking slightly nervous and aloof.

"Do you have a phone you can use to cancel your bank cards?" he asked.

Marsaili nodded and gestured to the landline - a retro 80s style novelty item with a pull-out antenna. Why did everything in her life suddenly seem so childish?

"Right then," Will said, rocking back on his heels. "I'd best be off. I was thinking…"

"Yes?"

"Maybe best if you take the rest of the week off? That's a nasty sprain; you don't want to be putting it under extra pressure by being on your feet all night. Rest up and let it heal. I'll make sure you're paid, of course," he hurried on, but Marsaili could see the true meaning behind his words. He didn't want to have to see her again for a while.

She nodded. "Good idea," she muttered quietly, reaching around him to open the door. "Goodbye. I'll get your clothes back to you as soon as I've washed them."

Will looked at her again, that same unreadable expression on his face, before turning swiftly through the door and jogging down the stairs. He didn't look back.

Marsaili closed the door and slumped against it. She knew there were many responsible, adult things she should be taking care of right now, but she couldn't face any of them. Instead she grabbed a packet of Jaffa cakes from the kitchen cupboard and retreated to the comfort of her duvet, hoping she would never need to come out from under it again.

CHAPTER 20

Marsaili wondered if it were possible to slip into a cheese induced coma. She might end up as some kind of medical first, she mused, as she sank deeper into the worn old armchair and popped another chunk of brie into her mouth.

It was the end of a Christmas Day that had actually turned out an awful lot better than she'd expected. Marsaili had marvelled at the meal Rowan managed to pull together, in between refereeing her meddling mother and mother-in-law and caring for a four-week-old baby. She was upstairs now putting Callie to bed, whilst the two grannies pottered in the kitchen and the men cleared the table to set up their annual Christmas evening game of Trivial Pursuit. Marsaili had just taken Fraoch for a quick walk, and was now back to picking at the leftovers of the buffet.

She looked up as the door to the living room creaked open, and smiled at the woman who joined her. She had been another unexpectedly pleasant surprise that this Christmas had brought.

Gayatri was nothing like Gregor's usual girlfriends. She was taller than him, for one, five years older for another, and Hindu. When he'd first brought her into the small kitchen at Marsaili's parents' home the night before, her father had struggled to hide his surprise. Not that he would have had any objections, there just wasn't a great deal of ethnic diversity in the North West Highlands and he hadn't been expecting it. He recovered himself quickly, however, and Gayatri was welcomed with the customary hugs and rounds of whisky, which she partook of enthusiastically. Marsaili had liked her immediately.

Gayatri helped herself to a generous chunk of brie and a pork pie, before flopping into the armchair opposite Marsaili. She sighed contentedly. "I wish I could eat like this every day," she said.

"Me too," Marsaili replied. "Are you ready for your first game of McKenzie family Trivial Pursuit?"

"Ready as I'll ever be," Gayatri replied with a smile. She was a lawyer like Gregor, and they'd met whilst arguing opposing sides of a case in court. Unlike most of his previous conquests, she didn't fawn over him; she teased him, albeit affectionately, and if anything, he was the one who appeared to be hopelessly smitten. Marsaili could see that he'd been telling the truth that day when they had lunch - Gayatri was special.

Marsaili had been home for nearly a week now, having taken Will at his word about the time off and deciding she'd be as well enjoying it with her family and friends, instead of moping around at home alone. Her ankle was feeling stronger, although it had come out in a rather lovely purple and yellow bruise, just as Will had predicted. Her bank cards had been cancelled and replacements were on their way, along with a new mobile phone. Her sim card was long gone, so she had no hope of recovering her number; Isla knew how to reach her at her parent's landline if required and sadly, she reflected, there was no one else in Glasgow to really miss her. Not now that things with her and Euan were officially done.

Forbes had popped in to see her the day after she'd fled the Christmas party, clearly concerned at her sudden exit. She explained everything that had happened with Euan, and even he'd struggled to put a positive spin on it. She didn't mention anything about her evening in Will's hotel room, however. She had no desire to open either of them up to Forbes' teasing and the inevitable innuendo that would follow. She hadn't even told Rowan about it, and for most of her life she and Rowan had shared *everything*.

The only person with the slightest inkling about that whole situation was Isla. She'd come back from her spa day to find the locks changed, so Marsaili hadn't had much choice but to fill her in. She'd also then found Will's clothes in their wash basket, and had raised a suspicious eyebrow.

"Whose are these?" she'd asked, holding out the male joggers a couple of days later. "Did Euan leave them here before..."

"No," Marsaili said, a little too sharply. "Will lent them to me," she explained with a sigh. "I really need to get them back to him before I head up North."

"I can do it," Isla volunteered. "You said he's at the Sheraton? I pass it on my way to work; I'll leave them at the front desk for him."

"Thanks," Marsaili was grateful. She didn't want to risk bumping into him right now. "Would you pop this in the bag too?" She'd taken the last £50 out of her bank account that morning. She had no idea how much breakfast and the locksmith would have cost, but hoped that would cover most of it.

And now Isla was spending Christmas down in Findlay's military digs, and Marsaili had had to explain to her expectant family why her mysterious new boyfriend was no longer joining them. She definitely didn't want to get into the whole thing with her mother of all people, so she had excused him on the pretence of illness. Shonagh looked disappointed, while her brothers looked suspicious. Marsaili had managed to avoid the issue so far, but knew that it was only a matter of time until one of them, or Rowan, called her out on it.

As she and Gayatri moved through to the dining room to join the others for the game, Marsaili found herself wondering what Will was doing today. She'd got the impression from their conversation that his relationship with his parents was somewhat strained; had he gone back down to England to see them, she wondered? She pictured him in an extravagant dining room seated around a huge table, Will staring at his plate as they ate in tense silence, the only noise the sound of silver cutlery clicking against fine bone china. Or maybe he was sitting in his hotel room, alone, eating room service in front of the telly? Or had the late-night phone call with his wife led to a reconciliation? Maybe she was with him instead, tangled up in the same sheets Marsaili had slept under just a few nights ago. She shook the image from her mind.

Marsaili took a seat around the dining table and gladly accepted the large measure of Knockando that Rowan's father pressed into her hand.

"Right then," Lachlan announced, rubbing his hands together. "I do hereby declare this year's game of Trivial Pursuit officially open! Teams?" he asked expectantly.

Marsaili followed his gaze around the table. Rowan sat to her husband's left, followed by her parents, then Marsaili's parents. Rowan's sister, Morven, and her partner Eilidh were next, then Gregor and Gayatri. And last but not least, Marsaili. Alone, again.

"Well we don't need to do couples…" Shonagh began uncomfortably.

"Boys Vs Girls," Gayatri said immediately, skooching her chair closer to Marsaili. She smiled at her, and Marsaili was grateful to see not a hint of pity in her eyes. "I can beat Gregor at most things," Gayatri continued playfully, "we'll just add this to the list."

As the game rolled on into the small hours of the morning,

Marsaili found that she was genuinely enjoying herself. Callie had unexpectedly joined them, having woken screaming at around midnight. Rowan had fed her and was now bouncing her around the table, nestled in a stretchy baby wrap against her mother's chest. She was proving to be something of a good luck charm; the girls were now only one green wedge away from making it to the middle of the board, when suddenly the phone rang. Everyone sat up and glanced at each other, with the slight panic that always accompanies an unexpected late-night phone call.

Lachlan answered it, his brown eyes concerned as he glanced around the table. The same unspoken thought passed between them all - the whole family were here; who could possibly be phoning?

However, his face relaxed almost instantly, when he obviously recognised the voice on the other end of the line. "It's for you," he said, holding the receiver out to Marsaili.

She got up and took it from his grasp eagerly. For a moment the thought flashed through her mind that it could be Will, but then she chided herself. She was pretty sure he wasn't thinking about her, and even if he was, he'd have no idea how to reach her.

As she placed the receiver to her ear, Isla's voice filled her head, bubbling with barely contained excitement. Marsaili felt a wave of relief; at least she knew it wasn't going to be bad news.

"I'm engaged!" Isla blurted out without further preamble, clearly unable to contain herself any longer.

Marsaili gasped as tears sprung to her eyes. She heard her mother exclaim behind her, and turned around to wave away her concern. She gave her a thumbs up and tried to blink away the tears.

"Oh, Isla I'm so happy for you!" she said, stretching the cord of the phone around the corner of the door and excusing herself into the hallway. "How did it happen?" she asked. Despite the abysmal state of her own love life, she was eager to hear the details of her friend's proposal.

"It was perfect," Isla began. "Findlay's digs are tiny, so he'd suggested that if it was a nice day, we should pack a picnic and take a drive to the Peak District, instead of having a normal Christmas lunch."

So far, this all sounded perfectly Isla and Findlay - she should have known he'd pop the question off the beaten track somewhere.

"He took me to this place called Dovedale, about an hour

from his barracks. So, he was carrying the picnic and we set off to climb this little hill. It was beautiful - no one else around, 'cos it was Christmas Day obviously, so we crossed the river over these little stepping stones and set off up the hill. Anyway, about halfway up I was bursting for a pee," Isla giggled, "so I did what we always do if we're in the great outdoors and disappeared off into the bushes. How was I supposed to know that ten minutes later we'd be at the top of the hill, looking at the most amazing view, and he'd be down on one knee!"

Marsaili laughed as Isla continued. "Honestly, I had no makeup on, my hair was scraped back in a headscarf, it was nothing like I imagined it'd be… but it was perfect."

"It sounds it," Marsaili agreed with a smile.

"Night out when you get home?" Isla asked.

"Definitely.'

They said their goodbyes, and Marsaili headed back into the dining room to share her friend's good news with her family.

CHAPTER 21

Boxing Day dawned, bright and clear. Feeling unusually refreshed, despite the overindulgence of the day before, Marsaili decided to start her day with a walk along the bay. As she was encouraging a reluctant Fraoch from her basket, she heard footsteps creaking down the old staircase above her head.

Gregor ducked into the room; his curly hair even more dishevelled than usual. "Morning," he croaked with a smile. "You're up early."

"So are you. Fancy a walk?"

And so, the pair of them found themselves winding their way along the single-track road towards Duirinish not long after 7am. The sky was still a dark navy, with wisps of pink promising sunrise was on its way. An invigorating breeze blew in from Loch Carron and the waves crashed along the shoreline in grey, foaming peaks. Fraoch ambled along behind them, sniffing the barren heather and half-heartedly eyeing up the occasional rabbit that hopped by, but lacking the enthusiasm to actually chase them. Marsaili and Gregor walked in silence for a while, wrapped up in their parents' old fleeces and soaking in the peacefulness of their childhood home. They'd spent years scampering around this coastline together, and Marsaili couldn't remember the last time they'd been out here just the two of them.

"I like Gayatri," Marsaili spoke, breaking their companionable silence. Gregor smiled in an unusually bashful manner, running a hand through his unruly dark curls.

"Me too," he said. "Do you think Mum and Dad like her?"

Marsaili nodded enthusiastically. "Definitely. Did you see Dad's face when she nailed that second Laphroaig? Ultimate seal of approval."

Gregor nodded, a coy smile playing on his lips. "I'm glad you think so. I told you she was different. And I'm hoping she'll be around for a while."

Marsaili stopped, spinning round to face him. "You don't mean…" She liked Gayatri, but she couldn't believe that Gregor would be contemplating making things official quite so soon. And, purely selfishly, she didn't think she could handle her serial dating, philandering brother marrying himself off at the same time as her flatmate.

Gregor shrugged. "I'm not talking about popping the question anytime soon," he said defensively. "But she's funny, she's smart, she's strong. For the first time I've found someone I actually want to hang out with, all the time. Not just, you know…"

Marsaili giggled, shaking her head as they resumed their walk. "You're smitten!" she teased, and he shoved her good naturedly.

"What about you?" Gregor asked after a while. "Loverboy recovered from his mystery illness?"

Marsaili looked at her feet, kicking a couple of stones along the path. "I don't know, I haven't spoken to him…"

"Because you've lost your phone?"

"That's right."

"So why not use the landline? Seems strange that he wouldn't at least call to wish you a merry Christmas. Did you give him the number?"

"Yes…" Marsaili sighed. Of all the people to quiz her about this, Gregor was the one she'd be least able to lie to. Aside from him being a lawyer, he had always been able to see right through her.

"Alright, no," she admitted. "I was seeing someone, but it ended. I just couldn't face the third degree from Mum."

Gregor nodded. Maybe it was part of the reason he'd made such a successful lawyer, Marsaili wondered, but he had a way of leaving gaps in conversations that seemed to invite people to fill them.

"He'd been lying to me," Marsaili explained. "I think he's been seeing someone else."

"Have you asked him?"

"No."

"So, you don't know for sure?"

"No, but…"

"Marsaili, you can't condemn him until you've heard his side of the story."

Marsaili bit her tongue. She knew that she'd run away without giving Euan a chance to explain that night, and everything since then had snowballed so quickly – the night in Will's hotel room, and the undeniable attraction to him which she was finding harder and harder to deny. But she knew that Gregor had a point; she at least owed Euan a chance to defend himself.

102

"It's not exactly the first time you've done this," Gregor said. "Remember Adam? You were convinced he was cheating. And Simon. In fact, just about every guy you've ever dated, ever since Matthew."

Marsaili stopped, playing for time by looking back over her shoulder and calling on Fraoch, who was currently half buried beneath a thorny bush. Gregor's remarks were hitting a little too close to the bone.

Matthew, her first boyfriend, had definitely cheated on her. She'd caught him kissing another girl behind the harbour wall when they were seventeen. She knew it was stupid - they'd just been kids. But ever since then, she'd always worried that she would never be enough; that no man could possibly be happy just with her and no one else.

Gregor pushed home his advantage. "I never knew Simon all that well, but Adam adored you. You were the only one who couldn't see it."

Marsaili was glad for the wind in her face; it gave her an excuse for the moistening of her eyes. Adam had been a good guy, she had to admit - kind, sweet, affectionate. He was a trainee paramedic - they'd actually met while he was on call, in Glasgow when one of her uni roommates passed out at a party and needed her stomach pumped. Marsaili had travelled with her in the back of the ambulance, and she and Adam had just clicked. It was so easy to start with; everyone loved him, especially her mum. However, the late nights and anti-social hours - not to mention the knowledge that he'd hit on her whilst on duty - did nothing to stave off Marsaili's inherent paranoia. Eventually she decided just to beat him to the punch and end things herself, in the interests of self-preservation.

"Give this one a chance," Gregor suggested. "He might turn out to be worth it."

Marsaili sighed and rubbed her eyes. "When did you get to be so bloody soppy?" she asked with a wry laugh. Her brother hugged her in response, before they turned and headed for home.

CHAPTER 22

Despite the fact that Christmas had come and gone, the bar was still packed with festive revellers. Marsaili and Isla were in one of their favourite haunts from their student days, downstairs in one of the many basement bars that lined Bath Street in the city centre. The decor was vintage and kitsch, with old sheet music lining the walls and the furniture made up of reclaimed sofas and upcycled tables refurbished in chalk paint. They ordered two large gins from the bar, and slipped into a pair of comfortable wing back chairs in the far corner. It was open mic night, and a band was just tuning up on the little stage.

They clinked their glasses together before taking a sip. "Congratulations!" Marsaili cheered. Isla looked so happy; the little diamond solitaire twinkled on her ring finger as she twirled the straw in her glass.

"Nope, that's enough," Isla said, when Marsaili tried to quiz her further about her wedding plans. "We've talked about my love life enough; what's going on with you? You haven't even mentioned Euan in weeks, and somehow your boss' clothes ended up in our wash basket. Something's up."

Marsaili decided it was time to give someone the full story. Gregor's words from their walk had echoed through her mind the last two days, and she needed a second opinion. So, she finally unloaded the full, unadulterated version of everything that had happened with Euan, and the events that had unfolded in Will's hotel room.

When she was finished, Isla regarded her carefully.

"So, let me get this straight," she said. "Gorgeous Euan has been telling fibs about where he was for an evening, and you think you might have been about to get off with your boss in his hotel room?"

Marsaili shrugged. "Sort of - I don't know. There was just this weird atmosphere... but he's going through a divorce. It's too complicated."

"And you haven't spoken to Euan?"

"Not since I found out. Do you think I should?"

Isla pursed her lips together thoughtfully. "It's up to you.

He's a really charming guy, but did you ever think… I don't know? Maybe he's a little *too* charming?"

Marsaili's shoulders slumped. It seemed everyone was going to give her conflicting advice. "I won't know until I go back to work tomorrow, I suppose. I can't avoid him forever. Maybe he is just a player. Anyway," she declared, downing the last of her gin. "I just want to enjoy myself tonight. Another?"

Isla nodded, and Marsaili fought her way across the room. The band had started now, and a small crowd of young groupies gathered around the stage. She pushed gently through them, one arm outstretched, to squeeze into a gap at the bar.

The band were surprisingly good - all floppy hair and teenage angst, but their song was catchy and Marsaili found herself bopping along to them as she waited her turn to order. The barman nodded in her direction, making it clear that he knew she was next. She didn't envy him; at least at the theatre, even on the busiest nights, the crowds only came in twenty-minute bursts.

She shouted her order in his ear just as the song came to an end and the bar was filled with clapping. The young groupies surrounding the band screamed and bounced around, flinging themselves at the musicians as they gathered together their instruments and exited the stage.

Their setup was quickly replaced by a single microphone stand and a tall black stool. The compere took to the stage just as Marsaili had retrieved her drinks, telling the barman to keep the change. She stopped in her tracks as she heard him announce the next act.

"Ladies and gentlemen, please welcome to the stage, Mr Will Hunter!"

The crowd clapped politely, as Marsaili stood frozen to the spot. Sure enough, Will stepped up onto the stage, his blonde head bowed and a guitar strung across his chest. He took a seat on the stool and cleared his throat, one long leg tucked up on the footrest as he settled himself.

Marsaili considered her options; she could stay where she was and hope he didn't see her, or she could try to creep back to her table in the corner, where she'd be more hidden. The only trouble with that option was that the path back to her seat led directly across the front of the stage, which was now devoid of the bopping groupies that might have provided her with some much-needed cover.

Will was checking the tuning on his guitar, and she decided to make a dash for it, hoping to get there before he looked up.

She was halfway across when the bar hushed ever so slightly, and Will launched into the opening chords of the song. She couldn't help herself; she stopped, and looked up.

Marsaili had recognised the song instantly - it was a cover, and one of her favourites. *Better Half of Me* by Tom Walker.

Will's voice was pleasantly gravelly and understated. He looked nervous, his eyes either closed as he sang or glancing down at his guitar. It wasn't until halfway through the second verse that he seemed to hit his stride and become more confident. He looked around the room, even seeming to enjoy himself a little, and his eyes suddenly alighted on Marsaili. There was a little twitch of recognition, but he didn't look away from her as he continued to sing.

Marsaili felt her pulse quicken. *You still fancy him then,* she thought ruefully. His eyes didn't leave hers for the remainder of the song, and she felt as if every other person in the bar must have been looking at her too.

As the strains of the final chord reverberated around the room, there was a smattering of applause. The spell was broken and Will looked away, giving a grateful nod and a wave to the audience as the compere came back on stage. Marsaili scurried back to her seat.

"What took you so long?" Isla asked, looking up from her phone. Clearly, she hadn't been as enthralled by Will's song as Marsaili.

"Did you see the guy up on stage?" Marsaili asked, handing her friend her drink and taking a long swig of her own. She suddenly wished she'd bought shots too.

"What about him?" Isla glanced over to the stage, but Will was gone, and a trio of female vocalists were now taking his place.

"That was Will," Marsaili explained, her voice hushed.

"No way!" Isla just about jumped out of her seat, eager to see him.

"Sit down!" Marsaili muttered through clenched teeth.

But it was too late. Will had emerged from the makeshift backstage area and was milling around the bar, his guitar bag in one hand and a pint in the other.

"The blonde guy, in the checked shirt?" Isla asked. Marsaili nodded, unable to help herself from turning around to take a glance. "You never said he was so handsome!" Isla oohed appreciatively.

Will looked over at just the same moment, and despite never having met him before, Isla waved. He saw Marsaili sitting across from her and raised his glass in response, looking self-conscious, before making his way through the crowd towards them.

Marsaili was glaring at her friend, eyes wide. "What did you do that for?" she muttered.

"I want to meet him" Isla explained with a shrug, a playful glint in her eyes. "I can hardly tell you which one I think you should go for unless I've met both the contenders."

"Hello," Will had reached them now, and stood uncertainly behind Marsaili's chair. "Fancy meeting you here."

Marsaili smiled and stood up to make the introductions, forcing herself to sound cheerful and accidentally overdoing it. "Will! This my flatmate, Isla." Isla reached out and shook his hand, before pulling over a spare seat from the table next to them and encouraging him to sit down.

Will perched on the proffered stool and placed his guitar on the ground.

"A man of hidden talents," Marsaili observed, gesturing to the instrument. Will scoffed modestly.

"It's just something to get me out, try to meet some new people. Better than sitting and staring at my hotel room walls."

"You were really good," Isla interjected. Marsaili shot her a look that clearly said *you weren't even listening!*

Will nodded his appreciation. "Thank you. Mum and Dad forked out for cello and piano lessons; I had to teach myself the guitar on the sly. Did you have a good Christmas?" he asked, changing the subject.

When he found out about Isla's recent engagement, Will was quick to congratulate her, before insisting on setting off to the bar to get a bottle of bubbly to toast the happy couple.

Isla smiled mischievously at Marsaili as he left. "He doesn't seem awkward at all!" she declared. "He seems very sweet."

"You've been in his company for all of thirty seconds," Marsaili muttered.

Will returned surprisingly quickly, an ice bucket, bottle of champagne and three glasses clasped in his arms. He deposited them on the little table and poured them all a generous glass.

"Cheers!" he declared, and they all drank. On top of the two large gins she'd already consumed, the bubbles made Marsaili feel alarmingly fuzzy.

"So, do you have plans for Hogmanay?" Isla asked.

It took Will a moment to figure out what she was asking. "Oh, you mean New Year's Eve?" He shrugged dismissively. "I never really celebrate it, to be honest. Just another night."

"Ah, but you're in Scotland now!" Isla continued. "Have you ever been to a ceilidh?"

Will shook his head. Marsaili didn't like where this was going.

"We always go to one on Hogmanay, at the bowling club just round from our flat. You should come!" Isla announced, as if the idea had just popped into her head. Marsaili strongly suspected otherwise.

Will gave Marsaili a sideways glance, uncertain. He started mumbling his excuses, but Isla spoke over him.

"No arguments! I insist; you can't spend Hogmanay on your own. You're coming with us." Isla finished her glass of fizz and excused herself to go to the bathroom, looking very pleased with herself.

As soon as they were alone, Will smiled at her. "I've been thinking about you," he said, suddenly shifting himself closer. "I'm so glad to bump into you. I wanted to apologise for how I behaved the last time I saw you. I … um…" He gave a nervous laugh. "I'm not very good at this, as you can see. But I haven't been able to get you out of my head…" His hand reached out for Marsaili's, and she pulled away.

"Did you get your clothes back?" she interrupted, forcing herself to repeat the mantra she'd been chanting silently in her head ever since he'd shown up so unexpectedly. *He's married, he's your boss…*

"Yes," Will answered. "And the money. You didn't need to do that…"

"I don't want to owe you anything," she interrupted again.

Will looked hurt. "You didn't owe me anything. I was happy to help."

"So, did you see your wife over Christmas?"

"Em, no," Will answered, confused.

"Maybe you should invite her for Hogmanay," Marsaili continued. "New year, new start."

"I don't think she'd be interested. I don't think I'd be interested, for that matter. I'd much rather…"

"Or you could invite Caitriona? I bet she'd love to come with you."

Will frowned at her. "Why are you…?"

"I'm just looking out for you. As a friend."

"A friend?"

"Yes."

"Right," Will nodded to himself, his eyes downcast. Marsaili tried to quiet the little voice of regret at the back of her head; no matter how much she liked him, pursuing something with her not-yet-divorced boss could only lead to heartache. It was best to nip it in the bud.

"I understand," Will said, finishing his glass of champagne and standing up. "Tell Isla I said goodbye, will you? It was very nice to meet her. Enjoy the rest of your evening."

He hesitated, before giving her a quick, impulsive kiss on the cheek and squeezing back through the crowd, into the darkened street beyond.

CHAPTER 23

Marsaili knew she would have to face Euan next. She had to break up with him, properly, and then she'd be able to get back on track with focusing on her career without any more unnecessary distractions.

In the end, it happened before either of them had an opportunity to prepare themselves. She was opening the door into the staffroom, thinking that she'd try to catch him between performances, when she walked headlong into him. He had a pen in his hand, and had clearly been popping something through the door of one of the lockers.

"Marsaili!" he exclaimed, looking shocked. To her surprise, and before she could do anything to prevent it, he hugged her. "I'm so pleased to see you, I've been worried sick."

Marsaili regarded him coldly. He looked tired, with bags under his clear blue eyes and the stubble on his chin much thicker than usual. Against her better judgement, she felt herself softening a little. He did look genuinely upset, and when she remembered that he would just have spent his Christmas alone, she couldn't help but feel sorry for him.

"What are you doing in here?" she asked.

"I asked your manager, Bruce, is it? He said you were in today, so I was waiting for you. I needed to head round to make up now though, so I just slipped a note in your locker," he said, gesturing behind him.

"That's not mine," Marsaili said.

"Oh," Euan looked confused. "Sorry - Caitriona pointed it out to me."

Marsaili rolled her eyes. That made sense, at least. She didn't imagine Caitriona would have been terribly keen for them to make up.

"Look," Euan took both of her hands in his, and looked into her eyes earnestly. "I know there's a tonne of stuff we need to talk about, and I have a lot I need to explain. And apologise for. Will you hear me out? I've missed you."

He was rubbing the back of her hand with his thumb. Marsaili found herself picturing all the happy couples sitting around

110

the dinner table on Christmas day, and couldn't help but imagine how different it might have been if he'd been there with her; if she'd never stormed out of the party and never ended up back in that hotel room with Will.

Euan was smiling at her hopefully. He was easy, and fun, and he made her feel good about herself.

"We can talk," she agreed at last.

Euan breathed a sigh of relief. "Thank you," he whispered, kissing her briefly on the lips. "I'll make it all up to you, I promise."

She met him at stage door that night, and they walked together back to her flat, arm in arm. It felt comfortable and familiar, and Marsaili knew before he'd even started talking that whatever his explanation, she was probably going to forgive him.

They made their way quietly into the flat, where Marsaili made them both coffee, deliberately steering away from the booze. They sat across from each other on her bed, and Euan looked suitably tense.

"So, what's the story then?" Marsaili asked. Although she was warming up to him, she wasn't about to make things too easy on him.

Euan took a deep breath. "I lied about being at the hospital that night. I think you already know that." Marsaili nodded mutely.

"I'm sorry; I panicked, and I just didn't know what to say." He looked down at the mug in his hands before continuing. "I was seeing someone before I met you. One of the dancers in the show."

Suddenly Marsaili remembered - the dark-haired girl who had glared so viciously at her at stage door, the morning after their first date.

"We'd never discussed being exclusive," Euan hurried on, "so when I met you, and I liked you, I didn't think there was any harm in going for a drink. I didn't think things would move as quickly as they did."

Marsaili remembered how eager he had been that night in the darkened booth - if things had moved quickly, it certainly wasn't because she had been the one instigating them.

"I didn't expect to like you so much," Euan was saying, his blue eyes watching her earnestly. He really did look thoroughly ashamed of himself. "After we slept together, I knew I had to call things off with Gemma. That's where I was that night. I went around to see her and tell her it was over. I should have told you at the time, but I was so worried you'd be angry, and I didn't want things to end."

He took her hand across the duvet, and Marsaili let him. Piecing it together, she did have to admit that it made sense. She didn't particularly like it, but it was better than what she'd been imagining in her head.

"It's really over?" she asked quietly, wrapping her fingers around his. He sensed her softening, and put his coffee cup down on the bedside table before coming around and enveloping her in his arms.

"I promise," he muttered into her hair, his voice thick. "I can't help seeing her at work, but other than that I won't have anything to do with her, or anyone else, I swear." He smiled. "I only want you."

Marsaili smiled back. It felt nice to hear him say that. And he was here, warm, in her bed, now free of any other baggage or complications.

"So, are we exclusive now?" she teased, feeling like a teenager again.

"Boyfriend and girlfriend?" Euan smiled, his hand creeping up her back as he nudged closer. "You bet."

He kissed her gently, and Marsaili slid softly into the oblivion of his embrace.

Later that night, Euan woke her with a kiss. She curled into him in response, wrapping her arm around his torso, stroking the dark hair that covered his taut belly.

"What time is it?" she mumbled.

"Just after three. Sorry, Beautiful, but I need to take off. I wish I could stay, but we've got an early performance tomorrow and I need to get some clean clothes from home."

"Can't you stay just a little longer? It's so early." She leaned back to look at him. The orange glow of the streetlight outside her window lit up half of his face, giving him an eerie glow.

"I'd love to, but I can't sleep anyway. Thought I could hit the 24 hours gym, instead of tossing and turning for hours. Don't get up," he urged, seeing Marsaili begin to sit up in bed. "I didn't want to wake you, but I didn't want to sneak off either." He kissed her again. "I'll call you tomorrow. Get some rest."

Marsaili watched as he slipped out into the hallway, and listened for the click of the latch on the door as it swung shut behind him.

Marsaili awoke to find Isla in the kitchen, wrapped up in her dressing gown. She was humming softly to herself as she boiled the kettle and buttered toast. Sometimes, when Marsaili looked at her blissfully doing chores like this, she half expected forest creatures to start frolicking around her.

"Morning," she yawned from the hallway, running a hand through her tousled hair. Isla gave her a sharp look that said more than words possibly could.

"What?" Marsaili asked innocently.

"Don't 'what' me," Isla replied. "I heard you sneaking in last night, with a deep-voiced man, having whispered discussions in your bedroom." She peered at her again, gesturing with a butter knife in her hand.

"So, which one was it?" she asked. "Mr Smooth, or Mr Baggage? Or have we thrown a third one into the mix?"

For a second, Marsaili had a very real insight into what it must have been like to be a pupil in Isla's class. She wouldn't have stepped out of line, that's for sure. Then she remembered that she was actually a fully-grown woman, and not a twelve-year-old girl.

"Euan came over," she said, with as much confidence as she could muster. "We sorted everything out."

"And how did you do that, exactly?"

So Marsaili explained everything that had happened, with Gemma the dancer and the slight 'overlap' in their relationships with Euan. "He was just trying to do the right thing," she said. "He ended it with her once we'd slept together. And we're official now - in an actual proper, functioning, adult relationship." Marsaili wasn't sure if she was trying to convince Isla or herself.

Her friend sighed, putting down the slightly threatening butter knife. "I'm sorry," she said. "It's your life, and if you really like this guy then that's great. Just... don't let him mess you about again, ok? There are good guys out there - you don't need to put up with being lied to."

"It was a one off," Marsaili assured her. "It won't happen again."

CHAPTER 24

A few days later, on Hogmanay, Marsaili found herself waiting outside the doors of her local bowling club, staring anxiously into the frosty night. Euan had agreed to meet her there as soon as the show finished, which should have been by half ten at the latest. It was now after eleven, and a familiar, anxious voice was piping up in the back of her head.

Rubbing her arms against the cold, she hurried back inside. She'd check her phone again; maybe he'd have called to say he was on his way.

The party night was in full swing, the ceilidh band having been on stage since 8pm, and the dance floor was packed with people flinging themselves enthusiastically around to the Virginia Reel. It wasn't exactly a fancy night out, but the drinks were cheap, you could bring your own party food and the regulars had some good craic. Marsaili shimmied through the crowd back towards her table, where Isla, Findlay, Gregor and Gayatri were seated with some of their other friends. Marsaili was glad her brother and his girlfriend had made the trip through for the night. All six of them - herself and Euan included - would be staying the night back at Marsaili and Isla's flat. It would be a little squashed, but she was excited for her brother and Euan to meet at last. If he ever gets here, that is, she thought darkly.

Will had also arrived, much to Marsaili's surprise. She wasn't sure he'd take Isla up on her offer. She was even more surprised to find that he'd brought Caitriona with him, who was easily the most overdressed woman in attendance. She was wearing a sparkly, short party dress, boobs and legs out on full display, in stark contrast to the sea of 'jeans-and-a-nice top' that surrounded her. Marsaili fought down the little bubble of jealousy in her chest when she first saw them together; after all, it had been her who'd suggested he bring her in the first place.

Will had steadfastly ignored her for most of the evening, whether by design or due to the fact that Caitriona had cornered him at a small table on the opposite side of the room Marsaili didn't know. However, he must have managed to escape, because as she went back inside, he was standing at the bar. Plastering a smile on her face, she decided it was time to stop being so ridiculous and head over to say hello.

He was dressed once again in his trademark off-duty uniform - checked shirt, ironed jeans and polished brown shoes - and carrying a pint and a glass of red wine. He turned as she approached and smiled warmly.

"Evening," Will said. He looked carefree, perhaps loosened up slightly by the multiple pints of ale he'd obviously already consumed. Marsaili nodded over to where he'd been sitting in the corner.

"You've escaped then?"

"Ah yes," Will slurred slightly, and gave her a lopsided smile. "Between you and me, I think she's rather keen."

"Keeping you all to herself, is she?" Marsaili asked with a smile.

"She certainly doesn't want me talking to you, that's for sure," he said. He stumbled slightly, and Marsaili put out a hand to steady him.

"She's in the loo," Will whispered conspiratorially. "Don't suppose you drink red?" He held up the glass of wine in his hand. "Fancy sneaking off before she gets back?"

Marsaili looked at him, knowing it probably wasn't a good idea but considering it nonetheless. She knew she should be looking out for Euan, but if he couldn't be bothered to turn up on time, why should she waste her evening waiting for him?

They stumbled down a darkened corridor, like two school kids playing truant, and found themselves in the men's cloakroom. There were lockers and coat hooks lining the walls, and it smelled strongly of deodorant and aftershave. Will placed the drinks down on a low bench, before sitting himself and passing Marsaili the large glass of red.

"Fuck me, it's a relief to be away from her!" He said with a sigh, laughing at the shocked expression on her face. She'd never heard him swear before. He ran his hands through his hair, fixing Marsaili with a look of utter disbelief. "I'm sorry if she's your friend, but why did you think I should bring her exactly? All she's done is talk about herself and her bloody 'career'." He put the word in air quotes, using the first two fingers of each hand. "I think she's under the impression that sleeping with me is going to help her get another rung up the ladder; she is sorely mistaken on that front." He paused, taking a long swig from his pint glass.

Marsaili couldn't help but ask the question. "Which part?"

"What do you mean?"

"Which part is she mistaken about - you helping her climb the career ladder, or you sleeping with her?"

Will suddenly looked serious. He bit his lip, taking a minute and inhaling deeply before speaking. "Marsaili, you can't have it both ways. You can't turn me down and then keep tabs on who I may or may not choose to have a relationship with." Drink had obviously made him more candid than he would usually be, and Marsaili rushed to apologise.

"I haven't done that with you," he continued. "I know you're back with Euan and that's your decision, it's none of my business. You're a grown woman and I have no right to interfere with your life, no matter…"

"No matter what?"

He was standing now, pacing the room and clearly frustrated. He looked at her again, with an intensity that both surprised and scared her, and for a moment Marsaili found herself wishing he would stop being so infuriatingly polite and just take her in his arms and kiss her.

"Lovers' tiff?" The teasing voice that interrupted them was annoyingly familiar. Marsaili tore herself away from Will's gaze to find her brother, peering round the door with a glint in his eyes.

"I was looking for the loo," Gregor continued, entering the room with his hand outstretched and walking towards Will. "Euan, I presume? Don't worry about me walking in on your wee spat. Believe me when I tell you, you're not the first to find my little sister's stubborn streak somewhat annoying."

"*Twin* sister," Marsaili corrected, scowling at him.

"Little by two minutes," Gregor shot back.

Will took Gregor's hand and shook it briefly, looking from one to the other in confusion. "She can be somewhat… irritating," he conceded. He recovered himself, and was all impeccable manners once more. "But I'm afraid I'm not Euan. My name's Will."

"My boss," Marsaili interjected, still glaring at her brother, and wondering what might have happened had he not interrupted them.

116

"Oh!" It was Gregor's turn to look confused now. "My mistake. Loos through here?" He excused himself, glancing at Marsaili with an inscrutable expression on his face.

Will was watching her still. "I'm sure your actual boyfriend will be here soon," he said quietly. "Mustn't keep him waiting."

"No, best not," Marsaili replied, slipping out of the door and returning to the hubbub of the party next door.

When she emerged back onto the dance floor, she realised it was getting close to midnight. Almost everyone was on their feet as the ceilidh band gave way to the DJ for the second portion of the night's entertainment, and he was hyping the crowd up into a frenzy before the bells. People were queued three deep at the bar to get their drinks in, ready for the big moment.

Marsaili noticed Caitriona, deep in conversation with another man. Irrationally, she felt a surge of protectiveness towards Will. Pretty ironic given the conversation they'd just been having; if anything, Caitriona ought to be the one annoyed at *her.*

Marsaili felt a hand on her waist and jumped. She was relieved when she turned to find her brother's identical brown eyes looking into her own.

"Well that was a bit bloody awkward!" Gregor declared.

"To put it mildly," Marsaili agreed.

"Sorry, sis. I just assumed with all that sexual tension flying around he must have been your mystery man. What's going on there? And don't fob me off; that was no ordinary employee-employer interaction."

Marsaili sighed. "It's a mess, Gregor, I don't want to get into it…"

He eyed her carefully. "Alright, but if he needs anyone to file a sexual harassment claim be sure to give him my card."

With that, he winked and slipped off into the crowd to find Gayatri.

Euan arrived just a couple of minutes before midnight. He was full of apologies, a routine Marsaili was beginning to find all too familiar. But she knew she'd hardly been a paragon of virtue herself that evening. She may not have done anything wrong, technically, but she'd certainly put herself in a somewhat incriminating situation. Not wanting to start the new year off on a bad foot, she gave him a half-hearted hug and managed to grab them both a drink before the countdown began.

10, 9, 8, 7, 6, 5, 4, 3, 2, 1… HAPPY NEW YEAR!

The cheer echoed around the small function suite, before everyone grabbed their respective partners in an embrace and a festival of general hugging and merriment broke out around the room. Euan kissed Marsaili firmly, one hand on each of her cheeks, and as they broke apart, she spotted Caitriona in a very similar embrace with Will. Obviously, his disdain for her self-obsessed conversation wasn't enough to get in the way of him thinking with his dick, like most men. Doing her best to ignore them, she dragged Euan off to introduce him to the rest of her friends.

There was the usual clump of autograph hunters to contend with, once word inevitably spread that a local celebrity was in the building. Thankfully tonight though, they were mostly in the form of middle aged and elderly ladies, who looked at Marsaili on his arm as if she were the luckiest girl in the world, and not as if they wanted to stab her in the eye with a fork.

As they were getting ready to leave, Marsaili was surprised to see Gregor speaking to Will. They were sharing a laugh over something, before Gregor scribbled on a slip of paper and handed it to him. Marsaili watched as Will slipped the paper in his shirt pocket, shook Gregor's hand, and the pair said their goodbyes.

Marsaili gave her brother a look as he approached. He shrugged. "What? Turns out he's into rock climbing, so I've recommended a few spots he might want to try out."

Marsaili snorted. Clearly all of her friends were going to find Will irresistibly charming.

"Weren't you the one who advised me to give Euan another go?" she asked, frustrated.

"Yeah, but that was before I met him," Gregor replied darkly. "There's something about him I can't take to." He eyed Euan carefully, as he stood some distance off saying goodnight to a couple of elderly fans. "He's too good to be wholesome."

"Well I like him," Marsaili argued back, "so make an effort with him, will you? For me?"

Gregor shrugged, as Euan jogged over to join them.

"Home time?" he asked jovially.

"Lead the way," Gregor replied, with an exaggerated sweep of his arm. Marsaili hoped his tone was only obvious to her.

CHAPTER 25

Despite the concerns of her brother and flatmate, Marsaili's relationship with Euan soon settled back into a steady rhythm. He'd sleep over at her place two or three nights a week, and in between performances they'd grab the occasional meal or coffee together. It wasn't the most exciting relationship, but it was comfortable and it was easy, and it kept inappropriate thoughts of Will from her mind. Most of the time, at least.

On the face of it, things with Will had returned to normal too, although she still occasionally caught sight of him unexpectedly and felt that somersault of attraction deep in her belly. It was just a crush, she told herself, and it would pass soon enough. And although she knew it was unfair – she was in a relationship herself, after all - she'd still been relieved to confirm that the Hogmanay kiss with Caitriona had been just a one off. The thought of the two of them being together had made her undeniably jealous.

They'd been working together, one quiet Thursday afternoon in the Upper Circle bar, when Caitriona casually dropped it into conversation. It was halfway through January now and the end of the panto would soon be upon them, along with the temporary closure and revamping of the theatre. Marsaili and Caitriona were taking advantage of the lull in activity to scrub the bar from head to toe. They'd cleared all the free-pour bottles and taken down the optics, and Marsaili was now perched on the raised bar, polishing the large mirror that covered the rear wall.

"Be careful up there." The male voice spoke from the doorway. Marsaili turned to see Will observing her carefully. "Not exactly in line with our health and safety practices, but I'll turn a blind eye for now." He gave her a little smile, which Marsaili returned before he continued on his way.

Caitriona humphed dramatically. "Weirdo," she said, throwing a resentful glance at Will's tall, straight back.

"What makes you say that?" Marsaili tried not to sound too interested, keeping her focus instead on rubbing a particularly stubborn smear on the glass.

"You know he asked me out for Hogmanay? We came to that ceilidh you'd suggested, at the bowling club?" Caitriona paused for a moment. She'd been mopping the floor and Marsaili could see her reflection in the mirror, standing on the far side of the room leaning on the mop, one hip popped out to the side.

"Well we'd been having a great time, chatting all night, so when the bells came around, I thought it was the perfect opportunity to go in for a little kiss. He seemed up for it, but then suddenly he was making excuses and putting me in a taxi." She resumed her mopping, flicking a shiny, smooth strand of blonde hair out of her face. "I think he's in the closet," she declared. Of course, Marsaili thought. Because obviously no hot-blooded, heterosexual male could possibly be immune to your charms, could he?

"Anyway," Caitriona continued, "No time for any of that nonsense! I've got another audition next week."

Marsaili scrubbed more furiously. Her smugness over Caitriona's failure to ensnare Will was quickly replaced by another wave of jealousy. Her headshot spree from a few weeks ago had yielded no results so far, and Euan's agent still hadn't got back to her either. She knew it had been the holidays, but still she had hoped something might have come from it by now.

"I have your boyfriend to thank for it, actually," Caitriona continued.

"For what?" Marsaili asked, suddenly uneasy.

"My audition. He passed my headshots along to his agent. The casting director for *Dear Green Place* agreed to see me straight away - apparently they have a role in the pipeline that she thinks I'd be *perfect* for."

Marsaili clambered down from the bar, gritting her teeth together. Caitriona was smiling at her, and she forced a grin in return.

"Isn't that *wonderful?!*" she enthused.

"Wonderful," Marsaili agreed.

Euan knew something was amiss the moment she met him at stage door. He kissed her on the cheek and she froze instantly at his touch.

"What's the matter?" he asked, his blue eyes concerned.

"We'll talk at home," she said coldly, marching off down the street ahead of him.

They walked in silence for a while, until eventually Marsaili could take it no longer and plonked herself down on a passing bench.

She crossed her legs and folded her arms over her chest, looking up at his amused face.

"When were you going to tell me about Caitriona?" she said.

Euan had the audacity to laugh; a brief snort of derision. "Caitriona? What about her?" He cocked his head to one side. "Don't tell me, you think I've been sleeping with her too?"

The thought hadn't actually occurred to her, until now. "Have you?" she retorted, wondering why that was the first scenario to come to his mind.

Euan threw his hands up in despair. "You know what Marsaili, I know I wasn't completely up front with you in the beginning, but I'm beginning to get a bit tired of this whole victim act."

"Victim?"

"Yes, victim! It doesn't matter what I do, in your eyes I will always be the bad guy, all because of one little mistake, and you will never trust me." Marsaili tried to answer, but he talked over her in a rush. She'd never seen him angry before. He pushed on, a leering grin on his face.

"You know I have girls throwing themselves at me every night, don't you? I could go home with a different one after every performance if I wanted to, but I don't. I come home with you, I go to sleep next to you, I make love to *you*!" He pointed at her furiously. "And you don't trust me."

"Did you give my headshots to your agent?" Marsaili asked, changing tack. That caught him off guard; obviously he'd assumed this was all about sex. He glanced from side to side nervously.

"Why are you asking about that?"

"Answer the question. Did you give my headshots to your agent?"

"Well, I was going to, but..."

"Did you give Caitriona's headshots to your agent?"

Euan exhaled sharply. "Yes! OK, yes, I passed along Caitriona's information. I thought she might be good for a part we have coming up."

Marsaili stared at him, vindicated. "And how exactly did you find the time to help out someone who apparently means nothing to you, but not your supposed girlfriend?"

Euan sat down heavily beside her, his head in his hands.

When he spoke his voice was quiet, but still frustrated.

"You want the truth? Fine. I didn't want to hurt your feelings, but I knew we didn't have anything coming up that you'd be right for. Caitriona on the other hand…"

"Was skinny enough and pretty enough to be on your precious show?" Marsaili finished for him.

"Is that what you want me to say?" he said quietly, his eyes defeated. "Yes, they wanted a slim, attractive, blonde. I knew you were too…"

"Fat?" She glared at him, daring him to confirm it.

There was silence for a moment, before Euan spoke again. "God, you really are impossible, you know that?"

Marsaili stood up, gathering her coat around herself. She thought she might have cried, but it turned out she was too angry even for tears.

"I think you've been perfectly clear. Goodnight, Euan."

With that, she turned and stalked down the street. Euan called after her, but she didn't look back.

CHAPTER 26

The following evening, with no word from Euan following their row, Marsaili resolved to distract herself by going out for tea with Isla. Her fury at him had abated somewhat, but the hurt still remained. He may not have said the words himself, but his opinion was clear - she was fun enough to sleep with, but nowhere near attractive enough to consider being on TV. Certainly no match for Caitriona.

Marsaili did her best to hold on to her anger - it was easier to be angry at him than hurt by him. And it held at bay any urge she might have otherwise had to contact him. They were definitely over this time.

She met Isla at a family pub around the corner from her school. It was 5pm and the place was crowded with parents and kids out for a Friday night treat. They were lucky to get a booth next to the windows, looking out over the river, and both ordered a glass of wine whilst looking through the menu.

"Good day?" Isla asked. Her tone was light, but her face looked tired. Marsaili hadn't told her what had happened with Euan yet; she wasn't ready to admit that her friend had been right to have her reservations.

"Not bad," she answered. "You?"

"So-so. I hate this term - dark mornings, dark nights, the kids are restless after Christmas... roll on spring," she said.

When the waitress returned Marsaili ordered a burger - no point worrying about her weight now, she figured - while Isla ordered grilled chicken and salad.

"Slimming for the dress?" Marsaili teased.

Isla wrinkled her nose. "Sort of, I suppose. Actually, I wanted to talk to you about the wedding..."

Marsaili sat up; Isla looked suddenly uncomfortable.

"You know how I said we weren't in any rush?" Isla began. "Well, there's been a change of plan..."

"Oh my God you're pregnant!" Marsaili blurted out. The people at the table next to them turned to stare at her outburst.

"No!" Isla declared, shushing her. "God no, not that." She took a deep breath. "Findlay got news that his posting is being changed. They're moving him to another base, up North - Lossiemouth. And because we're engaged now, they're willing to give him family digs, which means I can go with him."

Marsaili smiled. "But that's great news! Why do you look so upset about it?"

Isla shrugged. "I mean I am happy, it's just… I have to start looking for a new job. And obviously it means I'll be moving out of the flat."

Marsaili felt her shoulders slump. "Ah," she said simply. They both knew it; there was no way she could afford to stay there on her own. She'd either have to find another flat share, with strangers, or move into a smaller flat in a cheaper part of town. Or really admit defeat and move back home with her parents.

"Sorry," Isla said quietly.

"Don't be daft!" Marsaili said, forcing a cheeriness that she didn't really feel into her voice. She slid round the other side of the booth to put an arm around her friends' shoulder.

"I'm so happy for you," she said, and she meant it, deep down. "This is so exciting! You and Findlay in your first home; you've waited years for this."

Isla smiled, her hand on Marsaili's knee. "Maybe this will be a good thing for you, too?" she volunteered. "Things have been going well with you and Euan, haven't they? Maybe you two will end up shacked up together as well."

"Yeah, maybe." Marsaili replied quietly.

Isla picked up the tab when their bill came, despite Marsaili's protests. They left the restaurant and the smiling families behind, shrugging on their coats as they stepped into the damp night.

"Home?" Isla asked. "Or one for the road?"

Marsaili had her excuse prepared. "Oh, I said I'd catch up with Forbes for a quick drink. He's performing at the club tonight; said he'd squeeze me in before he starts his makeup."

Isla gave her a brief hug, and the two girls set off in opposite directions. But Marsaili wasn't going to see Forbes.

She'd tried his phone number a few times on the way there, and now she was waiting on the street outside. She rang the buzzer before trying his phone again - she knew it was the understudy's performance tonight, so in theory, Euan should have been home.

He owned a mews apartment on Park Circus. Marsaili had been there briefly, once or twice, when they'd popped by so he could collect some things. It was in a much more affluent part of town than Marsaili's rented flat, but he'd always claimed to prefer the cosiness of her place, and so they'd never spent the night there. The interior of his home was stark and modern, a feature he'd blamed on the interior designer he'd hired to decorate it, and the lack of a 'woman's touch' to make it more homely.

The intercom on the door buzzed into life, and Marsaili was surprised to hear a woman's voice answer it. She sounded impatient.

"Hello?"

"Hi," Marsaili said uncertainly. "Sorry I'm not sure if I've pressed the wrong buzzer… I'm looking for Euan? Euan Campbell?"

The woman sighed audibly. She had a broad, East End accent. "He's not in, love. Listen, I don't know how you've found our address, but don't come back, right? He has enough autograph hunters bothering him when he's out and about; we deserve some peace in our own home."

Marsaili smarted at the mention of 'our' home. She didn't think she was going to like what happened next, but she had to know for sure. "I'm not an autograph hunter," she explained, stumbling over her words. "I'm his girlfriend."

The woman's tone changed suddenly, from frustrated yet tolerant, to downright angry. "Wait there," she said tersely.

When she came to the door, she was every bit as glamorous as Marsaili would have expected. Even just lounging at home on a Friday evening, she was dressed in silk pyjamas and had her blonde hair carefully curled around her shoulders. Marsaili felt like an old tramp standing there before her, small and chubby and dishevelled on her doorstep.

The woman glared at her. "I don't know who you are, and I don't want to," she began, wagging a perfectly polished acrylic nail in Marsaili's face. "Euan Campbell is *my* fiancé, you understand? And I don't need whatever little whore's been sleeping with him coming around here trying to mess up our lives."

"I'm not a whore!" Marsaili protested. "He told me he was single!"

"Ha," the woman snorted, sneering as she looked Marsaili up and down. "You're one of his little experiments then." She crossed her arms across her chest and leaned against the doorway. "Go on - what sob story did he feed you? The orphaned, recovering drug addict? The child abuse survivor? Or has he come up with something more imaginative recently?"

Marsaili stared at her, open mouthed, as she continued her tirade.

"Oh, don't tell me you actually *believed* him!?" she giggled. "God, he must be getting better." At Marsaili's dumbfounded expression, she explained further. "'Honing his craft', that's what he calls it. Picking up pathetic, lonely women who haven't had a shag in months and seeing if he can sweet talk his way into their beds. How long did it take him to get into your knickers? One date? Two?"

Marsaili turned abruptly, not wanting to hear any more, furious tears burning the backs of her eyes. She set off down the street, thrusting her hands deep into the pockets of her coat. "Fuck off," the woman called after her, "and don't come back!"

CHAPTER 27

The news of Euan's engagement broke a couple of days later. Gregor was the first to phone her, having seen his face plastered across the front of the *Daily Record* at every newsstand in the train station on his way to work.

"I'm sorry, sis," he'd said simply. She was grateful, at least, that he hadn't gloated. "Call it a lucky escape, eh?" he tried, in an attempt to cheer her up. "Feel sorry for the poor girl who's marrying him - you're too good for that smug prick."

She knew he was right, of course. She wouldn't have wanted Euan back anyway, even if he'd begged her. But unfortunately, that didn't mean it hurt any less to see the effusive declarations of love for his bride-to-be spread over every newspaper, magazine and social media thread she encountered.

One saving grace, at least, was that the pantomime was nearly over. Marsaili had only one more week to endure, and then hopefully she would never have to see Euan Campbell's smarmy face ever again.

When at work, she seemed to be followed around by sympathetic glances and hushed words. Morag cuddled her, repeating Gregor's sentiments about her being 'too good for him', while Forbes threatened to castrate him with a pair of his size eleven stiletto heels. Even Caitriona looked uncharacteristically meek, as she folded her into a slightly awkward embrace. "He's a knob, Marsaili," she said. She held her at arm's length and looked earnestly into her eyes. "I promise, if I do get a part on his TV show, I won't speak to him. Not even a word... Well, unless we have to do a scene together. But I'm sure you can forgive me for that!"

The week dragged on, seemingly interminably, but the final performance eventually rolled around. Marsaili volunteered to work the after-show party. It would mean she might cross paths with Euan, but at least if she was behind the bar, she wouldn't risk getting trollied and saying - or doing - anything stupid.

In the end, Euan at least had the good sense to avoid her. He stayed in a corner of the bar at the back, and let his castmates fetch him drinks. He didn't even so much as glance in Marsaili's direction.

Morag was behind the bar with her, and Marsaili was glad of

the older woman's company. She prattled away amiably whilst they served, clearly hoping to distract her from Euan's presence. She was telling Marsaili about her teenage daughter's latest infatuation, a band called *Devil's Worship*, when Will unexpectedly entered the bar.

He hadn't been on shift that night, which meant he'd made a special effort to turn up. He could easily explain it as his opportunity to say farewell to the cast and thank them for their hard work, but when she saw him, part of Marsaili hoped he might have had another motive in choosing to attend tonight.

He approached the bar with a smile on his face, saying hello to people and shaking hands as he made his way through the crowd. He was wearing a dark blue lambswool sweater over his white shirt tonight, and looked as dashing as always.

"Evening ladies," he said, leaning on the bar. "Everything going OK?"

Morag nodded, placing her hands on her broad, motherly hips. "Pretty quiet, really, as these things go," she said, nodding to the sparsely populated bar. She was right; it was nowhere near as raucous as end of panto nights usually were.

Will looked at Marsaili, his eyes full of concern. "How about you?" he asked. "You OK?"

Morag put her arm around her before Marsaili had a chance to reply. She simultaneously squeezed her and scowled across the bar to where Euan was standing. "She's fine," she assured Will vigorously. "You're a tough one, aren't you lass? Not going to let a two-timing wee shite like him get you down."

Marsaili laughed in spite of herself. "That's me," she said, looking at Will as she spoke. "Tough as old boots!"

Will nodded. "That's my girl," he said with a smile.

It wasn't until much later, when the bar had emptied and Marsaili and Morag were busy cleaning and restocking, that Will re-appeared. He jangled the keys at them.

"I sent Bruce home," he explained. "He's got a wife and kids to get home to rather than an empty hotel room, so I thought I'd volunteer to lock up."

"That was nice of you," said Morag, with a smile.

"Speaking of family," he said to her, "shouldn't you be getting home too? Marsaili and I can finish off here."

Morag eyed him suspiciously, clearly torn between the desire to get home to see her kids before they went to bed, and her innate nosiness.

"It's fine, Morag," Marsaili said. "Get home to the wee ones."

"Not so wee now," Morag said, as she handed Will the bucket of hot water which she'd just finished filling. "Growing like weeds the pair of them! Thank you." Then, quietly, so only Will could hear, she whispered, "Don't you take advantage of her and her broken heart; she's had quite enough bother from you lot recently."

"I wouldn't dream of it," he whispered back with a wink.

Will plopped the mop into the bucket and started cleaning as Morag bustled out of the room. Marsaili continued working in silence, sliding bottles and cans into the empty spaces in the under-counter refrigerators. She found stock rotating strangely relaxing, like some kind of mindfulness exercise.

"I was sorry to hear about Euan," Will said eventually.

"You and I both."

"One thing I never understood though," Will said, pausing to look at her over the bar. "Why did you get back together with him in the first place? I thought you'd already found out about Erica?"

"Erica?"

"His fiancée."

Marsaili paused. "No," she said slowly. "He owned up to me about Gemma, one of the dancers. Said he'd been seeing her when we got together, but then he ended it."

"Ah, I see. My mistake. Never mind then…" Will went back to his mopping.

"No, wait a minute," Marsaili continued, finally piecing it all together. "That's what you meant, wasn't it, that night in your hotel room? When you said you'd tried to warn me? You knew he was *engaged?*"

Reluctantly, Will nodded. "I worked with her, down in London. She's an actress too, and we had her in with a touring company. She kept going on about how her boyfriend was some big deal on BBC Scotland. Anyway, she sent me a friend request on Facebook and I saw his photo on her profile picture. Took me a while to place him, mind you, and then when you started seeing him I… Well, I checked online to see if they were still together. And according to her Facebook page, they'd not long got engaged."

Marsaili could have kicked herself. Euan told her he didn't

use social media, and she was hardly a prolific poster herself; she hadn't ever thought to go looking for him.

"Why didn't you tell me?" she asked instead.

"I tried! You stormed out on me the first time, remember? And then I didn't want to push it in case you thought, you know…"

"What?"

"That I was just trying to split you up because I wanted you for myself."

Marsaili looked at him. He was sweating slightly, and ran his finger around the collar of his shirt nervously. She tried to laugh it off, turning her attention back to the half-filled fridge.

"Yeah right - who'd want me?" She asked with a shrug. "I'm stubborn, and clumsy, and short-tempered, and dumpy…"

"Don't do that," he said, quietly but firmly. "Don't talk yourself down and make out like you're less than you are. You're funny, and smart, and beautiful." In a sudden burst of decisiveness, Wil dropped the mop and crossed the room to her in three long strides, coming around the side of the bar. He stopped suddenly, seeming to hesitate. "Sorry. I know I'm your boss, and I'm in the middle of a bloody awful divorce, and the timing couldn't be worse. But I've been trying - very badly - to tell you for weeks. I like you. And not just as a colleague, or a friend."

Marsaili felt her mouth go dry. She'd wanted to hear him say it out loud for such a long time. Will took a step closer, his hand reaching out for hers. Briefly, their pinkie fingers intertwined, before she snapped back to reality.

"We can't," she said, stepping away. "It's just… It's too complicated. You're still married,"

"Separated," Will interrupted.

"I'm just out of a relationship," she continued. "Albeit a crappy one. And you're my boss."

"None of those things are dealbreakers," Will persisted. "Not for me."

"I'm sorry," Marsaili said, not wanting to look at him. "It can't happen."

Will nodded, deflated. "I understand," he said, stepping aside to let her pass. "It's late; you should get yourself home. I'll finish up here."

Marsaili swept past him, wishing him goodnight and striding

quickly out of the room, before her heart could overrule her head and send her tumbling into his arms.

CHAPTER 28

Marsaili stared gratefully out to the sea. It had been years since she'd last been on a boat. It was a clear, crisp, winter's day, with just a tiny hint of snow on the gentle breeze. The water was still and undisturbed, save for the cascading ripple furrowed through it by the prow of the boat.

It was a Sunday, and they were out on Lachlan's personal pleasure vessel. He'd dropped a couple of lobster creels, but they were there for the atmosphere more than the fishing. Rowan's mum was watching Callie and the three of them were spending the afternoon together. It was the first time Rowan had been away from her new daughter for longer than twenty minutes, but despite her nerves she was glad to be responsibility free for a couple of hours. Marsaili felt bad for gate-crashing what was supposed to be her brother and sister-in-law's first date since becoming parents, but when she'd arrived on her own parent's doorstep unannounced two days prior, they hadn't hesitated in inviting her along.

She had been due to come up the following weekend anyway. Not being religious, Rowan and Lachlan didn't want to have Callie christened, however they had decided to have a Naming Ceremony to officially welcome their little girl into the world. They assured Marsaili it wasn't going to be a big do - just close family and friends - and had asked her to act as a 'guide-parent'. Since the theatre was dark anyway, and in the light of her recent very public heartbreak, Bruce had agreed to let her take a week's unpaid leave and make the trip a slightly longer one. She got to come home to the bosom of her family while she re-evaluated things, and the struggling Pantheon didn't have to fork out her wages that week. It was a win-win for everyone.

Lachlan popped up from below deck, a bottle of beer in each hand, and passed one to each of the girls. Being in charge of the boat, he restricted himself to sipping from a bottle of Irn-Bru instead.

"Good to have you home, sis," he said, raising the plastic bottle in a toast. Marsaili sipped her beer and leaned back, enjoying the feel of the winter sun on her face. "It's good to be home," she agreed.

And it was. No matter how complicated and confusing her

life got, coming back to the simplicity of her rural home was always refreshing. In fact, every time she came home recently, the more reluctant she felt to leave again. Life here seemed easier and less stressful than in the city.

"It's been nice to see so much of you recently," Rowan said, as if she could read her thoughts. "You ever think of making the move back up here a permanent one?"

Marsaili sighed. "It's tempting right now," she admitted, before asking a question that had plagued her for years but she'd never had the courage to say out loud. "Am I mad for staying down there? For still trying to be an actor after all this time?"

"Not mad," Rowan reassured her quickly. She had never had the same urge as Marsaili to leave their childhood home; when Lachlan followed his father into fishing, Rowan followed her mother into floristry, and ever since then their focus had always been on building a life together. A small life; the kind of life which, Marsaili realised, she had always looked down on. Now, however, she could see the appeal. Rowan and Lachlan were part of something bigger than themselves, traditions that grounded them in the land and the community they came from. It was part of their bones.

"I admire you," Rowan was saying. "You've given it a really good go, but maybe there wouldn't be any harm in thinking about the next chapter?" Her friend looked at her consolingly. "What comes next? If the dream isn't going to come true, what do you really want out of life?"

Marsaili hadn't expected a full-on life-coaching session. "I just want to be happy," she said, "Isn't that what everyone wants?"

"And what do you think will make you happy?"

She contemplated the question for a moment. "A relationship; a family; and a job I enjoy."

"And if that job *isn't* acting?"

"I think I'd be OK with it," Marsaili admitted. It was the first time she'd said it out loud. She hadn't ever been an actor, not really; it was a hobby at best. And she didn't want to spend the rest of her life pouring drinks.

"So, the relationship stuff, that will all happen in its own time," Rowan said, glossing very diplomatically over how spectacularly everything with Euan had imploded. "But the job stuff - that we can do something about. Is there anything else you could see yourself doing?"

Marsaili considered the question for a moment, although she knew there was only one possible option that might bring her the kind of satisfaction she craved. It had been plaguing her thoughts for the last few weeks, and despite her reluctance to consider it before now, she couldn't forget how much she'd enjoyed that afternoon spent with the children at Isla's school. She'd got a buzz out of it; the kind of buzz she'd only ever felt before when she was performing.

"Teaching," she admitted. "I know I've always dismissed it before, but I think I'd enjoy it. And I might actually be good at it."

Rowan and Lachlan exchanged a knowing glance. "It makes sense," Rowan said. "You could still be involved in the creative activities you enjoy, but you'd have a steady pay check, and regular working hours. Plus, decent holidays. If you decided you ever wanted to start a family, that'd be a real bonus."

Marsaili knew she had the academic qualifications to get into teacher training. Plus, it wouldn't require her to live in the city anymore; if she wanted to be closer to home and family, there were schools up here too.

"I'll think about it," she said.

That night, crouched over her laptop in her old bedroom, Marsaili found herself surfing through university admissions websites. She browsed through a few courses that she knew she'd find interesting - archaeology, midwifery, Celtic studies. But either they wouldn't lead to a definitive job at the end of them, or they would require at least another 4 years of studying. Not that she was running out of time, but she didn't want to spend another half a decade waiting for her real life to begin. She'd wasted enough time chasing a dream; she wanted to get started on the next phase of her life *now*. Try as she might, she returned to teaching again and again.

Marsaili read through the admission policies for her top three choices - The University of the Highlands and Islands; Glasgow, where she'd done her undergraduate degree; or Strathclyde. All three required written applications, followed by two rounds of interviews. She was surprised by how competitive it was - she'd always thought of teaching as an easy backup option.

The more she read the more excited she became at the prospect. She would be qualified for primary or secondary, where she could focus on either English or Drama. It was currently late January, and the application deadlines were all in mid-March. If she was seriously thinking about this, she'd need to make up her mind quickly.

Her eyes tiring, Marsaili looked at the clock on her bedside table. It was after 10pm. She lay back on the quilted bedspread and stretched out, contemplating sleep. The house was quiet, so she assumed her parents were already in bed. She went to close over the lid on her laptop, resolving to think about it more in the morning, when a sudden thought entered her head. In spite of her better judgement, she found herself logging into Facebook for the first time in weeks.

She absentmindedly scrolled through her newsfeed for a moment or two. This was why she didn't bother with it normally, she thought - it was all humble brags and subtle boasting from people with whom she shared tenuous connections and would mostly avoid if she saw them out and about in real life. But she couldn't help herself - she clicked on the search bar at the top of the page.

Will Hunter, she typed carefully.

It turned out to be a fairly common name. She scrolled through the list of Wills, all varying ages, heights, weights and hair colours, until she saw one that looked like a possible match. The picture wasn't even of him - it was a sunrise, obviously taken from the top of a mountain somewhere. She clicked on it.

There was very little information on the page - no mutual friends, unsurprisingly. She flicked through the profile pictures until she eventually found one of him. It had obviously been taken without him knowing - he was dressed as smartly as ever, sitting at a table in a bar with his head turned to one side as he laughed at something. He looked happy.

She flicked to the next one and felt her stomach lurch. This time, he wasn't alone.

It was a black and white picture, clearly a professional image. It was his wedding day - Will was in a perfectly tailored morning suit, and his wife was in a stunning fishtail gown. She had dark hair that tumbled around her shoulders in loose, cascading waves and a crown of flowers on her head. It was springtime; they were walking through a field towards the camera, blossom hanging heavy on the branches of the trees, Will carrying his bride's train in his arms as they laughed at some shared joke. She was looking at the camera, but he was looking at her. The expression in his eyes was unmistakable - pure, simple, love.

Marsaili smiled sadly at his beautiful face. He may well like her, but he loved his wife. Probably still did. She could never compete with that.

With a sigh, she closed the lid and rolled over to go to sleep.

CHAPTER 29

In the days leading up to Callie's Naming Ceremony, Marsaili's home became a hive of activity. Rowan had given her own mother responsibility for providing the decorations, in the form of flowers and balloons, whilst Shonagh was tasked with baking the cake. Each granny was delighted to be involved and to have the chance to show off their own particular set of skills; Marsaili was just curious to see which would go the most over the top with their offerings.

As she descended the stairs into the kitchen, she suspected her own mother was in with a decent shout. Shonagh had obviously been up for hours, even though it was only just gone 7am. She was in her pinny, sleeves rolled up, her fawn coloured curls coated in a delicate dusting of flour. There wasn't a surface in the kitchen that wasn't covered in an assortment of baking tins, piping bags or mixing bowls, and in the air, there hung the sickly-sweet scent of icing sugar and melted chocolate.

"Morning mum," Marsaili called, halfway down the staircase. "Started on the cake then?"

Shonagh looked up, her expression harried. "Cakes, plural," she replied, slamming down the spatula in her hand and grabbing a whisk from the opposite counter. A dog eared and much scribbled-on recipe book, which must have been older than Marsaili herself, was open at her elbow. "Four tiers - one vanilla, one lemon, one chocolate and one fruit. Pass me the baking parchment, would you?"

Marsaili did as she was asked and surveyed the carnage in the room. In amongst the many dirty utensils, she could see two cakes cooling on racks by the windows. Another was in the oven, and the final one was obviously in the midst of being prepared. She may have been wrong, but she was pretty certain neither Rowan nor Lachlan would have requested this four-tier extravaganza.

"Mum, I thought this was only going to be a small party? How on earth are we going to eat all this?"

"Well they'll want some to pass on to the neighbours, or take into the shop for customers."

The concept of a 'small party' didn't sit well with Shonagh McKenzie. In her mind, Callie should be being baptised in the parish church and most, if not all, of the village ought to be in attendance. Whilst she'd never have said anything out loud, Marsaili knew she was wishing for a grander, and more public, welcoming for her granddaughter.

"Well let me do the dishes, at least," Marsaili said, crossing the room and filling the sink with hot, soapy water. Her mother silently squeezed her arm in thanks as she passed.

Whilst Marsaili scrubbed, rinsed and dried the various utensils her mother had used, Shonagh got the final cake in the oven and started looking out her decorating equipment. Each cake was to be covered in white fondant, with pink polka dots and ribbon to edge each tier. The top cake would have the addition of a handmade fondant cake topper in the shape of an elephant, along with Callie's name.

Shonagh was guddling in the back of the pantry when she let out a curse. Marsaili turned to her, her eyebrows raised questioningly.

"No black food colouring," she explained. "I need it to make grey fondant for the elephant."

"No worries," Marsaili replied. "We'll pop into town; the co-op should have some."

It wasn't even 9am yet, and Marsaili's father had shown no signs of emerging from his bed, so as they approached the jumbled whitewashed buildings that made up Kyle of Lochalsh, they decided to stop off at her old favourite for breakfast.

The Lochalsh Hotel sat on the waterfront, an imposing building painted in the same white as the rest of the town, looking out across the Inner Sound to Skye. Shonagh parked the little yellow car by the harbour wall, and as they clambered out and headed inside out of the damp breeze, Marsaili could see the bridge over to the famous island shrouded in early morning mist. She still remembered it being built, although only vaguely. They used to come through as small children, Marsaili on her father's shoulders, to eat fish and chips and watch the ferries traverse the short crossing. The bridge changed all that, and now tourists could pass straight through Lochalsh and onto the island without even stopping for a cup of tea.

A mixture of residents and locals were seated around the tables within, and when she saw them the waitress waved to Shonagh and Marsaili with a familiar smile. Her name was Jill, and she'd been a couple of years above Marsaili at school. Her parents owned the hotel, and she, like so many others, had obviously followed them into the family business.

"Morning ladies," she called. "Grab a table; I'll be with you soon as I can." With that, she rushed off to fetch another tray of cooked breakfasts for a group of German tourists who were sitting by the windows, watching the early morning sun cast shards of light through the clouds.

Marsaili and her mum found a table for two at the back and glanced over the menu. When Jill returned, they ordered two coffees and two bacon rolls, before conversation suddenly turned to Marsaili's personal life.

"So, what did happen with that boyfriend of yours?" Shonagh asked, without preamble.

Marsaili sighed and tried, unsuccessfully, not to roll her eyes. "I told you mum; we broke up."

"What went wrong this time?"

"He's marrying someone else. Kind of put a dampener on things."

"Oh." For once, Shonagh was quiet. Marsaili glanced around the room and found the complimentary newspaper stand nailed to the wall. She got up and rifled through the local publications and broadsheets, until she found a copy of the *Daily Record* from a couple of weeks ago. She plopped it down on the table in front of her mother, Euan's dazzling, blue eyed, dimpled smile staring up at them.

Realisation dawned. "*Him?*" Shonagh asked incredulously.

Great, Marsaili thought. Even my own mother can't believe he'd date me.

She nodded her head. "We met at work; he was Prince Charming in the panto. Turned out to be not quite so charming in real-life."

Her mum gazed at the image for a moment, taking in Erica's golden hair, ample bosom and sun kissed artificial tan. She was clinging onto Euan, her left hand placed proudly on his chest to display the enormous ring he'd given her. Suddenly Shonagh stood and crumpled up the newspaper, before marching across the room and tossing it in the bin. "Arsehole," she declared as she sat back down, leaning across the table and giving her daughter's hand a squeeze. "Chin up, love. Whit's fur ye'll no' go by ye."

Following breakfast, the two women walked over the road

behind the hotel and crossed the car park into the supermarket. The building's exterior had been refurbished, with fresh white paint and Gaelic signage across the entrance way, but inside the layout was the same as when Marsaili would accompany her mum to do the weekly shop as a child.

"Morning Shonagh!" The buxom lady behind the till greeted them with a smile. "And Marsaili! Home for the wee one's Christening?"

"*Naming Ceremony,*" Shonagh clarified, with a barely concealed roll of her eyes.

"Och, it'll be lovely," the shopkeeper replied. "Doing the baking for it are ye, Shonagh?" she asked, nodding at the items in their basket as she scanned them.

"Aye; I'll be sure to drop in some leftovers," Shonagh answered with a smile.

They paid and exited the shop, crossing the road and making their way back to the little yellow Beetle. It was shaping up to be a lovely morning for the time of year; still cool, but the warmth of the rising sun had melted away the mist and the sky was clearing.

As Shonagh unlocked the car and placed their shopping in the boot, Marsaili was distracted by a car that had appeared further along the road. It was gunmetal grey and clearly a classic of some kind, with an elongated bonnet and a small, upright driver's cabin and a fabric roof. Something about it was familiar, but Marsaili couldn't place it.

It wasn't until she was fastening her own seatbelt that she realised why she recognised it; it was the same make and model as Will's car, the one he'd driven her home in the morning after the Christmas party.

What are the chances? she thought, shaking her head at the coincidence, as her mother reversed out of their parking space and they headed towards home.

Murdo was awake by the time they got back, and the rest of the day passed in the rhythm Marsaili had become accustomed to since her return home - a walk along the cliffs with Fraoch in the morning, homemade soup warming on the Aga for lunch, and cups of tea round the kitchen table in the afternoon.

That was where they were sitting, her father reading the paper and her mother up to her elbows in icing sugar, carefully modelling the elephant topper for Callie's cake, when the phone rang. Marsaili answered it, pleased to hear the voice of her twin.

"Hi Gregor," she announced with a smile, gesturing to her mum, who waved in a way that made it clear she didn't want to be interrupted unless it was strictly necessary. "How's things?"

"Fine thanks; just wanting to confirm the plans for tomorrow. We're aiming to get on the road straight after work, should be with you about 8pm if that's ok?"

Marsaili relayed the message to her mum, who nodded brusquely. The Naming Ceremony would take place the day after, and Gregor and Gayatri were going to stay for the whole weekend.

"Looking forward to seeing you both," Marsaili said.

"And you," Gregor sounded impatient. "Can you put mum on?"

"She's mid bake off at the minute, I don't think she has a spare hand…"

Shonagh glanced over, tutting audibly before gesturing for Marsaili to place the receiver under her ear. She held it in place with one shoulder, before passing Marsaili the two balls of grey fondant she was currently trying to stick together. "Hold that," she whispered, and Marsaili pressed the two together gently but firmly, as instructed. Her mother paced over to the other side of the kitchen, her icing-covered hands outstretched so she wouldn't touch anything.

Marsaili wondered what could have been so urgent, or so private, that Gregor wasn't willing to relay it through her. She listened intently to her mother's side of the conversation, trying to piece it all together.

"Mmmhmmm," Shonagh nodded, her brows creased into a slight frown. "Oh of course that'd be fine… Aye, we've plenty space… OK… Aye, give him the address and tell him we'll see him later… OK, bye son, you too."

Shonagh kicked her husband's chair, urging him to take the receiver from her and replace it in the cradle, before she relieved Marsaili of her fondant duties.

"What was all that about?" she asked.

"Och. Gregor has a friend visiting the area; a hillwalker. His room's been double booked down in town so Gregor wanted to know if he could offer him a bed here for the weekend. Lachlan's room's free; would you mind popping up and putting some fresh sheets on for me?"

Marsaili nodded, rinsing the sticky residue from her fingers before heading upstairs.

Lachlan's childhood room was in the eaves, in between Marsaili's and Gregor's, while their parents slept downstairs in what would have originally been the dining room. The rooms were small, with coombed ceilings and dormer windows, but they'd never known any different. The headboard of Lachlan's old single bed still sat against the far wall, a small bedside table and lamp on one side and a narrow chest of drawers on the other. There was only just enough room for Marsaili to manoeuvre around it without bumping her head on the ceiling. Both of her brothers had spent the majority of their teenage years walking around with a crick in their necks.

There was a storage box under the bed containing spare bedding, which Marsaili hurriedly got out and gave a quick shake. The bare duvet and pillows were neatly folded on top of the mattress, so it didn't take her long to assemble everything. She plumped up the top pillow and finished it all by laying a crochet, patchwork bedspread over the top. Marsaili looked at it fondly; her granny had made it when Lachlan was born. They each had one; Lachlan's was varying shades of blue, whilst Marsaili's was yellow and Gregor's was red. They were just one of many items in their home that had been there for years, often handed down, washed and mended many times over.

The room smelt slightly fusty from disuse, so Marsaili opened the window and let in the cool breeze from outside. The curtains fluttered, disturbing a thin layer of dust on the deep-set windowsill. Knowing how busy her mother was, and not wanting her to be embarrassed in front of their unknown guest, Marsaili decided to finish sprucing the room up a bit more herself.

She fetched a cloth and wiped down all the surfaces, before polishing the little mirror that hung on the wall opposite the bed. Then she collected some fresh towels from the linen cupboard in the downstairs bathroom and folded them neatly at the foot of the bed, placing a hot water bottle with a fleecy cover on top. Marsaili finished it off by gathering a bundle of snowdrops from the garden, where they'd had an early bloom due to the unexpectedly fine weather, and arranging them in a little jug on the windowsill.

Marsaili stood back and looked at the overall effect; it was homely, if a bit dated, but fresh and clean and welcoming. More than adequate for one of Gregor's hillwalking pals, she was sure. And most importantly, it was one less thing for her mum to stress about.

The doorbell rang about an hour later, after Shonagh had set aside the fondant elephant to dry, and placed a chicken in the oven for tea. They were all seated around the fire in the little living room, a repeat of *Location, Location, Location* playing on the TV.

"Would you get it, love?" Shonagh asked, now absorbed in her latest knitting project - a little cardigan for Callie. It wasn't entirely clear who she'd been speaking to, but as Murdo had his feet up and was snoring soundly, Marsaili clambered out of her chair and padded to the front door in her slippers.

The polite smile Marsaili had prepared on her lips fell away when she opened the door and saw the tall figure standing there, dressed in walking boots and an expensive looking Mammut jacket, with a rucksack slung over one shoulder.

"*Will?*" she asked incredulously.

On the plus side, he looked every bit as shocked as she did. He stared at her wordlessly, and Marsaili was acutely aware of her unwashed hair, not to mention the oversized, home-knitted jumper and torn jeans she was wearing.

"I didn't know you'd be here," he managed eventually.

Marsaili didn't know what to say, so she settled for, "You'd better come in."

She led him through to the little living room, Will ducking to fit through the low cottage doors, and made the introductions. Murdo awoke with an abrupt snort, looking confused.

"You'll have a dram?" he said, not so much a question as an observation, rising from his chair and reaching for the decanter that resided permanently on the old oak sideboard.

Will hesitated, not wanting to be rude. "Maybe later," he said. "Thank you so much for having me."

"Marsaili will show you to your room so you can freshen up," Shonagh said with a barely concealed smile. "I'm roasting a chicken for dinner."

"Smells delicious," Will observed, his manners impeccable as always.

Shonagh grinned at Marsaili as she led Will out of the room, a twinkle in her eyes. Marsaili didn't like this one bit.

They climbed the stairs in silence, part of her wanting to laugh at the absurdity of it all, the other part wanting the ground to open up and swallow her whole.

She showed Will into his room, cringing at the sight of the snowdrops she'd arranged earlier, and suddenly embarrassed at the simplicity of her home. He was accustomed to posh hotel rooms and family manors. What would he make of her ramshackle little house?

They stood awkwardly for a moment, Will's tall frame blocking the doorway and Marsaili trapped between him, the bed and the low coombed ceiling.

"I really didn't know you'd be here," he repeated, looking genuinely abashed. "I'd never have taken Gregor up on his offer if I'd have realised. Honestly, the last thing I want is to make things awkward for you."

"So, you're really just up here hillwalking?"

He nodded. "Honest. Gregor recommended some routes when we were chatting at Hogmanay. I figured while I've got my weekends off, I'd make the most of it and do some exploring. Thought I might try the Five Sisters, if the weather holds."

Marsaili had to concede that it made sense. The Five Sisters of Kintail was one of the best-known walking routes in the area, ideal for more experienced climbers such as Will, taking in three Munros and some breath-taking views. "And your room was double booked?" she asked.

Now, however, Will's eyes narrowed in confusion. "What room?"

"At the hotel in town. The Lochalsh."

Will shook his head. "I never booked a hotel in town. I told Gregor I was planning to be in the area and he said his parents would put me up - he was quite insistent," Will rushed on, clearly seeing the look of rage that was passing over Marsaili's face. "He said I should experience some genuine Highland hospitality."

Marsaili took a deep breath. She hoped her brother's definition of 'highland hospitality' didn't include pimping out his sister.

"Are you ok?" Will asked. "I can go and find the hotel if you'd rather, it's no bother…"

"It's fine," Marsaili said tersely, taking a deep breath in before exhaling slowly. "It's not your fault; it's my meddling twat of brother that I'm mad at. I'll let you get settled in."

Will stepped aside to let her pass, bumping his head on the lintel as he did so. Marsaili crossed the hall into her room and shut the door behind her, cursing to herself. With any luck the celebrant that had been booked for Callie's Naming Ceremony could do funerals too, because when she next saw Gregor, she'd kill him.

CHAPTER 30

All things considered, dinner passed pleasantly enough, despite her mother's coy little smiles every time Marsaili and Will so much as looked at each other. She was sure now about the contents of the urgent conversation Gregor had had to have with their mother earlier that day, and could have happily throttled the pair of them.

Shonagh was quite obviously besotted with Will - whether it was his well-spoken accent, good looks or the fact that he offered to do the dishes after the meal Marsaili wasn't sure, but she was definitely weighing him up as potential son-in-law material already.

As they retired to the 'comfy seats' in the living room after their meal, Marsaili found herself and Will tactically manoeuvred next to each other on one small two-seater sofa, whilst her parents sat opposite. Will was encouraged to have the whisky he'd turned down earlier, and earned extra brownie points by not asking for water or ice with it. He sipped the twelve-year-old Glenfiddich appreciatively as they fell into a comfortable lull, the only sounds the crackling of the wood on the open fire and the gentle rumbling snore from Fraoch as she slept in her basket.

"So, you've no young lady in your life at the minute then, William?" Shonagh asked. Marsaili shot her a look across the room, but her mother was deliberately avoiding her gaze.

Will coughed his nervous cough. "Not at the moment, no," he agreed. "I'm actually in the middle of finalising a divorce."

"Och, shame," Shonagh replied, with an expression that did not exactly convey disappointment. "You've not even got your eye on anyone...?"

"Bloody hell Shonagh, gie the lad a break." As a general rule Murdo didn't say much, but when he did, he didn't mince his words. Marsaili could have kissed him.

"It's ok," Will assured her. "My, eh... situation's too complicated at the minute. Even if there was someone I was interested in, it wouldn't be fair on them to drag them into all this mess." He was looking down at the nosing glass clasped between his long fingers, but nonetheless Marsaili felt the implication of his words, and her cheeks flushed.

"Is your wife not making things easy then?" Shonagh asked.

"Not exactly," Will paused to take another sip of his whisky. "We've got a lot of assets to divide; to be honest I'm just trying to let the lawyers deal with it all."

"Best way to handle it, laddie - yer paying them enough for the privilege, I'm sure," Murdo said.

"And *I'm* sure Will doesn't want to discuss the ins and outs of his personal life with people he's only just met," Marsaili interjected as breezily as possible, raising her eyebrows pointedly at her mother. Mercifully, she backed off for now and changed the subject.

"What are your plans for tomorrow, William? Gregor said you had a walking route to explore?"

"Nothing too strenuous," Will replied. "I thought I might try a stretch of the coastal route - maybe to Drumbuie and back? That should be about six kilometres or so I think?"

Murdo nodded. "Aye it's a fine walk - nothing too rough. Good for this time of year when the weather's a bit unpredictable."

"Marsaili, you should go with him!" Shonagh suddenly declared, as if this were the best, most unbelievably original idea in the world.

Marsaili glared at her mother. "Will's come away for peace and quiet, mum," she said through gritted teeth. "I'm sure the last thing he wants is to have someone tagging along spoiling that for him."

"Actually, I wouldn't mind the company." Will looked at her for the first time since they'd sat down. "Some local knowledge would be nice as well." He was smiling at her, that same expression that always made her tummy go funny.

"Well that's it sorted then!" Shonagh announced with a clap of her hands. Marsaili could see her picking out a hat already.

They rose early the following day, a thick frost still lying on the grass outside and the sun only just starting to creep above the horizon. Marsaili was dressed warmly in jeans, hiking boots and a fleece lined jumper when she met Will in the kitchen. He was already filling a teapot and had put some bread in the toaster, and welcomed her with a friendly smile.

"Sleep well?" he enquired, pouring tea into a stoneware mug and adding a generous glug of milk. He stirred it and handed it to Marsaili.

"Once I got over the urge to strangle my brother," she replied, forcing a smile.

Will laughed. "One reason to be glad that I'm an only child," he said with a grin. "No meddling."

Marsaili was surprised by how at home Will had made himself; he was taking butter and jam from the fridge and spreading them on the toast as if he'd lived there all his life. She found herself watching him. He looked relaxed and comfortable. Marsaili even suspected that he might not have combed his hair that morning - the thick blonde locks stuck out haphazardly in places, like tufts of straw.

Will passed her a plate of toast and they sat together at the old kitchen table, discussing their plans for the day. His rucksack was already packed, with emergency equipment, a compass and maps. She reminded him that it was really just a casual stroll along the coastline, but he insisted on being fully prepared nonetheless. "And I've packed something for lunch," he added. Despite how irritated Marsaili was at her mother for interfering last night, she couldn't deny it; she was excited to spend the day with him.

Dishes deposited in the sink, they crept out before Shonagh or Murdo had emerged from their bed. The early morning light as they set out from the little croft house was stunning - a low orange sun was just peeking above the horizon, and the sky stretching endlessly above them was a myriad of pinks and reds. At its zenith, the stars were still visible, nestled in a carpet of deep navy blue.

"I could get used to it up here," Will said, pausing to look out across the water, his neck craning upwards. "Don't you miss it?"

"I never used to," Marsaili replied honestly, standing beside him and gazing at the view that had once been so mundane that she never even bothered to notice it. "But I do now. Every time I come home it gets a little harder to leave again."

"What made you go in the first place?"

Marsaili scoffed. "You grew up in London, right?" Will nodded, as they turned and headed down the path together. "Then you can't imagine what it was like to be a teenager here. It was great when I was little, don't get me wrong, but when you get to a certain age it just felt like there was nothing to do. And anything you did do got reported back to your parents. Forget Twitter - there's no more efficient spreader of dubious news than a small village gossip mill," she added with a grin.

Will laughed. "Well at least you had a chance to misbehave," he said. "Between school and tutors and extracurricular activities, any opportunity for a misspent youth sort of passed me by."

Marsaili glanced across at him. He had his eyes down, watching the path ahead of him, the first shards of morning sunlight cutting across his yellow hair. "You should be making up for lost time, in that case," she said.

He looked up, catching her eye. "Perhaps I should," he agreed.

They passed through a gate and onto the shore, before crossing a wooden bridge and following the signpost for 'Coastal Path to Drumbuie'.

"This is Port an Eorna," Marsaili explained. "Barley Port, in English."

"The Gaelic sounds much better," Will said with a smile. "Do you speak it?"

"A little - I did as a child, at home with Mum and Dad, but I'm a bit rusty now. Boats used to fish from here," she continued, resuming her role as tour guide, "but it's all owned by the National Trust now. That's the Applecross Peninsula across the water," she said, gesturing to the range of mountains that were just becoming more visible as the sun cast its light on the opposite shore, painting them in shades of purple and red. Marsaili and her brothers had walked this path many times during their childhood summer holidays, and it was nice to be exploring it again.

The grassy path turned inland for a while, taking them away from the coastline and along the edge of a field of scattered, hardy looking sheep. Marsaili remembered this section of the walk as being much boggier in the past, although it seemed the National Trust had taken measures to improve drainage in recent years. They crossed a boulder bridge over a little burn before clambering over a stile, walking on in silence as they both absorbed the view that the rising sun was affording them.

Gradually, the path curved back towards the coastline. "Those are the Cuillins," Marsaili said, pointing towards the mountain range across the water on the Isle of Skye.

"I know those," Will nodded. "Always wanted to climb them. Maybe on my next visit?" He cast her a sideways glance as they walked, a playful grin on his face.

"Who says you're invited back?" Marsaili teased. They laughed together; she couldn't deny how much she enjoyed his company, or the little flip she felt in her tummy every time he smiled at her.

"How are things going at work?" she asked. "Do you have great plans for transforming The Pantheon back into Glasgow's premier entertainment venue?"

Will sighed. "Can I be honest?"

"Yes."

"I don't think I even care anymore." He smirked as he said it, clearly trying to suppress a laugh. "God, that's the first time I've said it out loud!" He ran a hand through his hair. "I'm sorry, I know that's really not the attitude I should have, but I genuinely just don't care."

Marsaili laughed. "Well, that's definitely honest."

"I don't know;" Will sighed, "lately I just find myself wondering, does it really matter? Aren't there more worthwhile things to be stressing about than audience numbers and ticket sales and hobnobbing bloody obnoxious z-list celebrities."

Marsaili couldn't help but wonder if that particular jibe were aimed at Euan. "Theatres are important places if you ask me," she said. "They're a window, an escape. Part of our culture. Yes, it's not saving lives or preventing miscarriages of justice, but the arts inspire people and bring them comfort. Without theatres and concert halls and open mic nights," she flashed him a smile, which he returned warmly, "I think the world would be a much emptier place."

He sighed. "You're right," he said. "Maybe it's not really the job, maybe it's just me. I feel like I'm looking back on every major decision I've ever made in my life and wondering what the hell I was thinking."

"Well that's a feeling I do know," Marsaili said.

"How do you mean?" Will asked.

Marsaili shrugged her shoulders. "Just everything," she said. "How do you ever really know that you're making the right choice? You can follow your heart and get it broken, or you can make the sensible choice and still get screwed over."

"Which was it with Euan?" he asked. "Head or heart?"

"Neither," Marsaili admitted. "More boredom, and loneliness, I suppose. To be honest, I was flattered he'd even looked twice at me. How pathetic is that?" She let out a little self-deprecating laugh.

"It's not pathetic," Will said diplomatically. "You're only human, and he's a good-looking guy. Not my type," he added with a smile, as Marsaili shot him a grin. "But I can see how he swept you off your feet. Maybe if I'd been as forward, I could have done the same."

Marsaili walked on in silence, keeping her eyes steadfastly on the path ahead.

"Sorry," Will said. "Anyway, if you want to talk about doing something stupid, at least you didn't marry him. That's a mistake which is much, much harder to undo."

"Do you regret it?" she asked. "Getting married?"

"Yes and no," he said. " I thought I was certain, at the time. I thought I loved her. Now I wonder if it just felt safe. I've always done the sensible thing; I think now that maybe marrying Adelaide was just another sensible choice, really." Marsaili risked a glance at him. His hands were thrust deep in his pockets, the wind ruffling his hair. "It's what you do, isn't it? Our parents were best friends, we grew up together, started dating… it just got to the point where marriage was the next item on the agenda."

"So why didn't it work out?"

"I volunteered for the job in Glasgow, thought it would be an adventure; something we could do together, just us, without living in the shadow of our parents. She wanted to stay in London."

"And you couldn't do long distance?"

"We could have," Will admitted, "but I think realising that neither one of us wanted to make any sacrifices for the other highlighted the fact that we didn't really love each other that much after all. If we did, it wouldn't have mattered where we lived, would it? When we finally did decide to end it, neither one of us was even that upset."

In that case, Marsaili wondered, what on earth was she doing still phoning him in the wee small hours of the morning?

They continued along the shoreline, before climbing over a grassy headland and reaching another bay. Here the path disappeared and they had to cross over the beach itself, each concentrating on keeping their footing as they traversed the loose, uneven rocks. They re-joined the path at the other side, clambering up onto the edge of a grassy field. Will climbed first, before turning back and offering his hand, hauling Marsaili up behind him.

They turned right and headed inland, following the path along the edge of the field until they reached a railway bridge. As they crossed it, Marsaili pointed out the scattered rooftops of the hamlet of Drumbuie in the distance.

"We can carry on into the village if you like," she said, "although there's not very much there."

"Well how about we head back down to the shore instead, and have some lunch?"

They found a fairly even patch of rough grass by the edge of the pebbly beach. She was surprised to see Will unpack a tartan blanket, which he spread out on the ground before gesturing for her to sit. She did so gladly, as a flask of tea, tuna sandwiches, apples and a packet of chocolate biscuits followed. "Need to keep our energy up," Will said with a smile.

They ate in silence for a moment, listening to the distinctive "eek eek" cry of the oystercatchers as they swooped across the bay.

"My brothers and I used to come along here all the time as kids," Marsaili said. "During the school holidays mum would kick us out after breakfast and wouldn't expect us home until dinner. We'd spend all day out on the beach, or if we were lucky and we'd saved some pocket money we'd carry on into Drumbuie and buy ice lollies at the village shop."

"It sounds idyllic," Will said with a sigh. "like something out of a storybook."

"It was," Marsaili conceded. "That's always been my biggest concern about living in the city, to be honest. Don't get me wrong, I love it. I love being able to eat tapas whenever I feel like it, or go out for coffee at 10 o'clock at night. But if I ever do have kids, I'd want to give them the kind of childhood I had."

"Do you want kids someday?"

She nodded. "Someday. But I also wanted to be a Tony award winning actress by now, so who knows?"

Will laughed. "I'd like kids, in theory, but it terrifies me at the same time. What if I screw them up the same way my parents screwed me up? Or worse?" He shuddered.

"You seem to have turned out ok?"

"Are you kidding?" Will laughed. "I'm socially awkward, I never know what to say in any situation, and virtually every decision I've ever made has been based on doing whatever other people expect of me." He looked over at her, suddenly shy again. "Anyway, Adelaide never wanted kids so I'd kind of ruled it out. No chance of it happening now."

He was sitting upright, his knees pulled in towards his chest and his arms resting on top of them, squinting out across the water. Marsaili was overwhelmed with the desire to reach out and touch him, so she sat on her hands instead.

"Shall we head back?" Marsaili suggested. Will agreed, standing up and dusting crumbs from his long legs. He helped Marsaili to her feet, keeping hold of her hand as she stood, his eyes downcast.

"If things were different…" he began.

"Don't," Marsaili interrupted. "It's easier this way."

They both made an effort to keep the conversation light on their return, sticking to observations about the surrounding landscape and wildlife, or idle chit chat about their colleagues at work. They weren't far from Marsaili's home when she stopped suddenly, one hand instinctively grabbing Will's arm and the other shielding her eyes as she looked out to sea. The low winter sun was still glaringly bright, despite dusk being just a couple of hours away.

"What is it?" Will asked, glancing down at where her hand was clutching the crook of his elbow.

"Seals," she said, a grin on her face. "I just saw a head pop up. There!" she exclaimed again, pointing excitedly and jumping on the spot. It had been years, she realised, since she'd last seen them. "There's another one!"

Will looked, and this time he saw it - a little brown head, with glassy round eyes and flaring nostrils, peering around the surface of the water.

"There's another," Will said. Now that his eyes had located them, he was amazed to see that the water suddenly seemed to be full of them - in the water itself, and basking on exposed outcrops of rock, their bodies curved up in a distinctive arc with their heads and tails elevated. He couldn't believe he'd missed them before.

"It's amazing," he whispered.

"What is?"

"How something can be right in front of your eyes, and you don't even see it."

Marsaili looked up at him, the breeze ruffling his fair hair as he watched the animals frolicking in the waves. She wanted to kiss him, and she was pretty sure he wouldn't object. But he was her boss, and he was still married… it was a stupid idea.

"We should get back," she said instead, turning and leading the way back along the path. "It'll be dark soon."

Not long after they arrived home, to much interrogation from Marsaili's mother, they heard the rumble of a car approaching along the track. Marsaili excused herself in order to meet it, keen to greet her brother in private.

"What the hell do you think you're playing at?" she declared, advancing across the pitted ground towards him before he'd even got out of the car, arms folded across her chest.

"Pardon me?" Gregor asked, an amused smile on his face.

"Hi Marsaili," Gayatri said, exiting from the passenger side. "I did try to talk him out of it," she added with a shrug of her shoulders, "but he wouldn't listen."

"What exactly am I meant to have done?" Gregor asked again, his palms spread out in front of him in an expression of mock innocence.

"You're a meddling prick, and you know it," Marsaili said, eyebrows raised, glaring at him.

"Aw sis, don't be like that!" He laughed, looking extremely pleased with himself. "I saw you guys together at Hogmanay; I'm just giving you a little nudge." He winked and dug her in the ribs playfully with his elbow.

Marsaili spoke through gritted teeth. "There's nothing to nudge - he is my boss, he is in the middle of a divorce, and besides making things even more awkward between us your little interference has achieved nothing." Marsaili turned on her heels and stalked back into the house, hoping he believed her words more than she did.

Behind her, Gayatri came around the other side of the car and looked at Gregor sternly. "Told you she'd be pissed," she said.

In spite of her protestations to her brother, Marsaili knew that her own feelings for Will were only getting harder and harder to ignore. Having him here, in her home, getting on so well with her family, was doing nothing to change that.

They gathered around the dinner table once more, Will and Gregor chatting like old friends, and at the end of the meal when he once again offered to do the dishes Shonagh actually let him. That was a definite sign that he was being moved from the "guest" category to "part of the family".

The obligatory whiskies were poured, while Gregor and Gayatri went upstairs to unpack their things.

"No freshly picked flowers in our room, Mum," her brother observed as he came back into the living room. "Showing favouritism towards our guest?"

"It was Marsaili that set Will's room up, son, nothing to do with me," Shonagh replied with a smile.

Marsaili felt her cheeks flush.

"Oh, she'll be putting little chocolates on your pillow next, Will," Gregor teased.

Will cleared his throat, and smiled self-consciously. "It was a lovely gesture," he said.

Marsaili wanted to point out, once again, that she hadn't actually known the room would be for him. Instead, she excused herself and went to run a bath.

Sinking into the hot water, Marsaili sighed gratefully. Will's unexpected arrival had pushed everything else from her mind; she hadn't thought about the confusion over her career path, or where she'd live once Isla had moved away, in days. Having her family now seemingly on a campaign to set them up was the last thing she needed.

She wallowed in the water until it began to cool, before clambering out and drying herself off. She wrapped herself in a towel and headed upstairs, intending to get into her jammies and hide in her bedroom with a book for the rest of the evening. Somewhat antisocial perhaps, but it was the naming ceremony tomorrow and she'd have to put up with everyone all day; tonight, she just needed a break.

She climbed the stairs to her room, trying to make as little noise as possible on the creaky steps. As she reached her door, however, she heard a familiar, nervous cough behind her.

She turned, pulling the towel closer around herself. Her damp red curls were trickling water down her back, and her feet were bare. She felt acutely vulnerable, and Will looked suitably awkward as he eyed her, shifting uncomfortably from foot to foot.

"Sorry... I wasn't sure if you'd be coming back down. I just wanted to say - I've never said anything to encourage your brother. I know they're just teasing, but I don't want to make things uncomfortable for you."

"It's ok."

"I know we're just co-workers - maybe friends, if I'm lucky," he continued with a smile. "You've made it clear how you feel and I respect that, even if it's not what I was hoping for. I just want you to know that I'm not here trying to wear you down, or anything. Say the word and I'll leave, if that's what you want."

Marsaili felt her stomach turning itself over. He was looking at her earnestly, and she had to fight off the urge to drag him into her bedroom and throw away the towel.

"Of course I don't want you to leave," she said. That was the truth, at least.

He looked relieved. "Good. Because your mum's invited me to the naming ceremony tomorrow. Are you sure you don't mind me tagging along?"

It hardly came as a surprise. "Of course not," she replied with a smile. "Look, I'm tired," Marsaili said, making her excuses. "I'm going to get an early night."

Will nodded. "Goodnight."

CHAPTER 31

The unseasonable sunshine that had lingered for most of the week unfortunately didn't last. Marsaili opened her curtains on Saturday morning to be confronted with a thick haar; a sea fog that obscured virtually everything from her bedroom window. The shoreline, the water and the Applecross peninsula beyond had vanished. Marsaili came into the kitchen to find her mother, frantic, pacing the floor and chatting animatedly on the telephone.

Marsaili sat wordlessly at the kitchen table as the conversation ended, Shonagh sighing as she placed the receiver back in the cradle rather more firmly than necessary.

"Well, that's the outdoor ceremony out the window," she said.

Rowan and Lachlan had been hoping to have the ceremony by the shore next to the McKenzie's' croft, overlooking the sea. However, given the change in the weather they opted to hold it inside the cottage itself instead. Fortunately, they only needed room to accommodate and feed fourteen people, and with a bit of reorganisation it would be doable. Cosy, but doable.

The morning was spent moving furniture and hanging decorations, under Rowan's watchful eye. A fire was lit in the grate of the small living room, the kitchen was turned over to food prep and the dining table was moved out into the hallway and pushed against the wall in order to lay out the buffet. Marsaili and Will helped her father move the sofas in the living room, placing one at an angle on either side of the chimney breast facing into the room, and filling the vacated space with dining chairs and any other spare seats they could find dotted around the house. They laid them out in three short rows, four chairs in each, facing the fireplace. Once the ceremony was over, they could rearrange them for eating and drinking.

The finished effect was eclectic, but not unpleasant. By the time Rowan's mum had arrived and filled every surface with fresh flowers, including an elaborate display on top of the mantelpiece and a tall bundle of pink and rose gold balloons in the corner of the room, it was quite beautiful.

The finishing touch was a hand stitched row of bunting which Rowan had made, spelling out Callie's name on little flags. She pulled over two chairs, and she and Marsaili stood side by side to hang it across the old gilded mirror which sat above the fireplace.

"All set?" Marsaili asked. Callie was currently asleep in the travel cot in Shonagh and Murdo's room, completely unaware of the chaos that reigned around her as everyone prepared themselves for her special day.

Rowan smiled, surveying the room. "For saying it wasn't our first choice, I'm actually pretty pleased with how this has all turned out." Outside, the haar had cleared, but rain clouds had followed it inland, so that the small lead lined window panes of the croft house were now obscured instead by flowing rivulets of water. Marsaili thought she heard a distant rumble of thunder. Inside, with a warm fire lit, her family around her and delicious smells wafting from the kitchen, felt like a very good place to be indeed.

The two women followed the smells into the kitchen, to see if Shonagh needed any help. They had a couple of hours until the celebrant was due to arrive, and only Rowan's sister and her partner were still to appear. Rowan glanced nervously out of the window.

"You don't think it'll get much worse, do you?" she asked, eyeing up the encroaching storm.

"Of course not," Marsaili reassured her.

But an hour later, when Callie was awake and having a feed before Rowan put her into her new dress, no one was quite so relaxed. Morven and Eilidh had made it, although the rain had grown heavier and some of the roads from Plockton were only just passable. They were gathered in the living room/makeshift ceremony space while Lachlan paced by the window nervously, checking his phone as Shonagh and Rhona busied themselves providing everyone with cups of tea.

The celebrant was a lady named Janet, the same one who'd married Rowan and Lachlan just a couple of years before. They'd all kept in touch and she was starting to feel like a member of the family. Her lateness, and lack of communication, was unusual.

"Where is she coming from again?" Marsaili asked.

"Portree," Lachlan answered. Portree was the main settlement on the Isle of Skye, about forty miles away. It was a pleasant drive that should have taken about an hour on a clear day, but in this weather could be treacherous.

"I'm going looking for her," Lachlan said eventually. "She

should have been here by now, and if something was holding her up, she'd have pulled over and rung us."

Lachlan had an old, but solid and reliable, Landrover Defender. It had a winch on the front and high profile, thick, knobbly off-road tyres. If anything stood a chance of passing the roads, which were fast turning into rivers, it would.

"I'll come too," Will said, rising from his seat. "I've got a first aid kit and ropes and things in my hiking bag," he added. "Just in case."

The two men gathered up their coats, waterproof boots and the first aid supplies, as well as their mobile phones. Rowan gave Lachlan a concerned kiss before he left, although she didn't try to talk him out of it. "Take care," she said simply.

Marsaili hovered awkwardly at the front door, looking at Will. "You don't need to do this," she said.

"I know, but I want to help if I can."

Marsaili nodded. "Don't let him do anything stupid," she whispered, inclining her head surreptitiously towards her brother.

Will smiled. "I'll do my best," he replied, hauling a rucksack onto his shoulder before heading out into the rain.

Even though it wasn't long after noon, the storm brought with it dark clouds that blotted out the sun and made it feel much later. Will and Lachlan had agreed to drive the main road to Portree and back again, as long as it was passable - a journey that in fine weather should have taken no more than two hours. They were going to ring with an update when they got to Janet's house, before attempting the return trip. Given the conditions, everyone agreed that if they hadn't heard from them within a couple of hours at most, then they'd be ringing the emergency services themselves.

The time passed interminably slowly. Rhona and Shonagh tag teamed between tea making and bouncing Callie, as the rain rattled more furiously off the single glazed window panes and a howling wind shook the slate tiles on the roof. Murdo read the newspaper and made small talk with Rowan's dad over the football scores, while Gregor scrolled through his phone, looking for weather and traffic updates. Marsaili went to flick the local radio on in case they had any news, but changed her mind and opted for Radio 2 instead.

Gayatri sat next to her on the sofa, placing another log on the fire as she passed. Marsaili watched it disturb the embers and send up a cloud of fizzing little sparks. It had been almost an hour since the boys had left, and everyone was hoping for a phone call soon.

"They'll be fine," Gayatri said with a smile. As if on cue, an ominous roll of thunder sounded from above. Callie looked confused and let out a little cry, reaching instinctively for her mother.

"It was nice of Will to go with Lachlan," Gayatri continued. "Saved Gregor having to volunteer." Gregor looked up at the sound of his name, and she winked at her boyfriend from across the room. "He's a good guy, this Will," she finished.

"Oh, don't you start," Marsaili said, more forcefully than she'd intended. "Between my mum and Gregor there's been enough people banging that drum this weekend, thank you very much."

"And there's nothing to it?" Gayatri asked, innocently enough. "Gregor seemed to think he'd interrupted something between you two at Hogmanay?"

Marsaili sighed. "It was nothing; a drunken flirt, that's all. And besides, he's still married…"

"To a woman he's in the process of divorcing?"

"Yes… and she is beautiful, and elegant, and a million and one other things I'll never be."

Gayatri's eyes narrowed. "How do you know what she looks like?" she asked.

Marsaili's face flushed red, but she was rescued by the sudden ringing of the phone.

Rowan reached it first, Callie on one hip, phone grasped in the opposite hand.

"Hello?" she said breathlessly.

The rest of the room fell into a hushed silence as they listened, everyone focused on the changing expressions on Rowan's face.

"Oh, thank goodness!" she declared eventually. She smiled, nodding reassuringly to the rest of the room as the conversation continued.

"No, of course, of course. Take your time, OK, yep. Let me know when you get there. OK, love you too."

She hung up, and sighed with relief. "They've found her - she went off the road at Sligachan. Aquaplaned, by the looks of things." Everyone gave a collective gasp. Sligachan was on Skye; she obviously hadn't made it very far before the accident occurred.

Marsaili wondered how long she'd been awaiting rescue.

"She's fine; well, relatively fine," Rowan hurried on. "She knocked herself out, has a nasty concussion and what looks like a badly sprained wrist, but apart from being a bit battered and bruised she seems OK. They're waiting for the paramedics, then they'll follow her to the hospital and make sure she's alright."

It was another few hours before Lachlan and Will arrived home. Rowan's family had left not long after the phone call, on her insistence that they get home before the roads worsened. She and Lachlan and Callie would stay overnight here if required, she assured them. The storm had lessened now, though the rain still fell relentlessly, and the sky was a maze of dark blue streaked with deep pink.

Both men were sodden when they returned, covered in mud and with rain-soaked hair dripping in their eyes. Shonagh greeted them with towels, and shouted instructions to the others as she bustled around them. Rowan embraced her husband and helped him out of his wet anorak, whilst Marsaili somewhat self-consciously offered to take Will's.

Murdo gave them both a hearty pat on the back, sending droplets of water scattering over the flagstone hall floor.

"Well done, lads; that's a good day's work."

"It's Will who deserves the congratulations," Lachlan said, stepping out of his waterlogged boots. "He got her out of the car."

"What do you mean?" Shonagh asked. "She was trapped? I thought she just had a bump on the head?"

Will looked uncomfortable. "She did. It was nothing really…"

"The car was stuck - it had slid into a ditch," Lachlan continued, ignoring him. "She was half in the river when we found her, and unconscious. Driver's side door was in the water. Because of the angle we couldn't get the winch attached, so Will climbed down and carried her out. The water was rising fast. If he hadn't have spotted her, and got her out when he did, it could have been a lot worse."

Marsaili looked at him. He was looking at his feet, ruffling his rain-soaked hair with the towel. She wanted to hug him, but her mother beat her to it.

"Oh God bless you, laddie!" she cried, almost knocking him off his feet with the force of her embrace. "What a hero! And you too, son," she added as an afterthought, giving Lachlan a quick cuddle. He grinned at Marsaili over their mother's head.

"Marsaili, get a bath running, will you?" Shonagh instructed. "And Murdo get some more logs on the fire. These two need warming up!"

Marsaili did as she was asked, turning the old, creaking taps and unleashing a sputtering onslaught of slightly yellow, peaty water. It wasn't long before she heard footsteps padding along the hallway behind her.

"For Christ's sake Lachlan, give me a minute, will you?" She turned to find not her brother, but Will, peeling his wet jumper over his head as he went. He smiled when he saw her watching him.

"Sorry - I didn't mean to rush you. I can run my own bath," he shrugged. His damp t-shirt had ridden up his torso, affording Marsaili a glimpse of the lean, smooth stomach beneath it. She looked away self-consciously, busying herself with throwing in some Epsom salts.

"It really wasn't as dramatic as Lachlan's making out," he said, entering the room. His wet hair was standing up in tufts all over his head, and Marsaili once again had to fight the urge to reach out and run her fingers through it.

"Turns out you were the reckless one, then," she said, avoiding his eyes and keeping her voice light. "Scampering into flooded burns and rescuing damsels in distress."

He shrugged modestly. "I've said I'll take the sofa tonight - save Lachlan and Rowan travelling home with the little one in this weather."

Marsaili found herself becoming irrationally annoyed with him. Why did he have to be so bloody perfect all the time?

"Ever the gentleman," she said, hoping it would sound playful, but hearing it come out instead as snide and bitchy. She turned back to the bath, frothing up the bubbles with her hand.

"Have I done something wrong?" Will asked. He was leaning against the towel rail, one long leg crossed over the other at the ankles. He looked so at home here, and he was so beloved by everyone in her family, it was like he really was one of them. For reasons she couldn't quite put her finger on, Marsaili felt her irritation with him grow.

"Well, yes, you have actually."

"What?" Much to her surprise, he looked genuinely concerned. She was expecting him to get annoyed with her in return - after all, she knew she was being unreasonable - but here he was, all kindness and gentleness and polite consideration.

"That!" she exclaimed suddenly, pointing at him accusingly. "Being so bloody charming, and calm, and helpful. Why did you have to come here and be such a perfect bloody gentleman, and make my entire family fall in love with you, and then top it all off by going and rescuing a bloody minister!"

"I don't think she's technically a…"

"You know what I mean!" Marsaili retorted, her words bubbling forth before she really had a chance to think about them. "Why do you have to be so fucking perfect? You're just making it so much harder to…"

"What?" Will stood up, his tone suddenly different. His voice was low and his eyes narrow. "Harder to what?" he repeated.

Marsaili sighed, defeated. "Harder to get over you."

He took half a step towards her - still hesitant, but emboldened by her words. "Marsaili, you only have to get over someone if they don't want to be with you. Please believe me when I tell you, you have absolutely no need to get over me. You know how I feel about you."

They considered each other for a moment, until Will suddenly took the final step towards her, grabbed her by the waist and kissed her.

It was less gentle than she'd expected, both of them consumed by the need to finally give in to the temptation they'd been resisting for so long. She was pressed up against Will's sodden tee-shirt, as his hands snaked upwards into her hair, grasping the back of her neck desperately.

Suddenly, there was a cough in the corridor behind them, and Will and Marsaili both jumped. Lachlan was watching them, amused, one eyebrow raised and his eyes laughing as he towel dried his bushy ginger beard.

"I'll get a bath later," he said, winking at them before heading back along the hall to the living room.

The following morning, she found him, his hair ruffled and his face crinkly from sleep, still wrapped up in his sleeping bag on the living room sofa. He smiled as she padded in, wearing her jammies and slippers, and moved over on the sofa to make space for her.

"Morning," he said, stifling a yawn. Marsaili sat beside him and he took her hand gently in his. "I've been thinking of you all night," he said.

"Me too."

The smirked nervously at each other. Marsaili felt like a teenager again, as if she'd snuck a boy into her parents' house in the middle of the night.

"I was thinking," Will said, entwining her fingers in his. "I know you had your reservations, about us, with the divorce still being up in the air and everything. And I know you've been hurt before... I just want to reassure you. There's no one else I want to be with. I never expected to meet anyone so soon, but this feels right to me. I'm excited to see where it goes."

Marsaili smiled. "Me too."

"And when everything settles down a bit, I'd like to take you out for dinner, if that's OK with you. But maybe we should keep this just between us, for a bit?"

"You mean at work?" Marsaili certainly wouldn't object to that – the whole Euan debacle had unfolded in far too public a manner for her liking. She'd be glad to keep her private life private for a while.

"Just until the divorce is finalised." Will continued. "I know we're not doing anything wrong – my marriage is completely over, emotionally. But I'd be more comfortable if we didn't take things any further until the legal side of thing is sorted, too."

Marsaili finally got his meaning. "Oh," she said, surprised. "OK."

"This isn't about Adelaide," Will assured her. "It's not out of loyalty to her or anything. I just want to be done with that whole nightmare, and then you and I can give things a proper go. Without anything else hanging over us." He turned her to face him and stroked her hair, his eyes earnest. "Ever since that first night at work when you showed up late, and I was so rude to you... Every time I've seen you since then, I've made such an idiot of myself, when all I've really wanted is to get to know you better," he paused, searching for the right words. "I just want us to work things out in our own time. Is that ok?"

Marsaili nodded. He cupped her cheek in his hand and kissed her gently. "Can I drive you home tomorrow?" he asked. "I can't bear the thought of you stuck on the train, when I could have you to myself for four hours instead."

Marsaili smiled. "Yes please."

CHAPTER 32

The interior of Will's classic car was surprisingly comfortable, even over an extended journey. Marsaili relaxed into the leather upholstery as they cruised down the Eastern shore of Scotland's most ludicrously named body of water, Loch Lochy.

"You can't be serious?" Will said when she pointed it out, his eyebrows furrowed in an incredulous frown.

"Promise," Marsaili giggled. "They must have been running out of ideas by the time they got to that one."

The blue sky and sunshine that sparkled on the water belied the fact that it was only just above freezing outside. Will's hand rested on the gear stick beside her, occasionally drifting over to her thigh and squeezing it gently.

She watched him driving, the same carefree, relaxed expression on his face that she'd seen ever since he'd appeared so unexpectedly on her parent's doorstep. It was as if he'd become a different person; she no longer recognised that stoic, aloof man in the suit that she'd met on the opening night of the panto. So much had happened since then, Marsaili couldn't quite believe that only a couple of months had passed.

They stopped for lunch at a cafe in Fort William, enjoying the opportunity to be anonymous for a while longer. Without the prying eyes and ears of Marsaili's family, or the whispering gossip of their colleagues at work, they could hold hands across the table and steal kisses as they walked along the waterfront. They'd already agreed that once they were back at work, they would keep things under wraps, so for now Marsaili made the most of being able to touch him and kiss him whenever she wanted. Deep down, she suspected that it probably wouldn't last - that she was perhaps just a distraction from the stress of his divorce proceedings, and that she herself was on the rebound from the whole mess with Euan - but for now she was just happy to have him to herself, and he seemed to feel the same way.

He kissed her long and hard before they got back into the car, his hands firm on her waist and her back pressed up against the passenger door. Will exhaled deeply as he pulled away. "It's going to be hard not doing that every time I see you at work."

"You'll just have to try your best," Marsaili smiled, her hand stroking his cheek gently.

"I really appreciate you being so understanding," Will said. "I know it can't be easy starting a relationship with someone who's technically still married…"

"Relationship?" Marsaili asked teasingly. "Mr Hunter, you're getting ahead of yourself."

Will grinned. "You know what I mean. As soon as the whole mess with Adelaide is behind me, I'll be shouting it from the rooftops."

Marsaili tapped the side of her nose. "Discretion is my middle name," she said. There was something exciting about the thought of it all being just their little secret.

As they continued their long drive South, conversation turned increasingly personal. Marsaili told him of Findlay's redeployment, and Isla moving out.

"So, I'll need to start looking for somewhere else to live soon. Or a flatmate. But I've lived with Isla for years; I don't think I could deal with sharing with someone new. Or should I say I don't think anyone else could handle living with me."

Will laughed. "I'm sure you'd be delightful."

"Are you still at the hotel?" Marsaili asked.

"For now. I need to start looking myself, really. But until the financial stuff's sorted for the divorce settlement it's tricky to budget."

"Does that mean you're planning to stay? In Glasgow?" She didn't really want to ask it, but she couldn't help herself.

Will smiled and reached over for her hand, holding it in her lap as he glanced briefly away from the road. "I am," he said, smiling reassuringly. "I may not love the job, but I've got bills to pay. And I've found a rather lovely Scottish girl that I'd like to get to know better."

Marsaili smiled. "It's got me thinking, all of this," she said. "That maybe it's time to make a change. Do something different."

"How do you mean?"

She sighed. "Much as I don't want to admit it, I'm not really an actress. Never have been. And I don't want to pour drinks for strangers all my life. So, I thought I might try going back to uni."

Will smiled. "Good for you!" he said, patting her on the knee. "What do you want to do?"

Marsaili shrugged her shoulders, suddenly self-conscious and wondering if it was such a good idea after all. "I thought maybe teaching - it's the classic failed artist fall back isn't it? I could still be involved with some of the things I really love - literature, drama, that kind of thing."

"I think you'd be great at that," Will said, his tone genuine. "It takes a lot of guts to start over and do something new. I wish I could do the same."

"Be a teacher?"

"Good God no," Will said, clearly alarmed. "You'd be great at it, I'm sure," he continued. "Me, on the other hand - small children would eat me alive. But if I could go back in time, I certainly wouldn't study law."

"What would you do?"

Will thought for a moment. "Music, probably. It was always the thing I loved most. Mum and Dad were happy enough with it as a hobby, but they'd have lost the plot if I'd gone into *the arts*." Will shuddered, saying it in a way that made it sound like a dirty word.

Marsaili laughed. "But aren't you? In the arts, I mean? You do manage a theatre, after all."

"Ah, you see, working in the business side of the arts is fine - well, acceptable, at least - but having to admit their son was a performer of any kind... to my parents that'd be tantamount to declaring I was a liberal, socialist, Labour voter." He laughed bitterly. "At 18 I just did what they thought was best - I didn't even think to question it. So Law it was."

"It's never too late." Marsaili said.

Will shrugged. "Maybe."

They drove on in silence for a while longer, as the rocky landscape of the Highlands gradually gave way to the forests of Perthshire and, eventually, the rolling farmland of the Central Belt. They stopped for a coffee at a roadside service station and Will filled the car up with petrol, refusing Marsaili's attempts to pay. Before long, they were pulling up outside her flat, and she found that she didn't want to get out.

They looked at each other, the engine idling and the atmosphere between them suddenly awkward once again.

"Can I walk you upstairs?" Will asked. Much as Marsaili wanted to say yes, she knew what would probably happen once he set foot inside her flat. She shook her head.

"No, probably best," Will admitted. "Can I call you?"

"I'd like that."

Will grabbed her hand, his eyes earnest. "Marsaili, please believe me when I tell you I don't want to keep this a secret. Really, I don't. I just think it'll be simpler for now. Once my divorce is finalised, I'll take you out all over town, I promise."

Marsaili smiled, her thumb rubbing the back of his hand. "I'll hold you to that," she said.

Will leaned over the gear stick and kissed her. "Meeting you... you've brought me back to life," he said quietly.

"I'll speak to you soon," Marsaili said, giving him one more kiss before she climbed out of the car and up the steps to her door, forcing herself not to look back.

CHAPTER 33

The first person Marsaili saw as she made her way in through stage door the following day was Forbes. He was sorting through racks of costumes and bagging up the ones that needed to be washed or mended.

Instantly dropping what he was doing, he enveloped her in a hug before she had a chance to object. "How are you?" he asked, his face serious.

"I'm fine," Marsaili said, forgetting that he'd still be expecting her to be upset over Euan. She was astonished to find that she hadn't even thought about him in days.

"Fine?" Forbes repeated. "Your TV star boyfriend announces his engagement to a silicon and Botox infused trollop and you're 'fine'?" He had his eyebrows raised and one hand on his hip, a look on his face that quite clearly conveyed his disbelief.

Marsaili shrugged. "Just one of those things," she said. "I should have known better than to be taken in by him in the first place. Call it a lucky escape."

Forbes followed her to the staffroom as she went to drop off her coat and handbag, watching her suspiciously.

"I don't buy it," he said.

"Buy what?"

"This," he said, gesturing vaguely to all of her. "Why aren't you huddled in a ball sobbing your heart out and listening to Celine Dion?"

Marsaili laughed. "That's not how *everyone* mourns a break up. I'm fine Forbes, really. He was a dick, and now he's no longer in my life. Problem solved." She smiled and headed off to find Will to see what other mundane tasks had to be tackled that day, Forbes scampering along behind her.

"When did you get so philosophical?" he asked, still suspicious. "I thought at least you'd be filled with blood lust and seeking revenge."

"I've had a week at home with my family to gain some perspective," Marsaili said, knocking on the door to the office.

If she'd been worrying that she might suddenly throw herself at Will upon seeing him, she needn't have. As the two of them opened the door and stepped into the tiny room she saw that he was firmly back in work mode - three-piece suit, neatly combed hair, freshly shaved and with a stern, slightly harried expression on his face. He bore little resemblance to the person that had kissed her in her parents' bathroom, his hair wet and dishevelled and his golden stubble scratching his chin. It was like he had a rugged, laid back, identical twin.

He looked up, and when he saw her his eyes softened momentarily. The Will she'd come to know was still in there, beneath his business-like exterior.

"Morning," she said with a smile, making a conscious effort to keep her tone even. "Where would you like us?" she asked.

Will glanced at Forbes behind her. "I thought you were sorting out costumes?"

Forbes sighed melodramatically. "Needed a break," he explained, wafting his hands exaggeratedly around his face. "All that dust gave me a sneezing fit! It's a health and safety hazard, really," he continued in a low voice. "We ought to be provided with safety equipment."

Will squinted at him, clearly unsure if he was joking. Then he opened a drawer in his desk, pulled out a paper face mask and tossed it to him. "There you go," he said with a smirk. "Back to work."

Forbes tutted audibly, staring at the mask, before walking out with a haughty toss of his head.

Marsaili laughed. "It's not often Forbes is lost for words."

"It's been lying around in there since I got here, along with piles of other assorted crap - old paintbrushes and the like," Will said, slamming the drawer shut. "Glad I didn't throw it out now." He stopped, smiling at Marsaili the way he did when they were alone.

"You look lovely. Did you sleep well?"

Marsaili ran a hand over her dishevelled riot of curls, tucking it self-consciously behind her ears.

"Don't," Will said, rising from his seat and untucking it again so that it framed her face. "It's beautiful the way it is. Makes you look... wild."

She laughed, wanting him to kiss her but knowing that he wouldn't. He took her hand in his instead, before dropping it again and shaking his head in exasperation.

"God, I'm sorry, I'm terrible at this!"

"You're not so bad."

"I wish I could…"

"I know. Me too." She smiled at him. "All in good time."

"Indeed," he agreed, his brown eyes holding hers intently.

"Shall I help Forbes with the costumes?" Marsaili asked.

"Good idea," Will said with a playful smile, tossing her another face mask out of his bottom drawer.

Later that afternoon, as she was bundling bags of costumes into Forbes' car so they could take them to the launderette, her phone buzzed in her back pocket. Surprised, she looked down to see Will's number.

Oi, you! Get out of my head! I have work to do ;-)

Marsaili laughed, feeling an excited flutter in her chest.

"What's so funny?" Forbes asked, tossing the last bag in and slamming the boot shut before climbing into the driver's seat.

"Nothing," she replied, jumping at his voice and shoving the phone back in her pocket. She climbed into the passenger seat and Forbes gave her a sideways glance as he started the ignition.

"Hmmm… I believe you, thousands wouldn't," he said, before pulling out briskly into the city centre traffic.

As the week wore on, the fairy-tale bubble that had existed back up North seemed to dissipate more and more. Marsaili spent each day carrying out menial tasks around the theatre, and each night sitting in the glare of her laptop screen, working on her applications for the teacher training course. She'd decided to apply to all of the Glasgow universities, and the University of the Highlands and Islands, which had a satellite campus not far from her parents' house. All required a written application and references, followed by a two-stage interview process, assuming she made it that far. Marsaili was nervous, but with Isla's help she managed to pepper her forms with various educational buzzwords, and hoped it would be enough to get her a face-to-face meeting.

Will called most nights - he didn't really like to text, it turned out. Said he liked to hear her voice. Marsaili found that quite adorably old fashioned. They'd chat, discussing her uni applications, Will helping with grammar and proofreading. He was constantly reassuring her that he hadn't forgotten about her, seemingly nervous that she'd get fed up of waiting and move on. Part of her wanted to invite him over, or for him to invite her, but another part was glad that they weren't furtively sneaking around. Exciting as that might be, it would have made her feel like she really was a dirty little secret. At least this way she felt like he respected her. They were just pressing pause, she told herself. They'd pick up where they left off when the time was right.

As February rolled into March and blossom started to bud on the trees across from her flat in Alexandra Park, the postman still brought no news from her applications, and Will's divorce proceedings seemed to stagnate even further. She knew she needed something else to engage her mind and give her a sense of purpose. And that was how, with four weeks to go until Easter, she found herself once again volunteering in Isla's classroom.

Marsaili had met with the headteacher, a round, jolly man named Mr Anderson who bore a striking resemblance to the Fat Controller from Thomas the Tank engine. They were struggling for staff apparently, and although she couldn't be left with a class on her own, he was over the moon to have an extra pair of willing hands around. She was given a timetable for a few mornings a week, and shared her time between supporting reading groups, helping out in the playground and generally mucking in wherever the class teachers required assistance. She enjoyed it far more than she had expected to, and as the weeks went on found herself increasingly looking forward to her days there.

She was particularly excited when she was asked to assist with the staging of their Easter assembly. Isla's P7s were performing a retelling of the story of the Passion, and despite her reservations over twelve-year olds depicting the crucifixion, Marsaili was eager to get her teeth into something she really enjoyed.

She first met with the class on a Thursday afternoon. Isla was observing, but she'd agreed to let Marsaili have a go at running things, and that she'd only step in for support as and when required. Their aim for the afternoon was simply to re-familiarise everyone with the story and have a go at turning it into a script of some sort. How difficult could it be? Marsaili thought.

Two hours later, when the bell had finally rung, she had a newfound respect for what Isla had to deal with every day.

"And this is a really good class," Isla reminded her with a smile, as she circled the tables picking up stray pencils and throwing pieces of scrap paper in the bin.

"That was insane," Marsaili said, leaning against Isla's desk and feeling as if she'd just run a marathon. "How do you keep a lid on them?" she asked, incredulous.

Isla laughed. "It's harder when you're just popping in for the first time, or for the odd session here and there. You don't really get a chance to build up a relationship with them. But it'll come. You did really well."

"It didn't feel like it," Marsaili said. "I need a drink."

The session had started out pretty well, she thought - the occasional kid shouting out here and there, but they'd basically listened while they went through the outline of the story. Marsaili was even starting to feel quite in control of the whole thing. It was when they split into groups to start doing some writing that everything went wrong. Suddenly there were arguments breaking out, pencils flying across the room and one girl ended up in tears. Marsaili spent so much time putting out fires that she didn't feel like they really achieved anything productive, and before she knew it, it was quarter past three and she was gratefully throwing them all out of the door.

Isla was gathering up the sheets of paper that had been written on and cast her eyes over them briefly. "Some of these are actually pretty good," she said. "We can sit down tomorrow as a class and start piecing them together. Do you want me to take the lead?"

Marsaili considered it. It was tempting, but if she was actually going to make a go of this as a career then she had to toughen up. "No," she said. "It's fine. I can do it. Just jump in and rescue me if they form a lynch mob."

However, when the next afternoon rolled around and Marsaili found herself standing once again in front of the baying mob of twelve-year olds, she found that what Isla had said was right. It did get easier. Whether it was her sterner tone or more authoritative body language, or just the fact that she was no longer a stranger to them, the kids seemed more receptive. She managed to enjoy the odd bit of banter, without letting them walk all over her, and halfway through the lesson she noticed that Isla was sitting doing some marking at the back, seemingly oblivious to what was happening by the board. If that wasn't a sign of trust, Marsaili didn't know what was.

By the time the bell went, they had the bones of a script assembled on the whiteboard, and Marsaili had even managed to get the class packed up, tables tidied and waiting smartly behind their places to be dismissed. As they were walking out, she had to keep from jumping up and down on the spot with excitement.

"Check you out, Miss Mackenzie," Isla said with a smile. "You're a natural!"

"That was really good fun," Marsaili admitted.

"It can be, at times." Isla said. "You were really good with them. Authoritative but approachable; better than some third-year students I've had in."

"Do you think I stand a chance then? Of getting on the course?"

Isla shrugged. "As good a chance as anyone, I'd say."

Marsaili hoped so. The more time she spent in this place, seeing what it'd be like to do this job, the more it felt like this was what she should have been doing all along.

CHAPTER 34

The following weekend marked the re-opening of the theatre. In the weeks since the panto had finished it had been scrubbed and painted from top to bottom, and Marsaili spent that Saturday morning helping to set out the finishing touches before the inaugural performance. Will had been working flat out over the previous weeks and their nightly phone calls had been brief, although he never missed them. Marsaili could hear the stress in his voice and wished there was something she could do; while she was full of excitement and enthusiasm about her possible new career, Will appeared to be getting increasingly frustrated with his existing one. It didn't help that his wife was still holding out on the divorce settlement and refusing to sign the papers.

Marsaili was unpacking and laying out the new stools in the Upper Circle Bar when Will came to find her. Apart from the stage crew setting up for the evening's opening performance - a touring production of *The Importance of Being Earnest* - they were the only people in the building.

"Hi," he said quietly. Something in his expression made Marsaili want to hug him - he looked exhausted. He was dressed casually, in jeans and his Oxford University hoodie, his hair flat and his face crumpled.

"Are you OK?" she asked, advancing towards him before remembering where they were and stopping awkwardly.

"Oh, fuck it," Will said, crossing the room in three long strides and hugging her so tightly he lifted her off her feet. He exhaled deeply into her hair. "God I've missed you," he said, returning her to the floor. "Sorry, I know I shouldn't have…"

"It's OK," she said, squeezing his arm. "I've missed you too."

"I was up all night with Adelaide," he said, running his hands through his hair and sitting on one of the new stools. "Actually no, sorry, forget it - it's not fair to talk to you about this."

She shrugged. "I don't mind. Honestly."

Will sighed. "She'd had a drink, phones in the middle of the night to accuse me of all sorts. Cheating, being gay, marrying her for her money - you name it. I wish I could just be done with it all."

Marsaili sat on the stool next to him, one hand absentmindedly resting on his knee. "Can I assume she's still refusing to sign the papers?"

He nodded. "Says she's not going to make it easy for me. Wants me to suffer, for some reason."

"Why?"

"I don't know. She's used to getting things her own way. I don't think she likes the fact that I left her, technically. She doesn't want me back," he added in a hurry, "and I don't want her. I think she just wants to make it clear to everyone that *she's* dumping *me*, and she'll be doing it on her terms, thank you very much."

Marsaili stood up, wrapping her arms around his waist and cosying in against his chest. He rested his cheek on the top of her head. "I'm sorry," she whispered.

"Me too," Will said, placing a gentle kiss on her hair. For a second they both leaned into their desire to be close, before breaking reluctantly apart.

They spent the rest of the afternoon getting everything set up for opening night. Marsaili liked how he rolled his sleeves up and mucked in - he may have been the senior member of staff, but he didn't see anything as being beneath him. He helped her mop the floors and polish the brass, and insisted on carrying the heaviest boxes up from the storeroom.

"Showing off?" Marsaili asked, watching him pile another box of Becks on top of his already laden pile. He'd taken his jumper off and his tee-shirt was stuck to his back with sweat.

"Maybe," he answered with a smile, flexing his bicep at her with a wink.

Before they knew it, the afternoon had passed and it was after 5pm. They were in the Grand Circle Bar, everything shining and gleaming, the ice buckets filled and fridges fully stocked. Will looked at his watch.

"One hour until call time. Fancy some dinner?"

Marsaili nodded gratefully, her stomach rumbling. She hadn't realised how long it had been since she'd eaten.

Will told her to head down to his office and make herself comfortable, while he popped out to the Italian deli over the road. He returned with two pizzas, two cans of Italian lemonade and a tray of mixed salad.

His head popped round the door, smiling. "I know it's not a

proper date or anything," he said, holding out the food. "But it's the best I can do for now."

"It's lovely," Marsaili said.

Will sat opposite her, the same places they'd sat and drank coffee all those weeks before. He watched her as they ate. "I feel like I've known you for years, you know," he said.

"Is that your way of telling me you're fed up with me already?" Marsaili teased.

"Of course not. It's just, I don't feel comfortable around very many people. You make me feel like I can be myself. Like I don't have to worry so much about saying the wrong thing."

Marsaili laughed. "Oh, you do say the wrong things!" she said. "Very frequently, in fact. But I still like you."

"Good," his foot found hers under the table, and he hooked it around her ankle. She looked at him with a smile. "I wish this table weren't in our way," he said.

Marsaili glanced at the clock on the wall. "Our shift starts in fifteen minutes," she said.

"I can do a lot in fifteen minutes."

"Oh, is that right?" Marsaili asked, her eyebrows raised. Her foot was travelling up his leg now, rubbing his calf and making its way steadily North.

Suddenly the door into the office was flung open and Caitriona burst in. They both jumped, Marsaili bashing her knee off the underside of the table and Will almost toppling backwards in his chair. Caitriona looked back and forth between them, her eyes narrowed.

"Interrupting something?" she asked.

"Of course not," Will stuttered. "Just a working dinner."

Caitriona didn't look convinced. "Very cosy for a working dinner," she said, eyeing Marsaili carefully. "Anyway," she continued, "I just wanted to hand this in before our shift started."

She handed Will an envelope, continuing before he could open it. "It's my resignation notice," she said proudly, a smirk on her face as she glanced over at Marsaili again. "I'm leaving. I've got a recurring part on a soap opera!"

Marsaili grimaced. "Let me guess?" she asked. "*Dear Green Place?*"

"Yes! I'm sorry," she said, a rose pink, petted lip jutting out in false sympathy. "I know he wasn't very nice to you, but Euan has really come through for me. I'm going to be playing his girlfriend!"

Marsaili rolled her eyes. "Of course you are. Congratulations."

"No hard feelings! I'm sure you'll get your big break soon. And another boyfriend…" she added, eyeing Will as if to gauge his reaction.

He kept his face neutral, a professional smile on his lips. "I'm very happy for you, Caitriona. You'll be missed."

"And I'll miss this little place, too," she said, looking around her as if she were suddenly Meryl Streep and heading for the Oscars. "You'll both come for drinks after the show tonight? A little celebration *pour moi*?"

"Of course," Will said graciously. Caitriona smiled at him and threw Marsaili one last suspicious glance, before flouncing back out the door and off to the changing rooms.

CHAPTER 35

For a touring play, the opening night audience numbers were surprisingly healthy. Usually it was the big musicals and 'girls' night out' type of shows that attracted the crowds, but tonight the bar was packed. The Oscar Wilde crowd was typically polite and well behaved, but there were plenty of them and they were enjoying copious amounts of sherry and gin. Marsaili and Forbes were in the Grand Circle - the most expensive seats - and virtually everyone they served was pre-ordering their interval drinks. It should make for a relatively peaceful interval at least, Marsaili thought, but it meant that the time between curtain up and the thirsty audience making their way back out for refreshments would be manic.

As the overture started and the ushers saw the last remaining audience members to their seats, Marsaili and Forbes were already assessing the damage. They quickly threw as many glasses as possible in the dishwasher, before rushing down to the cellar to re-stock.

"Just as well you're so sturdy," Forbes said, as they stacked crate upon crate to minimise the required journeys.

"Just as well I'm not easily offended, more like," Marsaili retorted, hauling the loaded boxes into her arms with a grunt.

"Oh, you know I love you," Forbes said, swinging the door open for her and holding it with his foot. "Nothing wrong with a girl with a bit of meat on her bones. Will certainly isn't complaining, from what I hear."

Marsaili stopped in her tracks, feeling her cheeks flush. "What did you say?"

"You and Will - Caitriona caught you in the office. You're certainly working your way around the eligible men in this building! If I weren't gay, I'm sure you'd have had your wicked way with me by now too."

Marsaili felt the colour rise in her cheeks. "Nothing is going on with me and Will!" she protested weakly.

"Oh, come on, darling, don't lie to Uncle Forbes. He's been looking at you with barely repressed longing since the moment he arrived in the building, and now you're having cosy meals in his office and jumping out of your skin when you're unexpectedly interrupted. Doesn't take a rocket scientist to figure it all out."

Marsaili sighed, resting the boxes momentarily on her knee. She lowered her voice to a hushed whisper. "Fine - we kissed, OK?" Forbes eyes widened dramatically. "But it's nothing more than that. And keep it to yourself. I've had enough of people around here being privy to the ins and outs of my personal life."

Forbes looked delighted. "My lips are sealed," he said, bringing his hands up to his mouth, turning an imaginary key and tossing it over his shoulder.

The rumour mill wasn't helped when, on their way back up the stairs, they encountered Will and he insisted on taking some of the boxes from her pile and helping them into the bar. Forbes raised his eyebrows at her, watching Will intently as he smiled at Marsaili, helping her unload her other items onto the counter. "Nice to see chivalry isn't dead," he said teasingly.

Will looked guilty, as if he'd been caught out. "Just, um, trying to be helpful," he said sheepishly, before leaving quickly.

"'Just a kiss' my arse," Forbes muttered to his departing back.

Marsaili was grateful for the rush of interval orders, as it gave Forbes little chance for further probing. They hurriedly dried the glasses and worked through the pile of scribbled notes on carbon paper, pouring drinks and matching them up with the corresponding numbers on little brass plaques that lined the narrow bar running around the perimeter of the room. By the time they were finished, and the curtain was dropping on the first act, there was hardly any room left.

Marsaili quickly washed her hands and took her place behind the bar, hoping that the plethora of orders would result in very little actual serving. She was wrong; from the moment the first patrons walked through the doors they were kept busy, three deep at the bar and the rest of the room packed full.

Marsaili was in the middle of uncorking a bottle of red wine when she noticed someone gesticulating at her from the back of the queue. He looked annoyed. Very annoyed. His square face was puce and what little hair he had was sticking up in tufts from the top of his freckled head.

Waving her acknowledgement, Marsaili quickly placed four glasses on the counter to go with the red wine. The lady she was serving passed her a twenty-pound note. "Keep the change," she said with a smile. Marsaili thanked her, rang it through the till and dropped the £4 tip into the jar, before quickly catching Forbes' eye. "There's a problem out there," she said, pointing towards where the angry man was still glaring at her. "I'll be back in a minute." Forbes nodded absentmindedly as she excused herself, lifted up the flap at the far end of the bar, and disappeared out into the throng of customers.

The man saw her coming and started pushing his way, none too gently, towards the far side of the room, gesturing for her to follow. He stopped at the little brass plaque nearest the door, which read 37, and pointed at it angrily. The shelf next to it was empty.

"Can I help you?" Marsaili asked breathlessly as she finally caught up with him.

"Where the fuck are my drinks?"

"Pardon me?"

"Where. The fuck. Are. My. Drinks?" He repeated, slowly and deliberately.

"There's no need to swear, sir," Marsaili said, trying to sound bolder than she felt. She was aware of the curious glances of some other customers, who were watching the exchange warily.

"I'll speak to you however I like," he growled menacingly. It was clear that he'd had a few, and now that Marsaili was so close to him she was aware of how broad and muscular he was. He certainly didn't look like the average Oscar Wilde fan.

Keen to diffuse the situation, and realising how very far away she was from Forbes and any kind of back up, Marsaili tried to keep her voice calm and reasonable. "If there's a problem with your interval order sir I can easily replace them."

"Well what's the fucking point of my wife coming out here to order them if some bastard can just come along and nick them?"

"Please keep your voice down, sir, or I'll have to ask you to leave. If you have your order form, I'll replace them for you right away, you won't have to wait any longer."

The man harrumphed and grumbled, still glaring at her but rummaging in his pockets nonetheless. Finding nothing there did little to improve his mood.

"I don't have an order form," he said through gritted teeth.

Marsaili considered her options. Theatre policy was clear, but she didn't want this guy kicking off either.

"I'm very sorry sir, but without the original order form I'm not authorised to replace missing drinks. Perhaps your wife has it?"

He didn't take this well. He uncurled one stubby finger from the fists bunched by his side and pointed it at her, the chewed nail waggling in her face threateningly.

"Listen, sweetheart, I don't care what you're authorised to do. I paid for them, and I'll be having them. Get me my fucking drinks. Now."

Marsaili swallowed. There was no hiding the altercation now; the eyes of almost everyone other person in the bar were on them. She could see Forbes glancing over, still serving, his face concerned.

"I'm afraid swearing at me really isn't going to change anything, sir," Marsaili tried again.

"Is that right?" While they'd been talking, the man had blocked Marsaili's path, manoeuvring her so that she was trapped in a corner between the wall and the back of the open door. She saw a middle aged, sophisticated looking woman tapping her husband on the shoulder and gesturing towards them, seemingly concerned.

The man was still snarling at her. "Well how else could I *persuade* you," he asked, his clenched fist suddenly slamming down on the ledge next to her arm.

Marsaili jumped, but short of somehow pushing past his impressive bulk she had nowhere to go. The woman who'd alerted her husband to Marsaili's predicament was now frantically waving at Forbes, who had abandoned the bar and was attempting to push his way through the crowd to get to her. The husband was nowhere to be seen.

"I've tried asking nicely," the man growled, suddenly grabbing Marsaili by the arm. She wriggled to get away from him.

"Take your hands off me," she said, but her voice came out whimpering and afraid.

"Get me my drinks. I've paid for them fair and square." The man went to grab her other arm, presumably meaning to frogmarch her to the bar, but before he could a tall figure slammed into him. Despite his obvious strength, the man was caught off guard and his stocky arm was twisted forcibly up behind his back, as the figure who'd grabbed him forced him back against the wall next to Marsaili.

It took Marsaili a moment to realise her eyes were closed. "Get your hands off her," she heard someone mutter, the voice tight with barely constrained fury. She looked up to see Will, his hair dishevelled and his eyes blazing. The man was struggling in his grasp, but Will held him firm until Forbes arrived, and together they wrestled him out of the bar, flailing wildly and still shouting at the top of his lungs.

Marsaili stood, shaking, aware of the eyes of everyone in the bar on her. The woman she'd spotted earlier approached her.

"Are you alright?" she asked gently. Marsaili was rubbing her arm where the man had grabbed her.

"I'm fine," she said.

"You're pale as a sheet," the woman said, taking her hand and leading her through the crowd. "Come on, let's sit you down."

Marsaili allowed herself to be sat on one of the stools, while the lady and her husband, who had now reappeared, shooed people out of the bar and explained that it was closing.

"What an absolute brute," the lady said. She had a well-spoken Renfrewshire accent and was dressed in a smart skirt and blouse. Her heels click-clacked on the floor as she went behind the bar without asking and poured Marsaili a glass of water. "Honestly, what is the world coming to? Can't even enjoy a night at the theatre without some poor girl being assaulted."

Marsaili accepted the water gratefully, taking a sip. "Thank you," she said. "You didn't need to do that."

"Not at all," the lady said. Just then, the door creaked opened and Will and Forbes re-entered the room. Will rushed to her side, his brows furrowed and his eyes full of concern.

"Are you ok?" he asked, taking her gently by the arms and crouching to look in her eyes. "He didn't hurt you?"

"I'm fine," Marsaili said for the umpteenth time. "Where is he?"

"Jack Bauer here kicked him out," Forbes said with a glint in his eye, poking his thumb towards Will. "Quite an impressive display, really."

Will glanced warily at the two patrons still hovering in the bar, clearly concerned that he might have come on a bit heavy handed. "I merely used necessary physical force to remove him from the property, and suggested he ought not to return unless he wanted to spend the night in a police station. Fortunately, his wife persuaded him to make the sensible choice."

The well-spoken woman piped up. "No less than he

deserved, the hooligan. You were perfectly entitled to do what you did." She smiled at Will reassuringly. "And I would be perfectly willing to say so in a court of law, should it come to that," she added.

Marsaili glanced out of the window behind her. There he was; being hustled across the street by a skinny blonde woman in high heels, who was gesticulating wildly and periodically slapping him around the head.

Will stood up and started thanking the couple who'd helped her, shaking their hands and promising them complimentary tickets to a future performance of their choice.

"Forbes, could you get these fine people another drink and show them back to their seats? On the house, of course."

Forbes shut the door behind them, and as soon as they were alone Marsaili burst into tears. Will tenderly wrapped her in his arms, stroking her hair.

"Shhh, it's ok," he said gently. "I've got you."

Marsaili sniffled and blinked frantically, not wanting to leave marks on his nice suit jacket. "Thank you," she said.

"I'm just glad I was passing as that man came looking for help. When I saw his hands on you I… I just couldn't control myself," his voice cracked into a nervous laugh, and Marsaili noticed that he was trembling. "Adrenalin," he said. "I didn't even know what I was doing; I just did it."

"Well I'm glad you did," she said quietly.

Will squeezed her tighter and kissed her hair, before they were interrupted by Forbes letting himself back into the room. To Marsaili's surprise, Will didn't move away.

Forbes smiled, folding his arms across his chest as he regarded them. "Don't worry," he said with a melodramatic sigh. "Your secret's safe with me."

"It's not a secret," Will said. "Not anymore."

By the time the shift had ended, word had spread of all the excitement in the Grand Circle bar. Forbes, however, in a display of uncharacteristic discretion, had kept his promise, so that when Marsaili and Will walked into the pub hand in hand later that night, there was no shortage of murmurs. Marsaili almost wished she could have taken a picture of Caitriona's face - it hadn't been her intention to steal her thunder, but clearly that's what had happened.

185

"Well well well," Caitriona said, her voice overly chirpy. "You certainly get about." She looked Marsaili up and down with a sneer. "How long has this been going on?"

"Not long," Will answered with a smile, squeezing Marsaili's hand.

"I should hope not," Caitriona said with a coy giggle. "I'd hate to think you guys were involved when you kissed me on Hogmanay, Will?"

Will felt Marsaili bristle by his side. "Of course not," he said graciously. "And I think it was actually you who kissed me, if we're being pedantic"

Caitriona sniffed haughtily, while Marsaili suppressed a laugh. "Well thank you for coming anyway," she said, turning away from them and heading across to a table of fawning backstage technicians.

Marsaili and Will found their way to a booth at the back of the room, nodding to some of their colleagues as they passed. He fetched them a couple of drinks at the bar before sliding in beside her, his hand on her leg.

"Are you sure about this?" she asked, taking a sip of her wine. "Going public?"

He smiled. "Life's too short. When I thought that man was going to hurt you, I just... I lost it. I don't want to put my life on hold any longer. I want to be with you, now."

He kissed her then, his hand on her neck, in full view of anyone who cared to look.

Will walked her home that night, strolling through the darkened streets and stopping to kiss beneath the streetlights. When they eventually reached her doorstep, they stood for a moment, each pondering the unspoken question.

"Would you like to come up?" she asked.

Will sighed. "Yes," he laughed. "I would really, really love to come up. But I shouldn't."

"Oh. But I thought we were..."

"We are," Will took both of her hands in his. "And I want nothing more than to be with you. Properly. But there's no rush, is there? We can take our time."

Marsaili looked at him, perplexed. None of her previous partners had ever turned down an offer of guaranteed sex before. She nodded reluctantly, trying to quell the little niggling voice of doubt which had returned to the back of her mind.

He stood and waited on the doorstep until she'd climbed the stairs. Marsaili peered out of the living room window and saw his tall, straight-backed figure in the lamplight below, his blonde hair shining as if it were cast in solid gold. She waved to him, and watched as he turned and walked briskly back down the street.

CHAPTER 36

The following Monday, Marsaili found herself back in the now quite familiar and comforting surroundings of Isla's school. She spent the morning in the infant department, helping little ones count out their sums using multilink cubes and number lines, before tying endless shoelaces and helping them do up their ties following their PE lessons. She enjoyed talking to them, and hearing their unfiltered, innocent thoughts. She found herself thinking of Callie, and wishing she was closer so that she could see her grow up, and listen to her beautifully childish conversations.

In the afternoon she returned to Isla's class. They had cast the play now, and pretty much everyone was happy with their roles. The children who didn't want to be in the spotlight chose to work on the stage crew, whilst the extroverts gladly took on the principal characters. Marsaili took the actors down to the hall to start running through their lines and blocking out the scenes, while Isla stayed upstairs to work with the backstage crew.

The kids were enthusiastic and it didn't take long to run through things from start to finish. They had a couple of narrators to string together the main elements of the story, whilst the pupils playing Jesus, the disciples and Mary Magdalen had a few lines here and there. Pontius Pilate really got into his role as the villain of the piece, and they got around the crucifixion scene by deciding to portray it on a backdrop that would be rolled onto the stage. By the time they padded it out with a couple of hymns, Marsaili was confident that it would be a pretty decent wee show.

"Miss McKenzie?"

The voice belonged to Kieran, the little boy who was so relishing his role as Pontius Pilate. They were in the middle of tidying up the hall when he'd broken away from his classmates to talk to her.

"Yes?"

"Are we going to be doing this tomorrow?"

"Yeah we are, toots." Already she'd been picking up some teacherly terms of endearment. "Every afternoon until the performance next week."

His wee face lit up. He was all freckles and curly strawberry blonde hair, a good two or three inches shorter than most of his peers. A rather innocuous looking choice for the power-hungry ruler, but he played it perfectly.

"Aw good," he said, grinning. "I like when we have you. It's fun."

Marsaili smiled as he scampered back to his friends, feeling a little surge of pleasure deep inside her. It had been a long time since she'd done anything that really gave her a sense of pride; she never would have believed that a compliment from a freckly little boy would have made her so happy.

She told Will about it on the phone that night. He was on call for the performance and had rung just after the curtain went up, as she sat on her living room floor preparing resources for an activity she was planning for the next day. She'd even bought a laminator, at which Isla had laughed ruefully.

"Ah, I remember when I was young and enthusiastic like you," she said, as she ignored the pile of marking she'd dumped on the coffee table when she got home and headed out to a yoga class instead.

"I'm proud of you," Will was saying, and Marsaili could hear the smile in his voice.

"Me too," Marsaili admitted. "Now I've just got to get my resources ready for tomorrow - it's hard work this teaching lark!"

"Do you think you might be finished by the time the show ends?" Will asked hopefully. "I wondered if you might be free for a drink?"

Marsaili sighed. Much as she wanted to see him, looking at the pile of paper and clippings lying around her, she knew it was unlikely that she'd be finished and able to make herself presentable by the time the theatre was closing. She was already in her jammies, her freshly washed hair damp on her back.

"No problem," he said when she explained. "You're in tomorrow, aren't you? I'll see you then."

They said goodbye, Marsaili feeling a slight pang of regret at missing the opportunity to see him. She threw herself into her lesson prep instead, shouting a hello an hour or so later as she heard Isla return and head into the shower. She was just thinking about finishing up for the night when the buzzer suddenly went. She glanced at the clock on the mantelpiece - it was after 10pm.

There was no sound from Isla's room, so assuming she was

already asleep, Marsaili cautiously lifted the receiver to her ear.

"Hello?" she said.

"Pizza delivery," came the response, in a familiar, well spoken English accent.

"Will?"

She buzzed him up, and opened the door to find him, in his suit and smart long wool coat, carrying two pizza boxes and a bottle of wine.

"I wasn't sure if you'd have eaten? And I'm a dab hand with a pair of scissors, if you're still working?"

Marsaili smiled, kissing him lightly on the lips as she let him in.

They sat on the floor together, Marsaili in her pyjama shorts and tee-shirt, Will in his suit waistcoat with his tie loosened and his top button undone. They took it in turns to eat pizza and cut out number bond dominoes, sipping red wine from two mugs Marsaili had retrieved from the kitchen cupboard, the only clean receptacles she could find.

"Thank you for this," she said. "Although if I'd have known you were coming, I'd have gone to a little more effort."

"Well if I'm honest, my motives weren't entirely altruistic - I couldn't resist the temptation of seeing you in your pyjamas again," Will said with a smile, his eyes running over her, from her bare legs to her slightly frizzing hair. "However, I was thinking it was about time we did something a little bit more official. I believe I promised you dinner?"

"You did indeed."

"Are you free this weekend?" he asked. "Actually, don't answer that. I already know you are because I did the rotas. Bruce is on this Saturday night, and you and I both - entirely coincidentally, you understand - happen to have the evening off."

Marsaili smiled. He put down the scissors in his hand and added another little laminated card to the neat pile by his side. She slid closer to him, letting him pull her onto his lap. "What did you have in mind?" she asked, slipping her arms around his neck and running her fingers through his hair.

"Well, I thought I'd pick you up, and after that… you'll just have to trust me." He was looking into her eyes, his hands trailing up her legs and toying with the edges of her shorts.

"How will I know what to wear?" she asked. Will's lips brushed her own, teasing, but he didn't kiss her.

"You can wear whatever you like," he said. "You could wear a bin bag and you'd still be the most beautiful woman in the room." He did kiss her then, tenderly and slowly, his hands warm where they crept up her back, beneath her tee-shirt. "I'm hoping we might have something to celebrate by Saturday night," he said as they broke apart.

"Really?"

"I don't want to speak too soon, but I'm cautiously optimistic." Marsaili kissed him again, feeling her own desire start to overflow. For a moment they both gave into it, before Will pulled away, breathless and flushed.

"I should go," he said. "Or I won't be able to control myself."

"Me neither," Marsaili laughed, climbing out of his knee. He grabbed her hand as she stood up, pulling her back to kiss her one more time.

"Remind me again why we're taking things slowly?" he whispered.

"Because you don't want to be an adulterer, even if it's only on paper."

He grumbled, clambering to his feet and unfolding his long legs from beneath him. "It's not about me," he said, his expression serious as he pulled her closer. "I couldn't care less what anyone thinks about me. It's about you. When, or if, we... you know… I don't want to be in a relationship with anyone else but you. On paper or otherwise."

Marsaili leaned into his arms, resting her head on his chest. She sighed. "You're too bloody principled for your own good, you know that?"

He laughed, kissing the top of her head. She grabbed his coat off the back of the sofa and handed it to him. "Thank you again for the pizza," she said. "And for the help."

"My pleasure. Sweet dreams, my love."

CHAPTER 37

Marsaili paced the living room floor nervously. After countless outfit changes, she'd settled on skinny jeans, nude heels and an emerald green peplum style top. She left her hair loose and naturally curled - 'wild', like Will had said he liked it. Periodically peeking out of the window to look for his distinctive car, Marsaili felt her heart fluttering in her chest.

"Why are you so nervous?" Isla asked, curled up under a blanket watching *The Voice*. A bin man from Skegness was displaying his unlikely ability as a virtuoso opera singer. "You've spent loads of time with him; it's not like a blind date or anything."

"I know," Marsaili muttered, clenching her hands. "But this feels… proper. Like an actual date, dressed up, just the two of us. This isn't hillwalking or eating pizza in my jammies; this feels… grown up."

Isla snorted. "Marsaili, you're 33. You *are* a grown up."

"But not like him. He's so sophisticated, and educated, and bloody… *posh*. What if he takes me somewhere really fancy and then realises how ridiculous he's being, going out with some common wee lass from the Highlands?"

"You're the one being ridiculous," Isla chided. "Will's not like that and you know it. Even I can see he's besotted with you, and I barely know the man."

Marsaili sighed, unable to silence her internal demons. Just then, she heard the distinctive rumble of Will's car, and looked out to see the round headlights carving through the twilit street.

"Wish me luck," she said, grabbing her handbag and setting off down the stairs.

Will was standing on the street when she approached, leaning nonchalantly against the body of the car with his arms folded across his chest and a smile on his face. Marsaili was relieved to see that he wasn't overly dressed up - smart jeans, brown shoes and a white shirt beneath a tan blazer. He kissed her on the cheek and she breathed in the now familiar scent of his aftershave, before he opened the passenger door and helped her into the car.

"You look beautiful," he said, slipping into the seat beside her and fastening his seatbelt. "It's a bit of a drive, I'm afraid."

"Fine by me," Marsaili replied with a smile.

As they pulled out of the city and along the Great Western Road, slipping into Dunbartonshire and the rolling hills beyond, Marsaili began to have an inkling of where they might be headed. Will had obviously been doing some research.

They pulled into the car park of the country pub just after 8pm, bringing the car to rest beneath the boughs of a large old oak tree. They were right by the shores of Loch Lomond, and although they couldn't see it through the darkness, they could hear the lapping of the water at the shore. On the car park side the building looked like any other little country cottage - low slate roof, small windows and whitewashed walls - but Marsaili knew that on the other side there was a double height, glass-walled extension built out on stilts over the water. Will opened the door and led them through, speaking quietly to the waiter before they were shown to a private table for two, right in front of the glass.

Will pulled her seat out for her, suddenly looking nervous. "I requested a window seat for the view; didn't really occur to me that it'd be pitch black outside."

She smiled. "It's perfect. I love it here. Who told you?"

"Forbes. I wanted to take you somewhere special; he said Loch Lomond was your favourite place. He said it was the only place within reach of the city that reminded you of home."

Marsaili reached across the table and squeezed his hand. "Thank you."

When the waiter returned with their drinks, they ordered mussels in white wine and garlic sauce to share, followed by sea bass for Marsaili and a fillet steak for Will. Will poured his bottle of lager into a glass and raised it towards her.

"You know how I told you I was hoping to have some good news to share?" he asked. Marsaili nodded. "Well I do - Adelaide's lawyers called yesterday. We've reached an agreement, and she is going to sign the papers."

Marsaili smiled, clinking her glass with his. "That's brilliant! What made her change her mind?"

Will's face suddenly dropped. "I've… given in to some of her demands."

She frowned. "Money?"

He shook his head. "No, nothing like that. It's a 50:50 split

193

on that front, she hasn't contested that. And she's agreed to drop the spousal support claim, which is good seeing as she earns more than me anyway."

"So, what demands?"

"Just some of the particulars on the documents. She wants things worded a certain way, and I've gone along with it. It doesn't matter to me anymore," he said, taking Marsaili's hands across the table. "I just want it to be over with. I want to move on."

She smiled at him. "Well here's to moving on," she said, taking another sip from her wine.

When it came, the food was beautiful. They decided to share a chocolate fondant for dessert, Marsaili had a second glass of wine, and after he had paid the bill Will suggested that they take a walk along the shore of the loch.

It was cold, and as they stepped outside Marsaili realised that she hadn't brought a coat.

"Never fear," Will said, jogging across to his car and returning with his own. It was a long, single breasted dark wool trench coat that came down past her knees. He wrapped it around her, tying the belt and pulling up the collar. "There you go," he said, gently disentangling her hair from where it had got tucked in and draping it across her shoulders. He kissed her tenderly, before placing her hand in the crook of his arm and leading her down to the water's edge.

The shingle was loose underfoot, and Marsaili had to lean on him to avoid stumbling in her heels. Although it was dark, the light from the glass windows of the restaurant spilled out onto the shore and illuminated their way. They walked away from the building, towards the trees, until they were hidden from the view of any prying eyes.

Will stopped, pulling her into his arms. His blonde hair fell across his forehead, the moonlight streaking it with silver. "There's something else I want to tell you," he said, his expression serious.

"What is it?" Marsaili asked.

He faltered slightly, stumbling over the words. "I said something the other night. It just sort of slipped out…"

"Oh, it's OK," Marsaili laughed, relieved that it wasn't anything more serious. "The 'L' word? I figured you didn't really mean it, please don't worry about that." She grinned. "I'm not going to start googling wedding dresses or anything."

Will looked confused. "You thought I didn't mean it?"

"Well… you didn't. Did you?"

Will smiled, his face relaxing. "Oh, I meant it. My love." He stroked her cheek, tracing her jawline and down to her chin. "I love you. I think I've loved you ever since that day you shouted at me in my office." They laughed, and Marsaili snuggled closer in his arms. "I've never met anyone like you before."

He lowered his face to hers, kissing her, sending shivers of pleasure down her spine. "You don't need to say anything back," Will said. "I just wanted you to know."

Marsaili smiled, looking into his beautiful eyes.

"I love you too."

When Will dropped her off later that night, Marsaili felt as if she floated up the stairs in a bubble of happiness. He loved her. She wandered around the flat in a daze, exhausted but not wanting to sleep, taking her time removing her makeup and putting her clothes away as she recounted that moment beneath the trees over and over in her head.

It wasn't until she was putting the lights out and finally heading to bed that she noticed it - a little envelope propped up on the side table in the hallway, next to the lamp and the telephone. It had her name on it, and a post-it note on top written in Isla's immaculate handwriting.

Delivered downstairs by mistake! It said. Suspecting what it must be, Marsaili tore it open.

We are delighted to inform you that you have been selected for interview for PGDE (Primary) on Wednesday 23rd May. Please prepare a short lesson plan related to an aspect of Grammar, appropriate for a second level class, and bring along any associated resources. We look forward to meeting you then.

Marsaili's heart started to beat faster. It was the news she'd been hoping for; there was only one problem. The invitation was from the UHI - if she were successful, it would mean leaving Glasgow, and Will, behind.

CHAPTER 38

Will was ecstatic when she told him, over coffee in the West End the following day.

"That's fantastic news," he said, coming around from the other side of the table to hug her.

"It's just an interview," she said. "And if I did get in, then obviously it would mean me moving away?"

Will nodded. "I know," he said, a reassuring hand reaching for hers across the table. "But that wouldn't change anything, not for me at least. It wouldn't be my first choice, granted, but you could come down at weekends, and I could come up on my days off. We'd make it work."

She smiled. "Just need to get my head in gear for it now. I should have plenty to discuss at least, with all the voluntary work I've been doing at Isla's school."

"How's that going?" he asked.

"Really well, actually," she said, taking a sip from her latte. "The play's coming together, and the kids are enjoying it."

"And you?"

"I'm loving it," she admitted. "You know, it's funny - I spent so long getting annoyed whenever anyone suggested teaching as a career, like it was just the go-to fall back for the failed actor. Turns out they might have been right all along. I enjoy it."

"When's the play again?"

"Next Friday afternoon, during assembly. The rest of the school will be there, and the parents have been invited in."

"I thought I might pop along too," Will said. "If you wanted some moral support. Thought I could treat you to an early dinner after, before I have to be in work. A little celebration for you."

"Really?" Marsaili frowned. "You'd voluntarily come to a primary school assembly?"

"If it's important to you it's important to me," he said simply.

The day of the performance seemed to fly by at twice the usual speed. They spent the morning running through a dress rehearsal which was, of course, utterly dreadful. One of the narrators had developed a sore throat overnight, which had almost completely robbed her of her voice, Pontius Pilate forgot his lines and Judas Iscariot threw a strop over the fact that he'd have to kiss Jesus on the cheek. They'd agreed not to do it in the rehearsals, but it was kind of crucial for the performance itself.

"But you knew this was in the story when we assigned the parts," Marsaili tried to reason with him. "Why didn't you mention anything sooner?"

"I'm not gay," he said, ignoring her perfectly reasonable line of enquiry.

"No one's saying you are," Marsaili argued, "and even if you were there's nothing wrong with being gay," she added, amazed that the younger generation were still spouting such subconscious homophobia.

"Everyone will make fun of me," he admitted, and Marsaili saw that he was holding back tears. She pulled him out into the hallway, leaving Isla to supervise the rest of the class.
His name was Aaron - he was one of the popular kids, much admired amongst the girls. Tall and dark haired, with sparkling blue eyes and dimples, he played ice hockey and electric guitar. She never would have thought he'd have been a target for teasing, but then she supposed she'd forgotten how brutal primary school could be.

"Is that what this is all about?" she asked. He nodded sadly.

"OK," Marsaili said with a sigh. "How about we angle it so you don't actually have to kiss him. If he stands side on to the audience, and you lean in to the opposite side and just pretend to kiss his cheek?"

Aaron looked at her, considering it. "I wouldn't actually have to touch him, you know, with my lips?"

"You wouldn't have to touch him at all," she assured him.

He nodded reluctantly. She took him back into the hall and they ran through it a few times, while she loudly reminded the class that no one was *actually* kissing and it was all just part of the 'illusion' of the performance.

"Disaster averted," she said to Isla, as the bell rang and the pupils went out for their playtime, after being warned in no uncertain terms about the importance of making sure they kept their costumes clean.

"Producer, director, designer, hostage negotiator… all part of the job description," she replied with a smile.

There was going to be an early lunch that day, to accommodate the extended time needed in the afternoon for the performance, so the hour between break and lunch was spent playing maths games, watching *Newsround* and trying to keep a lid on the children's pent up excitement and giddiness. As she made her way down to the staffroom, Marsaili was surprised to find that her own stomach was bubbling up with nerves. She would be sitting on the floor in front of the stage with the script on her knee, giving prompts if required, while Isla corralled everyone backstage. In spite of the fact that she knew it was just a primary school assembly, she was really anxious for everything to go well.

As the bell went to signal the end of lunch, however, and parents and children began pouring into the building, Mrs Hodges from the office came scurrying along the corridor bearing bad news. She found Isla and Marsaili on their way back to the classroom. "I'm so sorry," she said, breathlessly. "That was Mrs McLeod on the phone, the music teacher. She can't make it - her wee boy's had a fall at school and bumped his head. She's had to go and meet him at the hospital."

Marsaili's heart dropped. The play was peppered with a few hymns, for which Mrs McLeod had agreed to play the piano. As far as she was aware, there were no other pianists on the staff.

"What do we do?" she turned to Isla, panicking.

"It'll be fine," Isla reassured her. "They can do it unaccompanied, I'm sure."

Just then, Marsaili recognised a tall figure making his way through the crowds. She also noticed a few of the mums eyeing him up; in his three-piece suit and with his hair swept back, he was decidedly conspicuous in a primary school corridor.

Will smiled as he approached, kissing her on the cheek and shaking Isla's hand warmly. "Good to see you again," he said. "How are things going? All set for the big performance?"

"Er, not quite, actually," Marsaili said. "We've just lost our accompanist."

"Oh," he replied. "What was she supposed to be accompanying?"

"Just some hymns," Isla said. "The kids know them well enough; we can manage without."

"Do you have the sheet music? The chords?" Will asked.

"Yes…"

"I can take a look at it, if you like. Can't promise it'll be much, but I could probably vamp along, give them something to keep them together if nothing else."

Marsaili felt a wave of relief wash over her. "Are you sure? You wouldn't mind?"

"Of course not."

Whilst Isla got the class organised and lined up to make their way downstairs, Marsaili led Will to the piano that had already been set up in the hall. He took off his suit jacket, undid his cufflinks and rolled up his sleeves, before casting a careful eye over the music and softly playing a few chords. "Are you sure you don't mind doing this?" she asked.

"Of course not. I can't promise it'll be perfect, mind you; I'm far from a pianist. But it'll be better than nothing," he said modestly.

Marsaili thanked him once more, leaving him an extra copy of the script so that he could follow and see when he would be needed, before taking her place at the foot of the stage. The headteacher arrived, made a short introductory speech welcoming the parents to the school, and then the lights dimmed and the action began.

It went better than Marsaili could have hoped. The kids remembered everything she'd told them, speaking loudly and clearly, taking their time and facing the audience. Aaron staged his fake kiss without any further drama, and Will did them proud, vamping along with the songs and giving them enough support to encourage them to sing out with confidence. When Marsaili looked over at him he seemed, once again, to be in his element. He was smiling and relaxed, his long, elegant fingers dancing over the keys with little effort. It was clear that he was a natural musician, and Marsaili felt sad for him that he'd never got to pursue it further.

The show ended to rapturous applause from the assembled parents, and Mr Anderson took to the stage once more to issue the thank yous. Marsaili was touched when not only was her name included, but Sophie, the narrator who'd almost lost her voice, came down and presented her with a bunch of tulips. Isla got one too, and they were both forced to reveal themselves and take a little bow with the children.

"And last but not least," Mr Anderson continued, "I must thank our last-minute musician who gamely stepped in to accompany the children with their wonderful singing. Mr... ehm..."

"Hunter," Marsaili volunteered, smiling over at him as he blushed at the unexpected recognition.

"Ah yes, Mr Hunter! Please, take a bow."

Will was ushered to his feet and gave a self-conscious wave to the audience, as Sophie stepped down and presented him with the flowers that had obviously been intended for Mrs McLeod.

He caught Marsaili's eye as he sat back down and grinned at her. It was far from glamorous, or exciting, or romantic. But in that moment Marsaili was just about as happy, and as proud of herself, as she had ever been in her life.

CHAPTER 39

The train wound its way through the mountains, passing rugged crags and carving its way across desolate moors. If she'd cared to look, Marsaili might have spotted a red deer stag grazing between the trees, or an osprey swooping overhead. But she didn't; she daren't tear her eyes away from the pile of papers on the table in front of her as she frantically tried to cram in as much last-minute preparation as possible before her interview the following day.

It was being held at the university's main campus, in Inverness, so she'd booked herself a cheap room in a Premier Inn for the night. It'd give her more peace to study than being in her parent's house, and it was one less stress as she didn't have to factor in travel time in the morning. She could get up, shower, treat herself to a hotel breakfast and check out at the last possible minute, before walking the short distance to the campus just around the corner. Her mother had agreed to get the train through to join her for lunch after her interview, before she caught her train back to Glasgow.

Marsaili stared at all the scribbled notes in front of her, feeling like if she didn't know it now, she never would, but also lacking the confidence to stop studying and just relax. She'd prepared her lesson plan, with Isla's assistance - a grammar activity on identifying words as nouns, verbs, or adjectives, but including some, like 'duck', that could come under more than one category depending on context. She had an exemplar of the resources she would use for the group activity - three neatly labelled plastic cups, with words to be sorted written on lollipop sticks - and a list of questions that she would use to challenge or extend understanding. Last but not least she had a print out of some PowerPoint slides she'd made to support the lesson, along with a worksheet to be used as an individual task, and some exit passes to assess understanding during the plenary.

"Don't you think it's obvious I've had a lot of help?" she'd asked Isla the night before, as the two of them sat on their living room floor poring over her preparation notes.

"Don't worry about that - just be honest. Explain that you know some teachers and sought their advice, and really emphasise the fact that you've been spending a lot of time in a primary school. Show them that you're not under any illusions about the reality of the job; that you don't think you're going to be finger painting all day and sauntering out the door at 3pm. They won't mind knowing that you've had a bit of assistance. They're looking for commitment and potential, and you've got bags of both."

Isla's other piece of advice had been to show them her personality, and try to link her existing experience to the demands of the job - the communication skills required to deal with difficult customers at the theatre could be easily transferred to dealing with unhappy parents, for example, and her ability to perform in front of an audience gave her the confidence to speak in front of a class and command their attention.

Marsaili sighed, glancing over her various mind maps and highlighting words, seemingly at random, hoping that somehow all this information would be in her head if they asked her anything related to it. She was happy with her lesson, at least, and felt she could discuss that confidently. She just had to hope that nerves didn't get in the way of letting her personality shine through and hopefully convincing them that she was a kind, approachable, friendly person who could be entrusted with the wellbeing of the next generation.

They pulled into Inverness not long after lunchtime. Marsaili gathered her things and decided to take her mind off the interview for a couple of hours with a wander around the shops. She'd brought an interview outfit that she was happy enough with, but there was no harm in having a look around the sales in case anything else caught her eye.

She took a walk around New Look, Dorothy Perkins and H&M, before finally trying Marks and Spencer's. As always seemed to be the case, on the rare occasion when she was actually in the market for buying something the shops were completely devoid of anything she actually liked. Deciding to take a walk along the river bank instead, Marsaili popped into Caffe Nero, grabbed a takeaway latte and made her way along the high street towards the River Ness.

The spring sunshine had brought with it the first tourists of the season, and Marsaili wound her way through groups of Japanese visitors on a walking tour, past shops bedecked in tartan and a piper in full Highland dress, skirling away outside the gothic facade of the Victorian town hall. Marsaili had forgotten how much she liked it here - she always felt Inverness struck the perfect balance of metropolitan hubbub whilst still having a familiar, small town atmosphere.

She found a bench near the water's edge and sat to drink her coffee, enjoying the warmth of the sun on her face and indulging in a spot of people watching. Hiding behind her sunglasses, she found herself imagining the individual stories of the people who passed her - the young couple in the middle of an argument; a harassed looking mother with a toddler and a baby in a buggy; an elderly man on his own. She'd always been fascinated by the little chance encounters and unexpected events that wove together to make up a person's life, and found herself wondering if one day she would look back on the events that brought her here, and marvel at how life had unravelled in a way she hadn't exactly planned. She'd heard a saying once - 'We make plans and God laughs'. Or to quote a famous compatriot, 'The best laid plans gang aft agley.' Marsaili wasn't sure if she believed in God, but any plans she'd ever made for herself certainly had a habit of going 'agley'. All she could do was go along for the ride and hope that things would eventually work out alright in the end.

Marsaili stood and threw her coffee cup in the bin, before setting off in the direction of her hotel. Whatever life had in store for her, professionally or personally, she wasn't going to spend any more time sitting around waiting for what she wanted to fall into her lap. It was time to go out and make it happen.

After a quick dinner in the hotel restaurant, a bath and a pep talk on the phone with Will, Marsaili managed a relatively restful night's sleep. She awoke around 4am, tossing and turning and running over questions in her mind, but she must have managed to get back off again because the next thing she knew it was half past six and her phone alarm was beeping. She leaned over to switch it off, her vision still blurred by sleep, when she noticed that she already had a text from Will.

I love you. Show them what you're made of xxx

Marsaili smiled, swinging her legs out of bed and determined to give this her very best shot.

And five hours later, as she wandered out of the university education department, she was pretty pleased with herself. They seemed to have liked the concept of her lesson, and she'd been able to answer their questions fairly thoroughly, despite the dryness in her throat and the fact that her tongue kept threatening to stick to the roof of her mouth. They seemed encouraged when she mentioned her voluntary work at Isla's school, although she had stumbled over the last question - *What do you think are the greatest challenges facing education in the 21st Century?* She'd waffled on about technology, and social media, and how to prepare pupils for the changing demands of the job market, but she wasn't convinced she'd answered it fully enough.

Despite that, Marsaili still walked down the street to meet her mum with a spring in her step. Even if she didn't get in, just going for the interview was good experience, she told herself. She could always try again next year, and maybe pick up some proper paid work as a classroom assistant in the meantime.

Shonagh was waiting for her in a restaurant attached to the train station. It was part of a hotel that encompassed most of the building; an old-fashioned affair where the waiters all wore waistcoats and looked like they'd just walked off the set of *Downton Abbey*.

"Sweetheart," Shonagh stood up to greet her, wrapping her in a hug. It was unusual to see her mother so dressed up - compared to the usual knitwear and jeans she wore around the croft, the smart trousers, blouse and bolero jacket made her look like a different person. Her curly bob was neatly styled, and Marsaili even swore she could see a hint of blusher on her cheeks.

"Got a hot date after this?" she teased.

"Och wheesht," Shonagh sat back down, calling the waiter over and ordering two gins and tonic. "Tell me all about it."

She filled her in, while they ordered club sandwiches and French fries, and her mother tutted about how busy the city was. Marsaili smirked; it had been years since her parents had visited her in Glasgow. If she thought Inverness on a Wednesday afternoon was busy, Marsaili could only imagine what she'd make of a Saturday on Argyle Street.

"So… how's William?" Shonagh asked with a grin, smiling up at her over the rim of her gin glass.

Marsaili pursed her lips, considering her mother for a moment. She and Will had already discussed it; although she hadn't met Will's parents yet, he knew hers and it seemed churlish to hide it from them. If anything, he was already looking forward to visiting them again.

"You know I don't speak to my parents all that often," he'd

said when the topic had come up, his expression nervous. "I'm not keeping you a secret, or anything. It's just they liked Adelaide, a lot, and her parents are their best friends… I don't think they're ready to hear that I've moved on. And I don't want them to hold that against you. When they do meet you, I want them to be able to see how wonderful you are."

Marsaili had smiled. In truth, it didn't matter to her what his parents thought. She had him; that was all she wanted.

She sighed, looking back at her mother's excited face. "Will is good," she started, "and before you explode with excitement, yes, we are seeing each other now. We have been for a few months."

"Oh, I knew it!" Shonagh almost burst out of her seat, clapping her hands in glee. "Oh Marsaili, he's such a lovely boy."

"Yes, I know he is," Marsaili agreed, trying not to roll her eyes or point out the fact that he was 37 and far from being a 'boy'.

"I just knew it when I saw you two together - I could see the way he looked at you. Yer old maw's meddling isn't so bad now is it?" Shonagh asked with a grin. Marsaili bit her tongue.

"Let's not gloat now, mother. I like him, it's going well, we're taking it slow. There's nothing else to report."

But Shonagh couldn't stop smiling. "Just don't take it too slow," she warned. "You're not getting any younger, you know."

Marsaili took a deep breath. "How's dad?" she asked, keen to change the subject. She was surprised to see a brief shadow pass over her mother's face, before she caught herself and smiled again.

"Och, he's fine," she said dismissively. "You know your father; nothing ever changes." Shonagh nibbled at a chip, not meeting her daughter's gaze.

"What aren't you telling me?" Marsaili asked.

Shonagh opened her mouth, then closed it again, before exhaling sharply.

"Mum?" Marsaili persisted.

"It'll be nothing," Shonagh said. "We didn't want to worry you. He's going to see his GP about it this week."

"About what?"

"Och he's had the odd dizzy spell lately. He's been sleeping lots. One of his hands goes a bit numb now and then." She waved her hand in the air dismissively, refusing to make eye contact with her daughter. "He's just getting older, that's all. I'm sure we're making a big fuss over nothing."

Marsaili looked at her mother, her eyes uncharacteristically dull, as she fidgeted with the napkin on her knees. She was clearly more concerned than she wanted to let on. Marsaili felt a little cold tendril of fear wind its way around her heart, but she pushed it away.

"You'll let me know how he gets on, won't you?"

Her mother nodded, before changing the subject and chattering on about Callie instead.

They said goodbye on the station platform, embracing quickly before they each had to board trains heading in opposite directions. Shonagh seemed to squeeze her tighter than usual.

"We're so proud of you," she whispered in Marsaili's ear. "You know that, don't you?"

Marsaili nodded warily; this wasn't the kind of thing her mother usually said.

"Good," Shonagh patted her brusquely on the back. "And tell that lovely boyfriend of yours we said hello."

"I will."

Shonagh stood and waved to her as the train pulled away, and Marsaili once again felt the familiar sensation of having to say a goodbye that she didn't really want to say.

CHAPTER 40

As May drew to a close, Marsaili and Isla finally did something they'd both been dreading, and handed in the notice on their flat. After much deliberation, and two rejection letters from her other university applications, Marsaili knew that it was make or break - either she'd get into the UHI and move home, or she'd need to suck it up and find another, cheaper, flat share elsewhere in the city.

"You don't think that you and Will might…?" Isla had asked on their way back from the letting agency.

"Oh no," Marsaili dismissed the suggestion instantly, not wanting to admit that the thought had actually, in her dreamier moments, crossed her mind. But it was ridiculous; it was far too soon for that. "We've only been going out for a couple of months. We've not even slept together yet."

Isla nodded. "Because he's still married?"

"*Technically*," Marsaili answered. "We agreed to take things slowly."

"That's pretty fucking slow," Isla said, her eyebrows raised. It wasn't like her to swear.

"I know," Marsaili sighed. "We get close, believe me. He just wants to wait until he's officially single before anything gets more serious."

Isla smiled. "I think it's nice," she said. "Unusual for you, granted,"

"What's that supposed to mean?"

"Just that you're normally a 'try before you buy' sort of girl. Nothing wrong with that," Isla hurried on, "but I think it's nice that you've actually fallen for someone and for all you know he could have a dick like a cocktail sausage. Its… old fashioned."

Marsaili scoffed. "Well we may not have had sex, but that doesn't mean I haven't checked out the merchandise. And I have no concerns on that front thank you very much."

Isla laughed. "Coffee?" she suggested, as they passed by the deli down the street from their flat. "We've only got one more month to enjoy being resident EastEnders, after all."

Marsaili agreed, and they slipped inside, finding a space in one of the booths by the windows. They each ordered a latte and some

207

homemade tiramisu to share.

Suddenly, Isla reached into her handbag and pulled out a little envelope. "Here," she said, handing it to Marsaili.

"I didn't realise we were meant to get each other cards?" Marsaili said. "Do Hallmark even do those? 'Congratulations on the dissolution of your joint tenancy agreement'?"

Isla rolled her eyes. "It's not for that. Open it."

Marsaili slid a finger under the envelope flap and pulled out the card. It was one of those personalised ones you order online - the cover was a collage of pictures of Isla and Marsaili together, going back to drunken nights out when they were Freshers, up to more recent ones of them mucking around with Snapchat filters in their living room.

Will you be my… it read at the top.

Marsaili opened it, as the penny started to drop and tears began to sting her eyes.

Mascara wiping
Dress holding
Guest wrangling
Confetti tossing
Ass kicking
BRIDESMAID?

Marsaili couldn't speak, nodding her head frantically as she choked back a sob.

"We don't have a date or anything yet," Isla said, "but I thought today would be a good day to ask." She squeezed her hand across the table. "We may not be flatmates for much longer, but we'll always be friends. There's no one I'd rather have by my side when I get married."

"I'd be honoured," Marsaili managed eventually.

"Good," Isla said with a smile. "Now enough mushy crap - how about we celebrate with a proper drink?"

One latte, half a portion of tiramisu, a bottle of red wine and a dish of olives later, Marsaili found herself stumbling towards a date with Will. He was playing another open mic night, this time at a trendy, hipster-filled late-night coffee bar, and she was coming along for moral support.

He was waiting for her outside, his guitar case in his hand, looking somewhat conspicuous in his chinos and jumper against a sea of skinny jeans, tattoos and hipster beards.

"Good evening," he said when he saw her, taking in her somewhat sozzled appearance. "You look like you've started without me." He kissed her warmly, not caring about her red wine breath.

"I think I need a strong coffee," Marsaili admitted.

"We don't need to stay," Will said, nuzzling her neck. "I can take you home and tuck you up in bed if you'd rather?"

Marsaili shook her head. "You're not getting out of it that easily," she said. "Come on - I've never been a groupie before."

They went inside, where Will gave his name at the counter and received a number in return, before finding them a sofa near the back. "I don't want you distracting me," he said with a smile. "When I saw you that night just after Christmas, I almost dropped my guitar."

He fetched them two coffees from the bar, and they settled down to watch the first acts. Marsaili slid in beside him on the sofa, his arm around her shoulders as he absentmindedly twisted her curls around his fingers.

"So how did it go today?" Will asked.

"Officially handed in our notice," Marsaili replied. "Four weeks to find somewhere to live."

"I'm sorry," Will said consolingly.

She shrugged. "It's not so bad. Time for a fresh start. And Isla asked me to be her bridesmaid, so that's exciting."

"Congratulations," Will said with a smile.

"How was your day?" Marsaili asked.

"I do have some news, actually," he said, as the first act - a James Bay wannabe with long hair and a statement hat - took to the stage. "I'm going to see a flat tomorrow."

"Really?" Marsaili sat up in shock. "Does that mean everything's been finalised?" Will had been adamant about not wanting to commit to a tenancy until all his finances were sorted out from the divorce.

"Not quite, but I'm fed up living out of a suitcase. I want a home." He looked nervous all of a sudden. "You know, if you're stuck… I know it's too soon, really, to be suggesting anything like this, but… if I find a place you know you'd always be welcome there. Even just temporarily, while you figure out what's happening with uni and everything."

Marsaili smiled and took his hand. "It's very kind of you, but

I'll be fine."

"Well, the offer's there if you want it." He shifted in his seat, suddenly looking uncomfortable.

The truth was, she did want it. She wanted it more than anything. Over the last few months she'd found herself imagining a future with Will, and quite frankly the thought of admitting it out loud terrified her. For the first time in her life she was starting to understand what people meant when they said things like 'you just know.' She'd known for a while know that she was in love with him; what she wasn't ready to admit was that she might actually *like* him - and trust him - enough to consider the possibility of being with him forever.

Marsaili finished her coffee and Will ordered her another, before suddenly it was his turn at the microphone.

She felt surprisingly nervous as she watched him adjust the strap on his guitar, combined with a quiet thrill as he smiled at the audience. He'd chosen a Ben Howard song tonight - *Only Love* - and despite his earlier words about not wanting to be distracted, as soon as he started singing his eyes were on hers.

Later, as he walked her home, Will seemed quieter than usual.

"Are you ok?" Marsaili asked.

"I'm fine," he replied, but still they wandered on in silence.

"Whereabouts is the flat?" she asked, in an attempt to kickstart some conversation.

"Just off Byres Road," he stopped suddenly, looking at her seriously. "I'm sorry if I've put too much pressure on you," he said. "I wasn't thinking of it as an official 'let's live together' thing. I just thought it might be practical, that's all." He smiled. "Not to sound dreadfully unromantic," he added.

Marsaili smiled back up at him, linking her arms around his waist. "It's ok," she said softly. "I know what you meant."

"Not that I don't love the idea of waking up to you every morning," he said, pulling her closer and kissing her. "It has two bedrooms though, if you didn't want to…" he trailed off nervously.

"I think it's time you stopped being such a gentleman," Marsaili replied, slipping her hands beneath his jumper and feeling his smooth, firm stomach.

"Don't tempt me," Will murmured, kissing her again.

They carried on to the steps outside her tenement, Marsaili

suddenly hopeful that tonight might be the night. However once again he kissed her, saw her safely in the door, and wished her goodnight.

"Sweet dreams, my love."

Marsaili sighed as she shut the door behind him. Going out with a 'nice boy' was proving to be more frustrating than she had imagined.

CHAPTER 41

The following day, while she was getting ready for work, Marsaili heard a letter plop onto the doormat. Dodging the piles of boxes that littered the hallway - Isla's were neatly organised and labelled, whilst Marsaili had just started dumping things haphazardly wherever they would fit - she lifted the manilla envelope and knew instantly what it contained. Her heart quickened in her chest. She'd been half-heartedly packing, not knowing whether her things were going to be heading North or if she'd be looking for a last-minute flat share in Glasgow. This letter held the answer.

She was tempted to leave it and ask Isla to open it when she got home, but in the end, she couldn't wait any longer. Impatiently, she tore the envelope open and her eyes scanned the page for the crucial words.

We are pleased to inform you that you have been accepted for a place on our PGDE (Primary) course commencing in September.

Marsaili felt a bubble of excitement building up inside her, and before she realised what she was doing found she was bouncing on the spot, both hands over her mouth.

"Yes!" she squealed, unable to contain her happiness. She called Will straight away.

"Hello?" he said, his voice impatient.

"It's me," she said. "Sorry, are you busy?"

"No, no, it's fine. Just drowning in paperwork." He sighed, and she could picture him, sitting at the desk in his tiny office, pressing the bridge of his nose the way he did when he was stressed. "What's up?"

"I got in!" she said. "I start in September!"

It took him a minute to catch up. "You got on the course?" he said eventually. "That's brilliant! Congratulations."

"Thank you."

"Can I take you out for a drink after work tonight?"

"Yes please," Marsaili agreed.

Will wasn't on shift that evening, so he met her outside as soon as she managed to get away. He was standing by the main entrance, dressed in navy chinos and an open necked shirt, the late-night spring sunshine dappling his hair with gold. He had a bunch of flowers in his hand.

Marsaili ran into his embrace and he lifted her off her feet, twirling her round before depositing her back on the ground.

"I'm so proud of you," he said, kissing her warmly.

"I'm proud of me too," she admitted.

They walked together down towards the river. "Where are we going?" Marsaili asked, as they turned away from the bars and pubs.

"Since it's such a nice night I thought we'd do something a little different," Will explained.

They walked along the waterside, where the city council had spent large sums of money rejuvenating the bridges and pathways in order to discourage clandestine class A drug use and instead attract more joggers and people out for an evening stroll. Much like Marsaili and Will.

They crossed the famous 'Squinty Bridge' and headed West into Partick, eventually stopping outside a block of red sandstone tenement flats.

"What do you think?" Will asked.

"They look nice," Marsaili agreed. Just then she noticed an estate agents 'FOR LET' sign on the top floor corner flat, one with a large, rounded bay window sticking out like half a turret. "Is that it?" she asked.

Will took both her hands in his. "I know when I brought it up last night it wasn't exactly the most appealing proposition. But hear me out - there's two bedrooms, so it'd be up to you where you want to sleep. And I know you're going to be moving in a few months anyway, but even once you're up there I'd hope you'd be coming down to stay with me at weekends and stuff, when you're able to." He looked into her eyes; his expression so earnestly adorable that Marsaili would have agreed to just about anything. "I know it's soon; I know there's a lot of reasons why this is probably a really, really stupid idea." She nodded, as he continued. " But these last few months are the happiest I've ever been - and I mean *ever* - and I know this is where I see things heading anyway, further down the line. Why don't we call it a trial period for now? Just until you start your course."

Marsaili smiled. "Have you taken it?"

"Not yet," he admitted. "I wanted to see if you liked it first." He took out his phone and scrolled through some photos. "It's furnished," he explained.

"And beautiful," Marsaili added, her eyes widening. It looked like something out of an interior design catalogue. "I don't think I could afford this," she said hesitantly.

"I don't expect you to pay half," Will insisted. "It's my flat, it'll be my name on the lease. You'd just be a temporary sub-tenant; you could walk out the door whenever you choose. I think you'll find my rates are very competitive."

He flashed her a cheeky grin, and she couldn't help but laugh. It was certainly more appealing than a scummy flat share with some impoverished graduates, which was the only other likely option to see her through the next few months. That, or moving home sooner than planned and missing out on time with him. "Ok," she agreed, "let's live together."

He swept her up into his arms again, kissing her once more.

"*Temporarily,*" Marsaili emphasised. "It's your flat, I'm just a guest."

However inside, unspoken, she thrilled at the knowledge that Will had been planning a future for them, too.

CHAPTER 42

From there, things moved surprisingly quickly. Will paid the deposit the next day, and within two weeks they had the keys. Marsaili was stunned when she was the one moving out before Isla.

"Told you so," Isla said with a grin, as she watched Marsaili toss her last few things into a box.

"It's not proper cohabiting," she argued. "Just a temporary arrangement."

"Yeah, yeah," Isla said. "Whatever you say - I'll be looking out a hat though, just in case."

Marsaili surveyed her meagre belongings. Ten years of her life here added up to surprisingly little. The flat had been furnished and kitted out with the basics when they'd first moved in, so all she had were her clothes, some books, her TV and a few bits and pieces of soft furnishings and framed pictures that she'd accumulated over the years. At least it wouldn't be a struggle to fit it all in Will's car.

He arrived to pick her up, and she hugged Isla tight. "This is so weird," she said, tears springing to her eyes.

"I'll see you soon," Isla said, in her usual no-nonsense style. "Stop being such a wuss."

They said their goodbyes, and Will drove them the short journey across town, from East End to West End. As she stepped into the flat for the first time, it felt like she was in another world.

Will had moved his things in the night before, although he didn't have much, either. Most of his personal belongings were still in the marital home down South, awaiting collection when the house was finally sold.

Excited, he gave her the tour. As they came in through the storm doors, entering a large, square hallway, the kitchen was on the right - a traditional long, narrow galley kitchen, like in most tenements, but beautifully finished in smooth, handle less white gloss units with a sparkling, solid black marble countertop. The living room was directly opposite, and housed a minimalist, modern, low-backed three-piece suite in tan leather and a wall mounted TV with recessed, underlit shelving either side of the chimney breast. There was a raised dais in the corner, where the room opened out into a semi-circular turret, with windows all round giving a beautiful view across the rooftops towards the university. Marsaili could see the iconic gothic tower dominating the skyline. A single wingback chair sat on the dais, positioned to make the most of the view, and opposite sat a cello in a stand. Will's, she presumed, although she'd never heard him play it.

The two bedrooms occupied the remaining two corners off the hall, with a bathroom in the middle, all finished in a similarly plush manner. Will was watching her, obviously gauging her reaction.

"Do you like it?" He asked.

"It's beautiful. Too beautiful for the likes of me," Marsaili replied with a self-deprecating laugh.

"Nonsense," Will came up behind her, his arms around her waist. "You deserve nothing but the best." He kissed her cheek. "I wasn't sure what to do about bedrooms? Which one do you want? I slept in that one last night," he said, gesturing to the one that looked down onto the back court, "but I don't mind swapping."

"I don't mind either," Marsaili said, confused - was she his live-in girlfriend, albeit temporarily, or his roommate?

She dumped a rucksack with her clothes in it on the bed in the vacant room, noticing as she did so that Will had taken the smaller of the two rooms, and wondering if that were deliberate.

Chivalrous as always, he carried up the remainder of her things for her, while she unpacked, slotting books into empty spaces and hanging her clothes in the vast, built in wardrobe. She made the bed, while Will popped out to get them some lunch, suggesting that later they should go to the supermarket and stock up properly.

While he was gone, Marsaili paced the floor, feeling uncomfortable and out of place. Maybe this wasn't such a good idea after all?

When Will returned, he brought fresh baguettes, cold meat, crisps, olives, a bottle of red wine and a bunch of flowers. Marsaili pushed her doubts to the back of her mind as he laid it all out on the coffee table and they sat together on the floor, eschewing the sofa.

"To us," Will said, raising his glass. Marsaili raised hers too and they kissed briefly. It was clear Will was excited, as he chatted happily over their picnic lunch, but Marsaili was finding it harder and harder to suppress the rising feeling of disquiet in her chest. Before long, she blurted it out, just as Will was telling her about a Netflix documentary he fancied watching that evening.

"What are we doing?" she asked.

"Eating lunch?" he replied, his mouth full and his expression confused.

"That's not what I mean. What is this? Are we roommates? Are we a couple? What's going on?"

Will swallowed. "We're… both, for now, I guess," he said hesitantly.

"And sleeping in separate rooms?"

"Well I didn't want you to feel under any pressure…"

"Will, it's been nearly three months!"

He flinched at her tone. They hadn't had a proper fight yet, not since they'd started dating, and here she was barrelling headfirst into it while he just looked confused.

"I thought you understood…" Will stammered.

"I understood when you were still legally married, but you said weeks ago that she was signing the papers, and now we're going to be sleeping under the same roof every night… do you just not want to have sex with me? Do you not fancy me, is that it?"

"Marsaili, how could you think that?" He moved closer, the confusion in his eyes replaced with remorse. "I'm so sorry if I've made you feel that I don't want to be with you." He slid closer to her and pulled her into his arms. She resisted, refusing to relax in his embrace.

"It's not like I'm imagining it, Will. There's been plenty of opportunities and you always make excuses."

He sighed, pulling away and running a hand through his hair. "I know," he said. "You're right. I have been putting it off."

Well here we go, Marsaili thought, steeling herself for the impending break up speech, and imagining Isla's face when she turned up back on their doorstep on the same day she'd supposedly moved out.

"It probably sounds silly," Will continued, "but I'm… Scared."

Marsaili almost laughed, but caught herself just in time. She'd heard it all now. "Scared?" she repeated incredulously. "Will, you were *married*. It's not like you're a virgin."

Sighing, Will pushed himself up on to his feet, his head lowered as he paced restlessly. "Of course I'm not. It's just… I know men are supposed to be at it every chance they get, but that's never been me. I'm a one-woman kind of guy. And I've only ever been with one woman…" he trailed off.

"Just Adelaide?" Marsaili asked.

"Yup," Will nodded, looking embarrassed, and she was overcome with a wave of guilt. Here she was acting like some insecure nympho and it was all because he was having a crisis of confidence. "I was worried you'd think it was… weird."

Marsaili stood and walked over to him, taking his face in her hands. "I don't think you're weird. I think you're incredibly sweet. And loyal. And kind." She kissed him. "So, you do fancy me?" she asked with a smile.

"Like you wouldn't believe," he said, lifting her off the ground and into his arms so that she was straddling him, his hands cupping her bum. He squeezed it playfully as he kissed her again.

"I think it's time for you to add another notch to your bedpost," Marsaili said.

Will flopped down onto the sofa, Marsaili on top of him as she ran her hand down his chest and over the front of his trousers. She began to undo his fly, untucking his shirt and kissing his neck as she went. He stopped her suddenly, sensing what she was about to do, and lifted her face up to look at him. "I love you," he said.

Marsaili smiled back. "I love you too."

Marsaili always enjoyed the sense of power that came with giving someone else pleasure. She heard Will's gentle moans and felt his body twitch as she brought him closer to climax, running her hands over the taut muscles of his stomach as she did so. Just before she thought he was going to come, she felt strong hands grab her under her arms and lift her up.

"Not yet," he gasped, his face flushed and his eyes burning with desire. "Your turn first."

He flipped her back onto the sofa and leant over her, kissing her on the mouth before working his way down to her neck, nibbling her ears and making her tingle with pleasure. He cupped her breasts in his hands and worked his way lower, kissing her stomach and eventually peeling off her knickers, until Marsaili herself was lost in a frenzy of pleasure.

She came once, then again, until eventually she was giggling and wriggling away from his touch. "No, stop," she pleaded.

His head popped up, concerned. "I'm sorry; did I hurt you?"

"No," she assured him. "I just need to catch my breath."

He smiled, relieved, and kissed her again. "I want to make love to you in *our* bedroom," he whispered, before gathering her up into his arms and carrying her through to the room Marsaili had claimed earlier.

He laid her on the bed, undressing her fully this time, and slowly. She returned the favour, taking in for the first time the downy, golden hair on his chest, so fair that from a distance it looked as though there was nothing there at all. He was toned and lean but solid, the muscles on his arms lightly defined as he climbed on top of her.

He ran his fingers over her face, looking into her eyes before he entered her. Marsaili couldn't remember anyone ever looking at her like that before.

"I love you," he whispered again, kissing her as she felt him move inside her.

His eyes never left hers the whole time, his hands in her hair as she ran her own over his strong back, urging him deeper, closer. When he came, he clasped her tightly, his head buried in her neck as he exhaled, his teeth lightly digging into her skin.

He rolled off, breathing deeply. "Fuck me!" he exclaimed.

"I think I just did," Marsaili giggled. Will pulled her on top of him, her head on his chest as she listened to his heart slowly return to its normal rhythm, both of them slicked in sweat but neither wanting to move.

Eventually Will spoke. "I think I need a shower. Fancy joining me?"

Over the course of the afternoon, they christened pretty much every room in the flat. By the time the sun was setting they were both tangled up in a blanket on the sofa, exhausted and spent, looking out of the window at the city rooftops and a beautiful pink-streaked twilight sky.

"I've never heard you play the cello," Marsaili said, seeing the instrument in pride of place on the dais.

"Not much demand for open mic cellists," Will joked.

"Will you play it for me now?"

He shrugged. "If you like."

He wriggled out from under the blanket and found his

discarded boxers, slipping them on before stepping out in view of the open windows. He grabbed his jeans and put those on too, then sat down with the cello between his knees as he adjusted the tuning. Marsaili followed him over to the dais, wrapped up in the blanket to cover her nakedness, and curled up in the wingback to watch him.

"Ready?" Will asked, eyebrows raised, his bare arms flexed as he held the bow in one hand and the other hovered over the fretboard.

Marsaili nodded eagerly, enjoying the view of him bare-chested in the glow of the streetlights.

He drew the bow slowly over the strings, the opening note so low and sombre that it seemed to resonate through Marsaili's chest. As he played, he lost himself in the music, his head bowed and his eyes shut, his whole body in motion as he extracted each note from the instrument. The piece was sad, and seemed to Marsaili filled with longing. As she watched his elegant fingers run up and down the spine of the instrument, shaking and drawing out the beautiful vibrato, Marsaili was surprised to feel her eyes welling up. She snuggled deeper in the woollen throw, gathering it up around her shoulders and surreptitiously wiping her eyes.

Will stopped suddenly, the music coming to an abrupt end, his arms momentarily frozen above the cello as the final note echoed around the room.

"That was beautiful," Marsaili said, hoping be didn't hear the choke in her voice. Crying after sex was guaranteed to make her seem like an absolute psycho.

Will smiled modestly, placing the instrument back in its stand. He leaned over and kissed her on the forehead.

"I'm exhausted," he said.

"I'm not surprised," Marsaili laughed. "You've been busy."

"Shall we go to bed?"

"*Our* bed?"

Will nodded, before sweeping her up in his arms and carrying her once more across the hall.

CHAPTER 43

For the next few weeks Marsaili existed in a bubble of domestic bliss. She'd never lived with a boyfriend before, and she was surprised at how quickly they settled into a rhythm together. It felt natural and easy. She loved waking up with him, seeing his long ungainly limbs sprawled across the bed, the duvet tangled between his legs and his hair tousled. He slept like a child, his body crumpled haphazardly as if sleep had enveloped him suddenly and without warning.

She discovered that he was a morning person, unlike her, and would wake at dawn with a smile, before going out for a short run and making espresso on the stove. He was always the first to leave for work, and so Marsaili would sit with him on the sofa in her jammies, drinking coffee and watching the news. Marsaili learned that he shaved with an open blade, which he kept in a little leather pouch with a bar of soap and an old-fashioned brush that he used to lather it up.

He'd kiss her goodbye every morning, and on the days when they were both working, they would walk home together at night, sometimes stopping off for some food or a drink on the way. He enjoyed cooking, and was far better at it than her, so on the evenings when they were both home, he would invariably be the chef, while Marsaili poured them wine and chose the music. Occasionally he'd bring her home flowers, or she'd buy a bottle of whisky for them to sample together.

On Sunday mornings Will liked to read the broadsheets, and Marsaili would lie on the sofa, her feet in his lap while she watched *Real Housewives* or *Love Island* on catch up. It was too perfect to last, Marsaili suspected, and they both knew things wouldn't be this way forever. But while this was their life, they intended to enjoy every single minute together.

Shonagh, of course, had been deliriously happy when she learned of Marsaili's new living arrangements.

"It's only temporary, mum," Marsaili reminded her. "Just so I can keep working right up until I move home and start uni." Her parents had already dismissed her offer to pay rent when she returned home, but nonetheless Marsaili was trying to work and save as much as she could just now to allow her to focus purely on her studies. It was only a year, and after that she'd have a guaranteed year's pay as a probationer, but still she didn't want to be leeching off of them, or Will. She'd even signed on to a few temping agencies, and was picking up some extra days in call centres and data entry companies to add to her evenings at the theatre.

"Oh, but it's a step in the right direction," Shonagh cooed. "With Gregor and Gayatri moving in too, I could have you all married off soon!"

Marsaili smiled. Her twin had called her the week before to fill her in on that particular development, as well as to gloat and pat himself on the back for the role he'd played in 'nudging' her and Will together.

"How's Dad?" Marsaili asked, keen to change the subject.

Her mother breathed in deeply; Marsaili could hear her sucking the air in between clenched teeth. "He's fine," she said, in an overly jovial tone. "The GP is sending him to hospital for some tests, but it's nothing to worry about. Just ruling some things out."

Marsaili pursed her lips. One perk of living at home, at least, was that it would be easier for her to keep tabs on them both. Her father rarely spoke to her on the phone, always deferring to his wife on that front, but when they were both living under the same roof, he wouldn't be able to escape her.

She was unable to end the call without assuring her mum that Will would be coming with her when she moved her stuff up in a couple of months' time.

"Tell him I'll make tablet," Shonagh squeezed in, right before Marsaili hung up, rolling her eyes.

It was a Friday night, and Will was on call for the performance at work. It was a musical this week, *Five Guys Named Moe*. Marsaili had the night off, and she was planning a little surprise for him when he returned.

She started with a long soak in the bath, shaving her legs carefully and rubbing moisturiser over every inch of her body. She left her hair to dry naturally, in the wild curls Will liked best, before putting on some makeup and unwrapping the expensive lingerie she'd purchased the day before. It was nothing too extravagant - a black lace bodysuit with a low plunging neckline and a tie up halter neck fastening at the back - but she'd never dressed up for him before, and she couldn't wait to see his face. Resisting the temptation to send him a photo, Marsaili slipped a red floral tea dress over the top and decided to keep it as a surprise instead.

Shaking out her still damp hair, she wandered through to the kitchen. It was 7pm; Will wouldn't be home for a good few hours yet. She gathered the items she needed from the fridge - olives, salad veg and two steaks - and opened the bottle of red wine to let it breathe. She'd put some frozen chips in the oven later, and had a couple of slices of cheesecake and fresh berries still chilling in the fridge. It wasn't much, but it was about all her culinary skills could handle.

When she heard Will's key in the door later, she came to greet him with an apron over her dress, a pair of heels on her feet and a glass of wine in each hand. The late spring evening was warm and he had walked home in just his waistcoat, his jacket slung over one arm and his sleeves rolled up. He stopped, looking at her in surprise. "I was expecting to find you on the sofa in your pyjamas," he said, smiling appreciatively and taking the glass of wine that she handed out to him.

"Not tonight," Marsaili said, stretching up on tiptoes to kiss him, wrapping one arm around his neck.

"Do I smell food?" Will asked, his expression disbelieving.

"Don't get too excited," Marsaili cautioned, taking his coat and leading him into the living room.

"Sit down," she said, "make yourself comfortable. Dinner will be served shortly."

Will flopped into the sofa as instructed, but grabbed her hand as she turned to go, pulling Marsaili down into his lap. "Come here a second," he murmured, kissing her deeply and running his hand up her thigh. "Can dinner wait?" he asked. "You've not got a souffle in there that's about to collapse or anything, have you?"

Marsaili giggled. "Just steak and oven chips."

"Sound delicious," he said, his mouth on her neck as he gently pushed her hair aside and began kissing and nibbling his way down to her collarbone. "But I think I'm hungry for something else right now."

"Well I was actually planning on having that for dessert," Marsaili replied, her pulse quickening as his hand slid beneath the hem of her dress and found the lace teddy beneath. He stopped suddenly.

"What's this?" he asked.

"A surprise," Marsaili answered, her fingers playing with the hair at the nape of his neck. He suddenly looked like a little boy with a present to unwrap.

"Can I see it?" he asked, grinning.

So Marsaili stood up, twirled and slowly lifted the dress over her head and dropped it on the floor. She giggled, suddenly feeling self-conscious.

Will stood up, his hands on her hips as he leant back and admired her, before turning her round to appreciate the full effect.

"You like?" she asked eventually.

Will nodded eagerly in response. "Very much," he said, pulling her once again into his arms.

"Not so fast," Marsaili said, shaking her head and pulling away from him as his hand slipped insistently between her legs. "Tonight's meant to be about you."

"This is about me," he retorted. "This is about me wanting to make sure that you are fully satisfied."

As he scooped her into his arms and carried her through to the bedroom, Marsaili gave up arguing, and forgot all about the food.

Afterwards, wrapped up in the bedsheets and both feeling profoundly satisfied, they drank the wine and ate the strawberries that Marsaili had bought to serve with the cheesecakes. She'd had to open the windows in the kitchen to air out the smoke from the burned oven chips.

"I'm sorry you never got your steak," she said, holding a strawberry up to Will's mouth. She was lying on top of him, her belly against his and their faces inches apart.

"I'd rather have you any day," Will replied.

She kissed his stomach, running her fingers over the dusting of golden hair that led down to his crotch.

"You never got the other part of your treat either," she said, sliding further down his body, her hands pressed against his firm thighs.

"It's not too late," he replied with a smile, settling back on the pillow with one hand behind his head and the other holding his wine. Marsaili raised her eyebrows.

"So soon?" she asked.

"Try me."

And so, she did.

The following morning, they enjoyed a rare lie in. Neither one of them was working, and they awoke to the sound of birds chirping outside on their windowsill and the late morning sunshine streaming in through the blinds.

Will was tossed carelessly across the bed in his usual manner, and Marsaili rolled over, draping one arm around him and kissing his back.

"Morning," he grumbled sleepily, turning over and pulling her in against his chest. They lay there for a moment, entwined around one another, before Will started to stir and his hands started to wander.

"What time is it?" Marsaili asked.

"I don't care," Will replied, his long, elegant fingers now tracing the bumps of her rib cage before grazing around the edges of her nipples. He lowered his mouth and took one gently between his teeth, nibbling it in a way that made Marsaili's skin tingle.

He suddenly flipped her onto her back and climbed on top of her, his flaxen head burrowed between her breasts. His lips worked their way down her navel, delicately kissing her pale skin, until eventually he parted her thighs. Marsaili sank into the pillows and closed her eyes. It wasn't long before her breath was coming in short, ragged gasps and she was twisting the sheets around her fists, when suddenly there was a sharp rapping on the door.

Will paused briefly, but his head didn't move. For a moment all Marsaili could hear was her own shallow, fervent breathing. Just as he was about to resume his attentions, the knock came again, but this time longer, louder and more impatient.

Will sat up, frustrated, and rolled his eyes, before clambering over to give Marsaili a kiss. "Don't move," he said with a smile, his hair flopping into his eyes. "I'm not finished with you yet."

She giggled, equally frustrated but looking forward to his return, as Will pulled on a pair of joggers from the pile of clothes on a chair in the corner of the room. He didn't bother with a shirt, jogging to the door bare-chested to get rid of whichever unsuspecting delivery driver or door-to-door salesman had interrupted them.

He left the bedroom door ajar behind him, so Marsaili could quite clearly hear the annoyance in his voice as he began speaking before the storm door had even been unlatched.

"Whatever you're selling we're not interested, thank you," he was saying, before she heard the door creak on its hinges and he suddenly stopped.

The reply did not come from a Glaswegian salesman, delivery driver or postie. The voice that answered him was female, English and every bit as well-spoken as his own, dripping in barely-concealed disdain.

"We're not selling anything," the woman said, as Marsaili heard high heels clicking on the tiled floor. "Now let us in and put some bloody clothes on."

Next came the unmistakable sound of bags being dropped in the hallway, and a stumbling of half formed words and vague noises of protestation from Will.

Marsaili sat up in bed, pulling the duvet over her and wishing the door was shut. She could just see the woman from behind now, closely followed by a man, as they moved into the hall.

Will's parents had decided to pay him an unexpected visit.

CHAPTER 44

Will tried to herd them into the kitchen, where they would have managed to avoid seeing Marsaili and she could have at least pulled the door shut and put some clothes on before the inevitable meeting occurred. However, his mother, well into her 60s but with hair still every bit as blonde as his, sprayed and backcombed into an impressively voluminous bob, strutted straight across the hall in her high heels towards the open door of the living room.

"It's almost noon," she was saying, her tone severe and cutting. "What are you still doing lazing around half dressed..." Her voice trailed off as she glanced to her right and into the bedroom. Marsaili froze, the duvet pulled up over her breasts and her red curls wild around her wide-eyed, freckled face. The older woman looked her up and down, her nose wrinkling into an unimpressed sneer.

"This must be her; I suppose?" she said, her head ever so slightly inclining in Marsaili's direction.

Will quickly stepped between them, pulling the door shut behind him. Marsaili could hear him urging his mother into the living room. "I'll put the kettle on and then we can talk," he said tersely.

As the high heels click-clacked into the living room and became muffled on the carpet, followed by the shuffling footsteps of what Marsaili assumed was Will's father, he let himself into the bedroom and shut the door behind him. His face was flushed, so much so that even his chest was dappled with red. He looked like he was going to break out in hives.

"Your parents?" Marsaili whispered, appalled, as she jumped out of bed and grabbed the nearest clothes she could find.

"I'm so sorry," he said, following suit and quickly throwing on a tee-shirt. "I wrote to them last week to give them my new forwarding address. I wasn't thinking they'd just appear on the doorstep."

Marsaili paused, her jumper half over her head. "You *wrote* to them?" she asked in a muffled voice.

Will shrugged. "I told you. We don't talk very often."

Marsaili hopped into her jeans, pulling an old pair of knickers out of one of the legs as she did so. "And what did your mother mean by 'is that *her*'?"

Will sighed. "I'll explain later." He came over and kissed her firmly, cupping her face in his hands. He looked into her eyes. "Just remember how much I love you."

Uncertainly, Marsaili allowed herself to be led into the living room. Will held her hand as she forced a smile and came face to face with them for the first time.

His mother was heavily made up, with piercing blue eyes and strong, angular features, much like Will's. She was very slim, dressed in a navy pencil skirt and green blouse. His father, on the other hand, was rounded and soft, with a neck that jiggled over the collar of his shirt. His hairline was receding and he had a spot of blood on his chin from where he had obviously cut himself shaving. Marsaili found herself wondering if it was him who had taught Will to use an open blade.

Will cleared his throat nervously. "Well, this isn't exactly how I was hoping you'd meet, but… Mum, Dad; this is Marsaili. Marsaili these are my parents - Lydia and Gerald."

"Pleased to meet you," Marsaili offered her hand and Gerald received it, albeit with a great deal of harrumphing and muttering under his breath. Lydia, on the other hand, merely stared at her coldly until Marsaili's hand dropped, limp and pathetic, by her side. Will's mother raised one perfectly preened eyebrow at her and folded her bony arms across her chest.

"What sort of name is that?" she asked.

"Gaelic," Marsaili replied. "It means 'pearl'. My dad found one in an oyster the day before mum went into labour, so…" She didn't know why she was still talking, and evidently neither did they. Will's mother fixed her with an unblinking stare.

"Pardon me?"

"My dad's a fisherman…"

Lydia's icy stare moved to her son. "A fisherman's daughter? No wonder she got her claws into you; must have thought Christmas had come early. Proud of yourself, are you?" she asked, glancing back at Marsaili. "Found a wealthy man to take care of you, broke up his marriage - a marriage *we* spent years building, I might add."

Confused, Marsaili automatically looked to Will for support. "I'm sorry, I don't know what you mean…?"

"Mother, don't," Will warned, his voice low. "We can talk about this later."

"No, William, we'll talk about this now." Lydia stood up suddenly, pacing the room. "Your father and I have come all the way up here on that Godforsaken sleeper train to try and talk you out of throwing away your marriage over some jumped up little strumpet…"

"Strumpet?" Marsaili repeated, disbelief finally giving way to a fiery indignation.

"Lydia, darling, there's really no need to be rude," Gerald tried.

"Shut up, Gerald."

"Mum, stop it."

"Don't talk to your mother like that," Gerald interjected.

Marsaili looked from one Hunter to the next, amazed that she'd once been concerned that her family might be the embarrassing ones.

Will was breathing deeply, staring down at the mother he dwarfed, yet somehow still cowed by her presence. He kept one hand on Marsaili's elbow, but otherwise remained silent.

"You're throwing your whole life away," Lydia went on. "Everything we've worked for, everything you and Adelaide have built together. For this?" Lydia looked around her in disgust, as if the plush West End flat were a hobbit hole. Her eyes finally alighted once again on Marsaili, and she glared at her. "We've seen the papers, you know. Adelaide showed us. And we begged her not to sign them until we'd tried to talk some bloody sense into you."

Will sighed, his expression defeated.

"What does she mean, Will?" Marsaili asked.

"He admitted it," Lydia declared, not giving her son a chance to answer. "Adultery. That's why Adelaide's divorcing him."

Marsaili felt a flash of fury. "You *cheated* on her?" she said in disgust, before the penny suddenly dropped. "You said you cheated on her with *me*?" She felt as if she'd been slapped.

"No, I didn't," Will said. He looked desperately at Marsaili, taking both her hands in his. "Your name didn't come up, I swear. I agreed to putting it on the papers in return for her not contesting the divorce." He sighed, running his hands through his hair so it stood up in tufts. "I just wanted it to be over. I just wanted to get my life back. *My* life," he repeated, shooting his mother a glance.

"You admit it then," Lydia said. "You've been having your

end away with this little…"

"Her name is Marsaili," he said, his voice quiet but edged with rage. "And she has absolutely nothing to do with this. Not that it's any of your business anyway, but we didn't even meet until after Adelaide and I had ended things."

"You haven't 'ended things' yet," Lydia replied, her blue eyes almost grey. "You're still married in the eyes of the law, and the church, and your family. We're here to put an end to this. You've had your fun, now it's time to stop all this nonsense and come home to your wife."

"This *is* my home now," Will replied. "There's nothing left for me in London. I'm happy here."

Lydia laughed, a shrill, unpleasant sound. "Oh, you can't be serious? Gerald, please talk some sense into your son?"

A panicked expression passed over Gerald's face, as he realised that he was suddenly expected to make a contribution. "Ehm, yes… come on William, there's a good chap. Nothing wrong with enjoying a spot of, um, *recreational activities* while you're away. But you really must come home now. Um… enough's enough," he said, in one last ditch attempt at putting his foot down.

Marsaili couldn't handle much more of this, and being referred to as a *recreational activity* proved to be the last straw.

"Well this *strumpet* is going to leave you to it, since clearly I have absolutely no say in what's going on here," she said, fetching her coat from the hall cupboard. "I'll be back in a couple of hours and you can all let me know what you've decided then." With that, she picked up her handbag and swept out of the door.

She returned, as promised, just over two hours later, after walking off some of her rage up and down Byres Road and drinking an overpriced latte from one of the many coffee shops. She turned her key in the door and entered slowly; there were no suitcases in the hall, and no voices to be heard either.

"They've gone," Will said, his voice carrying through from the living room. He sounded exhausted.

Marsaili went in to find him sat in the wingback by the bay window, looking out over the street below. He turned as she entered.

"I'm so sorry," he said, rising to greet her and folding her into a hug. He held her, speaking softly into her hair. "I'm sorry Mum was so horrible to you, and I'm sorry for not telling you about the divorce papers."

"Why did you do it?" Marsaili's voice was muffled as she clung to his chest.

"I told you; I just wanted it to be over. Adelaide wanted someone to blame, and if it meant not having it drag on for years, I was happy to be the bad guy. She knows I never cheated on her; it was just the only thing I could 'confess' without having to say I'd abused her, or anything even more horrible."

Marsaili pulled away and looked up at him. "You didn't cheat then, before you moved up here?"

Will shook his head sadly. "No. Bloody hell you know how long it took me to build up the courage to make a move with you; do you honestly think I'd have it in me to juggle two women at once?"

Marsaili shook her head, as they moved to sit together on the sofa. He gently wrapped a blanket around her and kissed her on the head, before excusing himself to make them both a cup of tea.

"Where did your parents go?" Marsaili asked, when he had returned and she was cupping a steaming hot mug in both hands.

"A hotel for the night. They're getting the train home tomorrow."

"And you?"

"What do you mean?"

"Are you going with them?"

Will's face crumpled a little, his expression confused. "Of course not."

Marsaili fidgeted with the handle of her mug. She'd been thinking about this a lot on her walk, and had come to only one conclusion.

"They were right though," she said. "We're not exactly the same, you and me. Maybe you would be better back where you belong, back with… her?" Marsaili felt her lower lip start to wobble and concentrated on taking deep breaths, not looking Will in the eye.

He took a moment to respond. "Is that what you want?" he asked eventually.

Marsaili shook her head, blinking away the tears that were now spilling forth. "But I think maybe it's for the best," she said. "You married her Will; you did love her once. Things here, with me, they're different and they're exciting for now, maybe, but one day you'll get bored… who's to say you won't want to go back to the life you had before?"

Will took her hands in his, his eyes pleading and his voice thick. "Marsaili please don't do this - we're happy together. Don't let them spoil this."

Marsaili stood up, tearing her hands away from him. She couldn't bear to look at him, and if she gave in to his touch then her resolve would crumble once and for all.

"I'm sorry," she said, trying her hardest to keep the wobble from her voice. "This was a dream, Will. It was never going to last." She looked at her feet, her lips trembling and her chest shaking.

"I don't want this to end," Will said quietly. "I love you."

An anguished sob broke through, and Marsaili felt her shoulders start to heave. She didn't want this either, but seeing his parents had only emphasised how different they were, and suddenly the future she'd thought they might have together seemed utterly unattainable.

Marsaili went through to the bedroom and quickly threw some clothes in a holdall. Will followed her. "No, don't, please," he said, pulling himself together. "I'll leave; I don't want you out somewhere on your own."

"It's your name on the lease Will," Marsaili said. "I have to go; I'll be fine. I'll just go home a little sooner than planned." She smiled up at him, wanting to memorise the lines of his face. "I do love you," she said, her voice cracking.

Will nodded. "I know," he said, pulling her roughly against his chest. He kissed her, hard and urgent, his hands on her face and in her hair, the salty taste of tears in both of their mouths. He pressed his forehead against hers. "Please don't go," he pleaded.

"I'm sorry Will, I have to." Marsaili broke away from him, grabbing the half-packed holdall from the bed and heading for the door without looking back.

CHAPTER 45

Marsaili downed another shot and felt the heavy bass line reverberate through her chest. It was only apple sourz, but it was the best she could do. Tonight, she wanted to get thoroughly pissed, and cheap, artificially flavoured drinks loaded with e-numbers were, for her, the quickest and most cost-effective way to achieve that.

It had been almost a week since she'd walked out of Will's flat. With their previous flat gone and Isla now happily ensconced with Findlay in some cosy military digs up North, Marsaili didn't have many options for where to go.

"Darling," Forbes had opened the door to her in his pyjamas, welcoming her with a conciliatory hug. She'd rung ahead to warn him of her arrival, and briefly explain the circumstances.

He'd bundled her into the living room, made the obligatory cup of tea, before looking at her with a confused expression on his face.

"But why?" he asked.

Marsaili explained the encounter with Will's parents, and the sudden realisation that no matter how much she might want to, she couldn't see any way that they could possibly make things work long term.

Forbes frowned. "You broke up with him because his parents didn't like you?"

"No," Marsaili snorted. "I broke up with him because…" she paused, struggling to explain it. "We're nothing alike. I watch trashy daytime TV and he watches *Question Time*. He plays classical music on the cello for crying out loud; he even has different glasses for different types of wine. He owns a cheeseboard," she said, as if this were the final, irrefutable, nail in the coffin of their relationship.

Forbes laughed, placing a gentle hand on her knee. "Darling, none of those things are reasons to break up with someone. Not if you love them."

She sighed, feeling tears sting the back of her eyes again. She knew he was right. "I got scared," she said eventually, sniffling into the now empty mug she was still clutching in both hands. "I know it's not been long, but how on earth could we possibly contemplate a future - kids, marriage, anything like that - when his parents so obviously disapprove. Can you imagine how awful Christmas would be?"

"Isn't this something you and Will ought to be figuring out together? Maybe he wouldn't care."

Marsaili shook her head. "I can't ask him to give up his family for me. It's not fair."

Forbes leaned forward. "Darling, if he wants to be with you and his parents can't accept that, they're the ones giving up on him. Listen to someone who knows - if my parents couldn't handle me loving another man that's their loss. You're not asking Will to do anything; he's a grown man and he'll make his own choices." Forbes took her hands in his. "For years I've been listening to you bemoan your miserable love life and all the various knobheads you've dated; you've finally found a good guy. And you're throwing it away over worries about things that haven't even happened yet."

Marsaili sniffed again, suddenly feeling pathetic and stupid.

"Did Will stand up for you, when his parents appeared?" Forbes asked.

She nodded quietly. "He sent them away, and he apologised for what they'd said."

"Did he then change his mind, go chasing after them and agree to go back to his wife?"

"No."

Forbes smiled. "Then what are you doing crying on my sofa when a gorgeous man, who loves you and has given you no reason whatsoever to doubt what he's saying to you, is waiting for you at home?"

Suddenly seeing how silly she'd been, Marsaili had rushed home, hoping it wasn't too late to apologise. But then she'd let herself into the flat and heard that Will wasn't alone; he was with his parents in the living room.

"It's all for the best," his mother was saying. They hadn't heard Marsaili enter, and she left the front door ajar behind her, not wanting to risk shutting it and alerting them to her presence. The old saying about eavesdroppers never hearing anything good about themselves rang in her ears, but she crept closer and peered round the door nonetheless.

Will was sitting on the sofa, his head in his hands, his mother perched on the arm next to him and patting his back consolingly.

Marsaili could hear him sniffing and she suddenly wanted to run to him and hold him. His father paced awkwardly next to the window; his hands clasped behind his back.

"You can put all this nonsense behind you now and come home darling," Lydia continued. "One of Daddy's friends at the Palladium is looking for a new manager, and I'm sure Adelaide would be most forgiving, once we've spoken to her and straightened it all out."

Marsaili stood frozen on the spot, holding her breath as she waited for Will to turn them down, or declare that he was staying and going to win her back.

He did neither.

"I just need to sleep right now, mum," he said, lifting his tear-stained face and rising from his seat. "We can talk about this tomorrow." They obviously weren't leaving first thing after all. Marsaili shrunk back from the door. His mother stood too, reaching up and cupping his face in both of her hands. "Mummy will sort this, darling. There's no need to be sad."

Marsaili had heard enough. She slipped out of the door and raced down the stairs as fast as she could.

And now she was in a gay club, alone, awaiting the start of Forbes' drag show. Marsaili had persuaded him to hand in her notice at work on her behalf, not wanting any reason to have to see Will, and was planning on getting the train to her parents' house the following day. Her course didn't start for a while yet, but she didn't want to sleep on Forbes' sofa any longer.

When he realised that she really wasn't coming back, Will had packed her things into boxes, all neatly labelled and far more organised than when Marsaili had originally packed them herself, and dropped them off at Forbes' flat for her. Apart from that he'd made no attempt to contact her whatsoever.

Marsaili ordered another shot, followed by a cheap blended whisky drowned in coke, and moved over to a booth near the front of the stage, which Forbes had reserved for her. He had persuaded her that she needed a night out, but really this was the last place she wanted to be. She wanted to be with Will, and if she couldn't have that then she wanted to be at home - her childhood home - in her pyjamas, cuddling Fraoch in front of the fire.

Marsaili took her seat and pulled out her phone, whiling away the time until the performance started by scrolling blindly through Facebook, and hoping no one would attempt to speak to her. At least she was unlikely to get hit on here, she thought.

She jumped when the phone unexpectedly buzzed in her hand. Any hope that it might be Will was replaced by fear when she saw her mother's mobile number. It was almost 11 o'clock at night, and her mother rarely used her mobile at the best of times.

Marsaili stumbled outside, sliding the flashing icon on her screen to answer just as she passed the bouncers and left the din of the club behind her.

She knew instantly that her mother had been crying. Her voice was tight and constrained, and it echoed as if she were in a large hallway.

"Mum?" Marsaili could feel the tears coming before her mother had even spoken.

"It's OK," Shonagh said instantly. "We're fine." She took a deep breath. "I'm at the hospital with your father."

"What happened?" Marsaili was already scanning the street for taxis, her mind racing as she tried to figure out her quickest way home at this time of night.

"He took a turn," Shonagh replied. "Like before, but this time he passed out on the stairs. He's broken his wrist and they're going to run some tests, but he's fine."

"I'm coming home," Marsaili replied, ignoring her mother's protestations as she waved at a passing taxi. The driver tore past her regardless, splashing through a puddle.

"Marsaili?"

Her heart jumped at the familiar voice.

He looked almost unreal, standing amidst a sea of hair gel, eye liner and skinny fit tee-shirts outside the flashing lights and garish facade of the gay club. His hair was swept neatly to the side and his white shirt was tucked into a pair of charcoal grey trousers. He was frowning at her the way he did, his brown eyes full of concern and affection.

"Are you OK?"

Will stepped towards her, snapping her out of her daze. The confirmation that he was real was somehow more alarming than the thought that she might have imagined him, and Marsaili involuntarily shied away from him. Her mother's voice still echoed from the handset.

"I'm on my way," Marsaili said hurriedly, hanging up.

"What are you doing here?" she asked.

"I only wanted to talk." He had his arms outstretched, palms facing her, as if she were a rabid dog he had cornered in an alleyway. "Forbes told me you'd be here."

Well that explained his insistence that she come tonight, and the private booth, Marsaili thought.

"What's the matter? You don't look yourself?" he pressed.

Marsaili hesitated, knowing what he would do if she told him the real reason she was out here, waving at taxis in the drizzling rain, but at a loss for any other excuse to offer.

"I have to go," she said, finally meeting his gaze. "My dad's been taken to hospital."

Instinctively, Will reached out to touch her before drawing back. "We can take my car," he said.

"No," Marsaili insisted, desperately scanning the road for another passing taxi. "It's ok; I was meant to be getting the train home tomorrow afternoon anyway. I just need to get back to Forbes' place; if I can get to the station first thing, I can hopefully catch an earlier one. It's fine, honestly." She attempted to smile, but found that tears were welling up behind her eyes instead.

"No arguments," Will said, gently but firmly taking her by the elbow and steering her down the street. She could see the conspicuous outline of his soft top classic car parked in the shadows under the railway bridge, and briefly wondered at the naivety that made him trust it wasn't likely to get broken into or vandalised there.

"Where are they?" he asked.

"At the hospital in Inverness. Raigmore."

She text Forbes from the car, after they'd paid a fleeting visit to his flat so she could pick up her clothes. Thankfully she'd already packed a few basics; the rest she was planning to have picked up by the moving company in a couple of weeks. None of her plans had really worked out recently, she thought ruefully.

Will sat quietly, staring into the darkness ahead with one hand on the steering wheel. After the flurry of activity Marsaili felt suddenly self-conscious, and unsure of what she should say. Concern for her father was mingling with uncertainty at why Will had arrived so unexpectedly after almost a week of silence, and what she was doing letting him drive her such a long way home.

"Thank you for doing this," she said eventually, staring through her reflection in the passenger window. "You really didn't have to."

Will smiled briefly, taking his eyes off the road for a second to glance over at her. "It's nothing. You shouldn't be alone at a time like this. And besides, I wanted to talk to you - what better excuse than to have you stuck in my car for four hours?" He laughed awkwardly.

Marsaili forced a smile. "What did you want to talk about?"

He sighed deeply. "I miss you," he said. "I miss you more after three months together and a week apart than I've ever missed Adelaide."

"That's not a reason to get back together."

"Who said anything about getting back together?" he said in mock-innocence.

Marsaili raised her eyebrows at him, although she knew he couldn't see her expression. The lights of the city were slipping past them as they delved deeper into the countryside and headed North towards Perth.

"So that's not what you wanted to talk about?" she asked.

He sighed again. "Ok, maybe it was part of it. A big part." He took one hand off the wheel and rubbed it nervously on his thigh. "I love you Marsaili, and if you really don't want to be with me, I can accept that, but I couldn't let you go without a fight. I had to give it one last try."

Marsaili sighed and returned to staring out of the window. She was tired.

"Why?" she asked.

"Why what?"

"Why do you want to be with me?"

Will laughed. "I told you - I love you. You make me happy."

"Do you even know what makes you happy?"

He opened his mouth, then shut it again uncertainly. "That's not fair," he whispered.

Marsaili continued. "I think it's perfectly fair - you went to law school because your parents said you should; you married Adelaide because it was easy; you took the job at the theatre because

238

it was handed to you. Have you ever actually gone after something on your own, just because it's what *you* really want?"

The words had come out slightly harsher than she'd intended, but she meant them. Will looked hurt, his eyes downturned as he tightened his grip on the steering wheel, and she felt bad for a moment.

"I went after you," he said eventually. "More than once, despite you turning me down." He tried to smile, but it fell short of his eyes.

Marsaili sighed. "Will, I don't want to be another decision you made just because it was easy. I don't want to be something else you look back on in years to come and realise you were just going along with it all, and I certainly don't want to be an outlet for some sort of delayed rebellion against your parents, or a way for you to get over your divorce."

"That's not what this is about," he said, his tone frustrated. "I couldn't care less what my parents think, and the divorce was a relief, believe me. I love *you*, Marsaili. Why is that so difficult for you to understand?"

Marsaili felt her own temper rising. "Don't talk to me like I'm stupid," she snapped. "I might not have gone to Oxford, but I'm not an idiot"

"I don't think you're an idiot," Will said, lowering his voice. "I just want you to see that none of that matters to me."

"None of what? Me being a barmaid, or a fisherman's daughter, or fat…"

"Would you stop!?" It was the first time Marsaili had heard Will so much as raise his voice. He was always so placid, but now his face was flushed and she could see his rapid heartbeat pulsing at the base of his throat.

"Stop talking about yourself like that," he repeated, more quietly. "You know I think you're beautiful."

"Well, I'm no match for Adelaide. And with Mummy and Daddy whispering in your ear I'm sure you'll be running back to her in no time."

Will opened his mouth to respond, but paused, leaving it hanging half open. "How do you even know what Adelaide looks like?"

Marsaili felt her face flush. "I found you on Facebook," she admitted. "Back before anything had happened between us. I saw your wedding pictures."

Will shifted uncomfortably in his seat.

"*She's* beautiful," Marsaili insisted. "How can you go from that to some dumpy wee redhead? No wonder your mum was shocked when she saw me. I'm clearly not your type – I'm not elegant, or graceful, or…"

"Just because she looks elegant in a photograph doesn't mean that's how she was in real life. It's a split-second image of what she looks like on the outside; it doesn't show you anything that really matters about a person."

Marsaili slumped down in her seat. She knew he was right, but in that moment all her insecurities about their relationship came bubbling forth, and no matter how much she wanted to she couldn't stop them.

"Marsaili, I'm still here; not down in London, or getting back with my ex. I *chose* to come here tonight, because I wanted to see you and try to fix this bloody mess." Will raked the fingers of one hand through his hair, his expression helpless.

"I just… I don't know how to make you see how much you mean to me," he continued. "You've not been a distraction, or a game, or a rebellion. This is *real*, Marsaili… Or it is to me, at least." His voice broke then, and Marsaili felt a lump form in her own throat.

"It's too late," Marsaili replied, steeling her resolve and doing her best to ignore the overwhelming desire to reach out and touch him. "I need to be on my own for a while, and I think you do too. Maybe in another time, if things were different," she began, "but right now I would never know if you were with me because you really wanted to be, or just because it was the easiest way to escape a life you no longer wanted."

Will nodded, blinking back tears, his eyes suddenly vacant and defeated. "OK," he sighed. Marsaili watch him swallow deeply, his Adam's apple bobbing up and down against the collar of his shirt. "Can we keep in touch at least?" he asked.

"I think it's probably best if we don't."

He didn't reply. Will's gaze remained fixed on the road ahead, and they lapsed into an uncomfortable silence.

EPILOGUE

ONE YEAR LATER

The music started, the opening arpeggios of *Glasgow Love Theme* echoing through the air, and Marsaili instantly felt tears stinging her eyes. She blinked them away, conscious of her makeup and false eyelashes, and the fact that Isla would tolerate no such soppiness. Her best friend was behind her, resplendent in a flowing ivory gown that only just hinted at the burgeoning bump growing beneath it. Her blonde bob was shiny and thick, pinned half up at the sides and garnished, fittingly, with little white sprigs of Baby's Breath.

"Suck it up," Isla whispered through a grin, and Marsaili turned to see her with one hand resting on her father's arm, the other clutching a bouquet of blush pink roses and thistles. "Go!" she urged, flapping at Marsaili with the flowers.

With a deep breath, Marsaili swallowed the threatening tears and stepped into the church.

The music seemed to swell with the acoustics of the room, and the little bubble of emotion in her chest grew too. She smiled at the gathered happy faces, her eyes flitting over them without focusing too much on any one individual. It was a sea of hats and smiles and kilts, as she made her way slowly - and cautiously, in the 5-inch heels Isla had chosen for her - along the carpet runner. She saw Findlay at the end of the aisle, in his dress RAF uniform, resolutely facing the minister with his back to the congregation. Gregor, in his role as Findlay's best man, was smiling back at her. She was dimly aware of the rest of her family a couple of rows from the front, her mother dabbing her eyes with a handkerchief and Rowan jiggling a restless, almost two-year-old Callie on her knee while Lachlan dangled a doll in front of her.

Gratefully, Marsaili reached her spot at the front and looked up to watch not Isla, but Findlay. He had turned now, and was watching his bride make her way down the aisle with a look of such sheer astonishment and absolute happiness that it made Marsaili's heart burst. He looked like a man who just couldn't believe his luck.

The bride reached the front, placed a kiss on her father's

cheek and slipped her hand into that of her husband to be, as the minister welcomed them all and asked them to be seated.

The ceremony was being held in a church in Lossiemouth, where Isla and Findlay had spent the last year living as part of his deployment. Isla was working in a little school in a village along the coast, overlooking the sea just like she'd wanted, and soon they would have the family they'd been planning for so long.

Marsaili couldn't believe how quickly a year had passed. She had made the most of being enrolled at the UHI and over the past twelve months had enjoyed having her closest friends and family all in the one place for a change. She was still living with her parents, just a few hours away from Isla, and had been able to see Rowan most weeks and have the privilege of not only spending time with her friend, but also seeing her niece grow up. It was perfect, and she was content; more content than she'd ever been in her life. There was only one thing missing, she thought, as they stood for the first hymn and she watched Findlay and Isla steal a loving glance at one another.

Will was nothing if not a man of his word, she knew, and when they'd agreed not to make contact, he'd stuck to it resolutely. He was still in touch with Gregor, however, and the two had gone climbing and walking together a few times. That was the only reason she knew that he'd quit his job at the theatre, not long after they'd separated. Other than that, she had no idea where he was or what he was up to.

Far from pushing him from her mind, this seemed to only have fuelled her desire for him, and it felt as though she thought of him and missed him more with each passing day. She knew she could have swallowed her pride and called him herself, or asked Gregor to speak to him, but she wasn't ready yet to face the reality that he had most likely moved on. It was easier to imagine that he might still be out there somewhere, pining for her the way she was for him.

. Next week she would graduate, and in two months she would take up her first post as a Newly Qualified Teacher. To her surprise, she had made such a positive impression on one of her placements that the head teacher had actually requested to have her come back for her first year, and in August she would have a P7 class at the village school in Kyle of Lochalsh itself. The steady pay cheque meant she was even able to start looking at cottages to rent, although she didn't intend to move far from her parents, not after everything they'd been through.

A few days after Marsaili's early morning arrival at Raigmore hospital, courtesy of Will, the tests on her father had come back with some news. Relapsing and remitting MS wasn't the worst diagnosis on the list of possible conditions the doctors had suspected, but it wasn't exactly great, either.

She looked over at him now, seated beside her mother with one strong arm around her shoulders, his back straight and his head of salt and pepper hair thick and unruly. No one would have guessed that he was sick; right now, he still looked as healthy as ever, although Marsaili knew that could change at any moment. He looked over suddenly and caught her eye, smiling. Marsaili smiled back. Whatever time he had left, she intended to be around for as much of it as she could.

Isla and Findlay were exchanging their vows now, gold rings slipped carefully onto their fingers, before one more hymn was sung and suddenly *Everlasting Love* was playing and Marsaili was following her friend, now a wife and soon to be a mother, back down the aisle.

The summer sun was bright as they spilled out into the street and the waiting wedding cars, Marsaili and Gregor in a people carrier with Findlay and Isla's parents while the bride and groom were whisked away in a classic VW camper van. The remaining guests were walking to the hotel, just down the hill from the church, while the bridal party headed to the beach for photos.

Marsaili was glad Gregor was with her. Newly engaged himself, Gayatri had been entrusted to her future in-laws while he was on duty. Marsaili was happy for them.

"Your turn next," she said, nodding out of the car window to where Isla and Findlay were disembarking, Isla changing into wellies and preparing to cross the rickety wooden bridge that led over the Lossie estuary and to the white sand and dunes of the beach beyond.

Gregor smiled, helping her from the car. Thankfully Marsaili, too, had wellies for the outdoor photo shoot.

"What about you?" he asked. "Now that you're a career woman; time to settle down?"

Marsaili scoffed. "With who?" she said. "Kyle of Lochalsh isn't exactly overflowing with eligible bachelors."

Gregor offered her his arm as they walked towards the bridge, Marsaili bundling the long skirt of her dress up off the floor.

The sage green chiffon material had been floor length with the heels, but now that she was in flats in dragged on the ground.

"Actually, there's someone coming tonight I thought you'd like to meet," Gregor said, as the photographer urged them into position, their backs to the sea and the picture postcard view of the town behind them.

"Who?" Marsaili asked suspiciously.

"Just a guy Findlay and I know; a climbing friend. I think you'll like him."

Marsaili frowned. "I don't know..."

"Marsaili, it's time to get over Will," Gregor said bluntly. "It's been too long; you need to move on."

They were interrupted by the photographer repositioning them, snapping off a few more shots before moving Gregor and Marsaili aside to make room for just the happy couple and their parents.

"Has he?" she asked quietly. "Moved on?"

Gregor sighed. "Do you really want to know?"

Defeated, Marsaili shrugged her shoulders. "Probably not," she confessed.

"Chin up, sis," Gregor chirped, a conciliatory arm around her shoulders. "'Whit's fur ye'll no go by ye,' and all that."

They arrived back at the hotel to find the cocktail reception in full swing. Gregor still had his speech to worry about, but Marsaili's responsibilities were officially complete - one bride had been safely delivered to her wedding, she'd made it down the aisle without falling on her arse, and the necessary pictures had been taken. Now she could let her hair down. She helped herself to a glass of prosecco and some canapes from a passing waitress, before snaking her way through the crowd and out onto the terrace.

Marsaili found her parents and siblings gathered around a table in the sun, looking across the Moray firth and talking animatedly. Callie spotted her first, clambering off her mother's knee and excitedly pointing and babbling, until Rowan eventually took her daughter by the hand and helped her weave her way through the crowd and across the terrace. Marsaili swept her niece up into her arms, a bundle of giggling, wriggling arms and legs and soft brown curls.

They joined the others, Marsaili's parents each welcoming her with a warm embrace.

"You look lovely, sweetheart," her mother said.

"Aye, bonnie," her father concurred with a smile. Marsaili had to confess, she'd rather enjoyed having her hair and makeup done by a professional for the first time in her life. She felt like the very best version of herself, her complexion smooth and her long hair blow dried and then loosely curled so that it fell to her shoulder blades in tumbling waves.

The hotel where they were holding the reception sat on a clifftop on the outskirts of town, looking down over the golf course and out to the skerries and the sea beyond. Today the water was turquoise and the sky clear and cloudless. Marsaili enjoyed the warm sun on her skin as she sat and drank with her family, nibbling canapes and chatting, before they all gathered in the large conservatory for dinner. It was perfectly positioned to take advantage of the expansive views across the firth, and the late summer sun flooded the room in a natural golden glow.

Marsaili took her place at the head table with the rest of the bridal party, directly in front of the panoramic glass windows. Gregor and Findlay delivered their speeches to great aplomb, perfectly balancing the risqué with the heart-warming and the funny anecdotes with the touching ones, and the meal was served. Marsaili was seated beside Findlay's mum, and the evening passed in a blur of champagne and pleasant conversation. Before she knew it suddenly the ceilidh band had arrived, and they were being ushered into the bar so that the function room could be rearranged to set up for the evening reception.

She took the opportunity to step out for a moment, enjoying a breather on the balcony overlooking the sea. The cloudless sky had allowed the heat of the day to evaporate, so that now as the sun started to sink lower in the sky the air grew chilly. It made the hairs on her arms stand on end.

She heard footsteps behind her and turned, finding Gregor stepping out from the din and the light of the bar. The band were ready now, and the guests were being rounded back up in preparation for the first dance. Marsaili suddenly remembered that she did have one last duty - to join in with Gregor after the first verse, and encourage their fellow guests to do the same. Isla had been worried about the dance being awkward, and didn't want to be the centre of attention for too long.

"There you are," Gregor said, removing his kilt jacket and placing it over her shoulders without asking. Marsaili shrugged into it gratefully, pulling it closer around herself.

"That guy I was telling you about just arrived," he said, leaning beside her on the railings and following her gaze out to sea. "Came in on the bus from Elgin with the rest of the evening guests."

Marsaili sighed. "I don't know, Gregor."

"Come on - I may be your brother, but from an objective perspective you are looking rather beautiful tonight. Don't let it go to waste." He placed a hand on her forearm and squeezed. "Trust me."

Just then, another figure joined them on the balcony. In the glare of the disco lights from within Marsaili couldn't make out his features.

"There you are!" Gregor said. "I wanted you to meet my sister. This is…"

"Marsaili," a familiar voice said. "Like parsley."

Marsaili blinked furiously, convinced her ears were playing tricks on her. But there he was, as if he'd just walked out of her dreams.

"I remember," he said, taking a step towards her.

He looked the same, yet somehow different. He was tanned, and his hair was longer, although still combed into his customary side parting. It seemed blonder too. He was clean shaven, as usual, although his sideburns too were longer, and he was dressed in a light grey three-piece suit with an open necked pale blue shirt underneath. He smiled at her, his warm brown eyes crinkling at the corners the way she remembered.

"Hi," he breathed.

Marsaili felt her mouth go dry and her heart beat faster, as if it were climbing into her throat. She glanced at Gregor, who smiled coyly and slipped back into the party, slapping Will affectionately on the shoulder as he passed.

"You have a bit of a habit of showing up when I least expect you," Marsaili said, composing herself at last as he walked slowly over to her side.

"Sorry about that," Will answered with a smile, taking in her appearance. "You look well," he said.

"So do you," she replied.

They stood facing each other in silence for a moment. "Did you bring a date?" Marsaili asked. "Pity if you did - great place to pick up girls, weddings."

"Especially bridesmaids, so I'm told." Will reached out without thinking, as if they'd never been apart, and wrapped a long, red tendril of hair around his fingers. "God, I've missed you," he said.

He pulled his hand away abruptly, as Gregor suddenly stuck his head back out through the patio doors. Marsaili glared at him.

"Sorry to interrupt the reunion," he said, "but duty calls." Gregor gestured back into the function room where the crowds had gathered and the band were getting ready to begin. "You're needed inside."

As chivalrous as ever, Will stepped aside and held the door open for her as they followed Gregor back into the function room just in time for the opening strains of *Thinking Out Loud* by Ed Sheeran to drift out into the night air

They stood awkwardly side by side, watching Isla and Findlay sway together in time to the music, Isla's head on her husband's shoulder. Just as the first chorus kicked in, Marsaili turned to find her brother, only to see him slip onto the dancefloor with Gayatri already in his arms. She frowned at him, and he winked in response.

Will cleared his throat. "Aren't you supposed to be...?"

"Yes."

"Allow me." He offered her his arm, and without speaking, Marsaili let him lead her onto the floor. One hand was warm on the small of her back, while the other held her hand gently and turned her around the dancefloor.

They left a careful gap between their bodies, Will's head respectfully turned to one side. But as the music continued, they drifted gradually closer, until eventually Marsaili's head was on his chest, his chin resting on top of it like it used to, and his arm was wrapped entirely around her waist. Neither said a word. She closed her eyes, and when the music ended it took a moment for them to separate.

Marsaili looked around the room, aware that Will's arrival had not gone unnoticed. Her mother would pounce on him soon if she got half a chance.

"Shall we go back outside?" he suggested. Marsaili nodded,

and they slipped back out into the cool of the night.

Will looked at her, smiling nervously. "We've never danced together before," he observed. "I liked it."

"Why are you here?" Marsaili asked, no longer able to hold it in. "I haven't heard from you in a year, I've been getting on with my life - why now?"

Will paused for a second before answering. "I've spent the last 12 months doing everything I could possibly think of doing to take my mind off you," he said. "I quit my job; I finalised my divorce and sold my house in London. I busked, a lot. I spent almost all of my money on a belated gap year - a sad, single, almost middle-aged man travelling alone around Australia is not a good look, in case you were wondering. I dated - very badly," he laughed. "And eventually I realised that no matter where I went or what I did, there was still only one place I really wanted to be, and one person I really wanted to be with. In the middle of nowhere. With you."

His hand found hers now, and he pulled her closer, stroking her cheek tenderly with his thumb as he looked into her eyes. "You remember that story you told my parents about your name?" he asked. Marsaili cringed at the memory. "I've not been able to get it out of my head since. It's perfect - you are a pearl. You showed up in the most unlikely place, in the shittiest time of my life, and you had absolutely no idea how precious you were to me." Marsaili felt a lump forming in the back of her throat as he continued. "I've come back now to show you."

Gently, he slid one hand behind her neck and cupped her face to his. With his mouth inches from hers, he suddenly paused, watching her carefully, half a smile dancing on his lips. "If you'll have me, that is?"

Marsaili shrugged her shoulders, toying with the hair at the nape of his neck. "I suppose."

He kissed her then, and it was as if they had never been apart. Marsaili smiled, slipping her hands beneath his suit jacket and feeling the familiar contours of his back. "What do we do now?" she asked.

"I haven't got a bloody clue," Will laughed. "I should probably point out that I'm currently unemployed and technically homeless," he added with a shrug.

"Quite the catch," Marsaili replied, still smiling up at him.

He bowed his head to hers, his nose brushing her cheek. "So, what do you say? Do you think you could love an unemployed, divorced, homeless busker?" Will murmured, as his lips grazed her jawline.

"I already do," Marsaili breathed, nuzzling into his neck. "I always have."

Will pulled away suddenly. "You are talking about me?" he asked, looking down at her with that quizzical frown she loved so much.

Marsaili laughed. "Yes, I am, you bloody idiot," she replied, slipping her hands around his neck and pulling him to her, certain that this time, she would never let him go.

ABOUT THE AUTHOR

Elsie McArthur lives in the Highlands of Scotland with her husband, two children, two dogs and a cat. She is a part-time primary school teacher, part-time stay at home mum and full-time procrastinator. In her spare time, she enjoys walking, baking and eating too much cake. This is her first novel, and was mostly written whilst breastfeeding or being napped on by small children.

Elsie is active on social media and may be contacted via Facebook, Instagram and Twitter.

Reviews - which are always greatly appreciated - can be left at Amazon or Goodreads.

Elsie's second book, 'Love, on the Rocks' is now available as an ebook and paperback from Amazon.

PRAISE FOR ELSIE MCARTHUR

Elsie McArthur made it possible for her readers to connect with her main character on many levels and for that, I am giving this book 5 stars.

Stacy Hawk, Author

This was a beautifully written contemporary romance set in gorgeous Scotland. Throughout the story the emotions of the characters were palpable and evocative.

Wendy Bayne, Author

I really enjoyed this heartwarming story. I was hooked from the very first page. Can't wait to read more from this author.

Hayley Walsh, Author

This book delivered exactly what I was after — it was as funny and fierce as they come.

Caroline G, Amazon Reviewer

Printed in Great Britain
by Amazon